ACCLAIM FOR E

THE AMISH MATCHMAKERS

"Beth Wiseman's *The Amish Matchmakers* charmed me from the very first page in this novel about two spirited (and well-intentioned) Amish widows who think they know what's best for others but don't always know what's best for themselves. With romance sparking between Amish and *Englisch* characters, can love possibly prevail? Wiseman answers the question with respect, tenderness, and grace in a truly heartwarming story!"

—MYRA JOHNSON, AWARD-WINNING AUTHOR OF THE FLOWERS OF EDEN HISTORICAL ROMANCE SERIES

HOPEFULLY EVER AFTER

"Beth Wiseman has done it again—a story of love, hope, and rising above our circumstances. You don't want to miss this one."

—VANNETTA CHAPMAN, *USA TODAY* BESTSELLING AUTHOR OF THE INDIANA AMISH BRIDES SERIES

THE STORY OF LOVE

"Beth Wiseman's *The Story of Love* had me turning the pages as quickly as I could read them. Her compelling, unpredictable romance between two strong characters with complicated lives plays out beautifully, one unexpected turn after another. Beth has done it again."

—PATRICIA DAVIDS, *USA TODAY* BESTSELLING AUTHOR OF AMISH ROMANCE

THE BOOKSELLER'S PROMISE

"*The Bookseller's Promise* beautifully illustrates the power of love, family bonds, and the good news of the gospel . . . A captivating story of discovering faith and finding hope in the midst of despair."

—JENNIFER BECKSTRAND, AUTHOR OF THE MATCHMAKERS OF HUCKLEBERRY HILL SERIES

A SEASON OF CHANGE

"A beautiful story about love, forgiveness, and finding family in an unexpected place."

—KATHLEEN FULLER, *USA TODAY* BESTSELLING AUTHOR

AN UNLIKELY MATCH

"With multiple vibrant story lines, Wiseman's excellent tale will have readers anticipating the next. Any fan of Amish romance will love this."

—*PUBLISHERS WEEKLY*

"This was such a sweet story. I cheered on Evelyn and Jayce the whole way. Jayce is having issues with his difficult father, who's brought a Hollywood crew to Amish country to film a scene in a nearby cave. Evelyn has a strong, supportive family, so she feels for Jayce immediately. As they grow closer and help each other overcome fears and phobias, they know this can't last. But God and two persnickety Amish sisters, Lizzie and Esther, have other plans. Can a Hollywood boy fall for an Amish girl and make it work? Find out. Read this delightful, heartwarming story!"

—LENORA WORTH, AUTHOR OF *THEIR AMISH REUNION*

"Beth Wiseman's *An Unlikely Match* will keep you turning the pages as you are pulled into this heartwarming and unpredictable Amish romance story about Evelyn and Jayce, two interesting and compelling characters. Beth doesn't disappoint, keeping you guessing as to how this story will end."

—MOLLY JEBBER, BESTSELLING AMISH
INSPIRATIONAL HISTORICAL ROMANCE AUTHOR

A PICTURE OF LOVE

"This is a warm story of romance and second chances with some great characters that fans of the genre will love."

—PARKERSBURG NEWS & SENTINEL

"Beth Wiseman's A Picture of Love will delight readers of Amish fiction. Naomi and Amos's romance is a heartfelt story of love, forgiveness, and second chances. This book has everything readers love about a Beth Wiseman story—an authentic portrait of the Amish community, humor, the power of grace and hope, and, above all, faith in God's Word and His promises."

—AMY CLIPSTON, BESTSELLING AUTHOR
OF THE AMISH LEGACY SERIES

A BEAUTIFUL ARRANGEMENT

"A Beautiful Arrangement has everything you want in an escape novel."

—AMISH HEARTLAND

"Wiseman's delightful third installment of the Amish Journey series centers on the struggles and unexpected joys of a marriage of convenience . . . Series devotees and newcomers alike will find this engrossing romance hard to put down."

—PUBLISHERS WEEKLY

"A Beautiful Arrangement has so much heart, you won't want to put it down until you've read the last page. I love second-chance love stories, and Lydia and Samuel's story is heartbreaking and sweet with unexpected twists and turns that make their journey to love all the more satisfying. Beth's fans will cherish this book."

—JENNIFER BECKSTRAND, AUTHOR OF THE PETERSHEIM BROTHERS SERIES

LISTENING TO LOVE

"Wiseman is at her best in this surprising tale of love and faith."

—PUBLISHERS WEEKLY

"I always find Beth Wiseman's books to be both tenderly romantic and thought-provoking. She has a way of setting a scene that makes me feel like I'm part of an Amish community and visiting for supper. I loved the title of this book, the message about faith and God, and the heartfelt romance between Lucas and Natalie. *Listening to Love* has everything I love in a Beth Wiseman novel—a strong faith message, a touching romance, and a beautiful sense of place. Beth is such an incredibly gifted storyteller."

—SHELLEY SHEPARD GRAY, BESTSELLING AUTHOR

"*Listening to Love* is vintage Beth Wiseman . . . Clear your calendar because you're going to want to read this one in a single sitting."

—VANNETTA CHAPMAN, *USA TODAY* BESTSELLING AUTHOR OF THE INDIANA AMISH BRIDES SERIES

HEARTS IN HARMONY

"This is a sweet story, not only of romance, but of older generations and younger generations coming together in friendship. It's a tearjerker as well as an uplifting story."

—*PARKERSBURG NEWS & SENTINEL*

THE AMISH
MATCHMAKERS

Other Books by Beth Wiseman

The Amish Bookstore Novels
The Bookseller's Promise
The Story of Love
Hopefully Ever After

The Amish Inn Novels
A Picture of Love
An Unlikely Match
A Season of Change

The Amish Journey Novels
Hearts in Harmony
Listening to Love
A Beautiful Arrangement

The Amish Secrets Novels
Her Brother's Keeper
Love Bears All Things
Home All Along

The Land of Canaan Novels
Seek Me with All Your Heart
The Wonder of Your Love
His Love Endures Forever

The Daughters of the Promise Novels
Plain Perfect
Plain Pursuit
Plain Promise

THE AMISH MATCHMAKERS

BETH WISEMAN

ZONDERVAN

The Amish Matchmakers

Copyright © 2023 by Elizabeth Wiseman Mackey

Requests for information should be addressed to:

Zondervan, *3900 Sparks Dr. SE, Grand Rapids, Michigan 49546*

Library of Congress Cataloging-in-Publication Data

Names: Wiseman, Beth, 1962- author.
Title: The Amish matchmakers / Beth Wiseman.
Description: Grand Rapids, Michigan : Zondervan, [2023] | Summary:
   "Welcome back to the Peony Inn where love always blooms in this stand-
   alone novel that finds two Amish matchmakers vying for the heart of the
   same man"--Provided by publisher.
Identifiers: LCCN 2023011532 (print) | LCCN 2023011533 (ebook) | ISBN
   9780310365730 (paperback) | ISBN 9780310365761 (library binding) |
   ISBN 9780310365747 (epub) | ISBN 9780310365754
Subjects: LCGFT: Novels. | Romance fiction. | Christian fiction.
Classification: LCC PS3623.I83 A65 2023 (print) | LCC PS3623.I83 (ebook)
   | DDC 813/.6--dc23/eng/20230313
LC record available at https://lccn.loc.gov/2023011532
LC ebook record available at https://lccn.loc.gov/2023011533

Zondervan titles may be purchased in bulk for educational, business,
fundraising, or sales promotional use. For information, please email
SpecialMarkets@Zondervan.com.

Printed in the United States of America

23 24 25 26 27 LBC 5 4 3 2 1

To Sam Hanners, rest in peace my friend.

Glossary

———❍———

ab im kopp: crazy (lit: "addled in the head")
ach: [exclamation]
boppli: baby
bruder: brother
daadi: father
daadi haus: small parents' house on property
danki: thanks
Die Kelt is farichderlich den winder: The cold is terrible
   this winter.
Deitsch: Dutch
dochder: daughter
Englisch: non-Amish folk/English language
Er dutt mir leed: I'm sorry
fraa: wife
Gott: God
grossdaadi: grandfather

gut: good

kaffi: coffee

kind/kinner: child/children

lieb: love

maed: girls, young women

maedel: girl, young woman

mamm: mom

mei: my

mudder: mother

nee: no

onkul: uncle

Ordnung: the unwritten rules of the Amish

rumschpringe: adolescent rite of passage (lit: "jumping around")

schweeger: brother-in-law

schweschder/schweschdere: sister/sisters

sohn: son

urgrossvadder: great-grandfather

Wie bischt: Hello/how are you

wunderbar: wonderful

ya: yes

I

———— ✄ ————

Esther shuffled across the living room in her socked feet, stopping to peer over her sister's shoulder—an easy enough task since Lizzie was a tiny woman. She squinted against the glare of the morning sun, then gently reached for the binoculars her sister had pressed to her eyes.

"What have I told you about spying on that poor man?" Esther set the binoculars on the coffee table, straightened, put her hands on her hips, and waited for Lizzie to turn around.

Her sister spun to face her and huffed before shifting her dentures back and forth in her mouth, a compulsion that had become as much a part of Lizzie as the air she breathed.

"It's not normal for an *Englisch* man to rent a small cottage without electricity," Lizzie said. "He never leaves the *haus*, even though he has a fancy automobile parked out front. And I saw a young woman pull up yesterday in a little red car. She had a bunch of bags and looked like she was delivering groceries to him." Lizzie shook her head, causing strands of gray hair to fall from beneath her prayer covering.

Esther ambled to one of the rocking chairs and sat. Her knees had been swelling since she woke up this morning, which was usually a sign that rain was coming. Or that she'd been on her feet too much the day before.

"We've had several people rent the cottage who weren't Amish," she said. "He signed a lease for six months, and this is November. He'll likely be gone before the summer heat arrives. He's only been here a week, so maybe he is just getting settled."

She rubbed her hands on her knees, trying to recall if she had any of the cream left that the doctor had prescribed for her arthritis, before she locked eyes with her sister. Esther often wondered how they shared the same genes. Lizzie was seventy-five, but she was as spry as any fifty-year-old Esther knew, and the woman didn't have any known ailments. She had no issues with high cholesterol, she'd been spared arthritis, her blood sugar was normal—despite the ridiculous amounts of sweets she ate—and Esther had recently seen her running after a rooster by the chicken coop.

Running. Like a teenager.

Lizzie scowled. "I just don't know about him."

Esther folded her hands in her lap, kicked the rocker into motion, and sighed. "*Ya*, exactly. You've never even met the fellow." She waved a hand toward their guest cottage. She and Lizzie had plenty of rooms for rent in the main house—the Peony Inn where they resided—but the older man had specifically requested the cottage for six months. "Why don't you just go over there, introduce yourself, and stop spying and chattering about him?"

Lizzie pointed a finger at Esther, maintaining her frown. "I don't go inside that cottage anymore." She lowered her arm and raised both eyebrows. "And you know why."

Esther chuckled. "*Ya*, I know why, and it's silly, Lizzie. The cottage isn't haunted. We don't believe in such things."

"Maybe you don't. But you're not the one Gus is haunting." Lizzie stomped a foot. "I knew that man would find a way to spook me even after his passing."

Grumpy Gus, as they'd lovingly referred to him, had been a thorn in Lizzie's side right up until the end of his life. Gus felt the same way about Lizzie, but the two adversaries had made their peace before Gus died.

"Gus is not haunting you." Esther rolled her eyes. "And if you'd been here when Dr. Stoltzfus checked in, you would have seen that he is a very nice, retired dentist. He might even be able to help you with your dentures." Esther doubted it. Lizzie had been to countless dentists, none of whom could find anything wrong with the way the dentures fit. "He's actually quite handsome."

Esther felt herself blushing, surprised at herself for verbalizing the thought.

Lizzie ignored the comment, her finger pointed at

Esther again as she wagged it fiercely while drawing her eyebrows into a frown. "And that's another thing. 'Stoltzfus' is an Amish name. Why does an *Englisch* doctor have an Amish name?"

Esther shrugged. "I have no idea. On his rental application, he provided plenty of good references, and he appeared to be a respected member of his community until he retired ten years ago. When did you become so suspicious of people? You've never behaved like this in the past."

"We've never had a stranger rent the cottage. It's always been locals, even after Gus died. The same thing with the other house that's unoccupied at the moment. We've always known the folks renting it." She scratched her jaw. "And what has the dentist been doing for the last ten years?" Lizzie lowered her arm but raised her chin.

Esther rubbed her eyes, buying a little time to think of something to pacify her sister's concerns. "Lizzie, we run a bed-and-breakfast inn. We have strangers in and out all the time, and we've never had a problem we couldn't handle. It's none of our business why Dr. Stoltzfus is here. He paid for all six months in advance. If you want to know more about him, then you need to march over there and introduce yourself."

"Hmph." Lizzie kept her chin up as she pounded her way to the kitchen, shaking the wood floor with all ninety-five pounds of her tiny frame.

Esther slowly lifted her much larger and wider self to a standing position, stretching her arms above her head before she made her way to the fireplace to add another log. Then she stepped into a pair of slippers nearby. Life at the inn was casual this week since they had no tenants, but they would have a houseful coming on Friday.

She stopped at the window, briefly peered at the other house they often rented on the property, currently un-occupied, then set her eyes on the small cottage. Lizzie was right that their new guest had stayed mostly to himself. But Esther thought of that as a bonus. The man didn't complain about anything, and he had paid up front. What had caught her off guard was the man's looks. He had been extremely charming, well-dressed in English clothes, and very hand-some with a full head of gray hair and a clean-shaven face. He didn't look like he was in his mid-seventies, which Esther had estimated him to be based on his rental application and work history.

Lizzie had a mouthful of chocolate-chip cookie when Esther walked into the kitchen.

"How is that you can eat a dozen of those, not gain a pound, and your glucose is never high?" Esther sighed as she sat across from her sister at the table. "My blood sugar goes up if I even look at cookies or other sweets." Esther was only two years older than Lizzie, and it seemed unfair that Esther couldn't indulge without consequences. She'd tried losing weight and ate the right foods—most of the time—but her diabetes remained.

"I baked you some sugar-free cookies." Lizzie said through a mouthful as she pointed to a cookie jar on the counter.

As Lizzie had grown increasingly unfond of cooking and baking, Esther appreciated her sister's efforts. "*Danki* for that, but you know they don't taste the same." She decided to throw caution to the wind and reached for one of the smaller normal cookies on the platter. After a dainty bite, savoring the flavor, she said, "Don't forget, we have six women coming Friday afternoon."

Lizzie nodded as she snatched another cookie. "*Ya*, I know. The cleaning service will be here tomorrow to remake the beds and tidy up the rooms. I've already checked inventory for food. We're set."

Esther and Lizzie had hired unwed Amish girls to help with the Peony Inn in the past, but most of the young women in their small Montgomery, Indiana, community had married. They'd hired an English cleaning service last year when help became too hard to find. Esther could barely get up and down the stairs these days. Lizzie often took them two at a time, on the way up and back down again. Still, although Esther and her sister didn't always agree on things, they'd agreed it was too big a house for them to handle on their own. Lizzie was spunky, but she tired the same way Esther did. It just took her longer.

Esther plopped the last bit of cookie into her mouth. "Maybe I should invite our new tenant here for a meal since you are caught up in ghostly nonsense and choose not to go meet him at the cottage."

"You can call it 'ghostly nonsense' or whatever you like. Things fall off shelves when I'm there. The battery-operated can opener comes on whenever it feels like it. And the place smells weird."

Knowing Lizzie really did believe Gus was haunting her, Esther stifled a gut-busting laugh. She cleared her throat. "Things fall because the cottage needs leveling. The can opener probably needs new batteries. And if it smells *weird*—as you put it—it was probably from being closed up and unoccupied part of the summer."

"Well, don't invite that man here. Ghosts can attach themselves to people, and the old dentist might bring Gus along with him over here to haunt me."

"*Ach*, Lizzie!" This time Esther couldn't hold back as she laughed aloud. "That is all such nonsense. You need to go back to your clean and wholesome romance novels. You're reading too many books about silly things. I know you try to hide some of the novels you bring home, but you left one on your bed about murderers. That type of literature is affecting your ability to think clearly, and the bishop would not approve of them or your way of thinking. Neither would *Gott*. That type of reading is making you act irrationally."

Lizzie groaned before she got up and left the kitchen.

Esther shook her head. Lizzie was the quirkiest person she knew, and Esther couldn't love her more if she tried. But Esther had a secret. She and Lizzie had spent years playing matchmaker for others since they had opened the Peony Inn after the deaths of their husbands. Both men had died much too young, and she and Lizzie had struggled to fill the voids. Turning their childhood home into a bed-and-breakfast had

BETH WISEMAN

occupied their minds and helped them work through their grief. They'd slipped into the roles of matchmakers easily. She and Lizzie had loved deeply, and they rejoiced each time an opportunity presented itself to nudge two deserving people into a romantic relationship. But they'd never played matchmaker for each other. It seemed nonsensical at their age.

Until Esther met the handsome and charming English man renting their cottage.

Esther was overweight and had a long list of ailments, some which had worsened over the past year. In her heart she was sure God would call her home first, and Lizzie would be devastated. It would be easier for her sister if she weren't alone. And Esther had a plan.

———◆———

Lizzie went to her bedroom and closed the door. A few minutes later, she heard Esther's bedroom door close. They occupied the only two downstairs bedrooms. The other rooms were upstairs for guests. Lizzie and her sister were like clockwork when it came to naps. Two o'clock, every day. But Lizzie wasn't tired today.

She waited until she heard Esther snoring on the other side of the wall that separated them, then she tiptoed to the living room and picked up the binoculars.

After she padded back to her bedroom in her black socks, she went to the only window in her room with a view of the cottage. A view partially obstructed by an overgrown tree outside. She made a mental note to ask the young man who took care of the property to trim back the branches. For now, she leaned as far to one side as she could, the binoculars up and ready. She watched for a good ten minutes before she decided this was a waste of time. What were the chances the reclusive mystery dentist would step outside when she was watching?

"Ugh." She tossed the binoculars onto her bed and went to the candy bowl she kept on her bedside table. She unwrapped two Hershey Kisses and popped them in her mouth, tempted to take out her stupid teeth and gum the candy into submission. If none of the fancy dentists in Bloomington had been able to fix her teeth, she doubted an old, retired dentist would have any new tricks up his sleeve.

Lizzie had her reasons for wanting to know more about their renter. She had an idea, and for her to execute her plan, she had to make sure the man wasn't a serial killer who'd faked his references and was just biding his time until he would sneak over to the inn and slice them both up. Maybe he would hide their bodies in the deep freeze and say they'd gone missing, citing dementia or some other mind-altering affliction.

And the name Stoltzfus was about as Amish as you could get. Had the dentist been Amish in his youth, before he went to medical school?

Or maybe he's really an Amish man in hiding, pretending to be a retired dentist. If so, why is he hiding?

Her mind drifted back to the serial-killer theory. Then she shook her head and reached for two more pieces of candy. She shivered, realizing her thought process was off-kilter. Esther was right . . . She needed to go back to her romance books. They always had a happy ending. Her reading choices of late had been about ghosts and murderers and all things unpleasant. The bishop definitely would not approve.

Lizzie opened the bottom drawer of her nightstand and picked up the latest books she'd bought at a used bookstore on one of her trips to Bedford via a driver she'd hired. Jake Lantz certainly wouldn't carry any of those type of books at his bookstore here in Montgomery. Nor did she want anyone knowing she was reading such torrid tales. If Gus hadn't started haunting her, she would have never picked up the first book. Esther would be shocked to know how far her reading habits had gone right down the toilet since then—much worse than the one book her sister had spotted on the bed.

She placed her five latest books on the bed and eyed the titles.

How to Know When a House Is Haunted.

The Most Notorious Killers in History.

When Your Neighbor Is Not Your Friend. She raised her eyebrows and took a deep breath before she glanced at the other titles.

Spirits Among Us.

And last, but not least . . . *Unsolved Murders.* No

wonder she was spooked and suspicious all the time. When had she become someone who read this kind of stuff?

She needed to donate the books to a library or the Donation Spot, a local place that took just about anything, like a Goodwill organization. She briefly considered burning them in the fireplace, but that didn't feel right. She promised herself she was back to her happily-ever-after romances. Lizzie preferred romance, but leave it to Gus to scare her senseless and set her on the wrong path.

She gathered up her books and looked up at the ceiling. "Nice try, Gus, trying to sway me to the dark side." Then she dumped them back into the drawer and sat on the bed, dangling her feet since they didn't reach the floor.

One way or another, she was going to have to find out about their new renter. But she wasn't going inside that cottage.

Lizzie chuckled softly. Maybe Esther was right. How much harm could a man in his seventies—his presumed age, according to Esther—cause anyway? Yawning, she tossed back her covers and decided maybe she needed that nap after all. But not before one final peep out the window—

She stiffened all over, paralyzed, when she saw movement on the cottage porch. When she snapped out of it, she took the binoculars and brought them to her face so fast that she hit her nose, hard enough that she almost cried out. Biting her lip to silence herself, she hoped her racing heart would slow down as she adjusted the focus on the binoculars.

"Oh my," she said in a whisper. She'd been trying all week to get a peep at their new tenant. She'd heard Esther say earlier today that he was handsome. Her sister probably didn't realize she had mentioned his good looks before, after first meeting him. Her comment was what had sparked Lizzie's idea. Esther had a gleam in her eye every time she spoke about Dr. Stoltzfus. Lizzie just had to make sure he was honorable.

At first glance she could no longer imagine him as any type of criminal or someone living a secret life. Dr. Stoltzfus was a tall man. A tall and handsome hunk. She'd learned that word from her romance novels. He had a full head of gray hair, was proportionally built, and she'd bet money he had good teeth since he was a dentist, which seemed more plausible now that she was able to have a good look at him. He wore blue jeans and running shoes, and she saw the hint of a white shirt beneath his blue jacket.

Please, dear Gott, *don't let him be a bad man. I pray he is a* gut *man. I pray he is a kind man.*

Lizzie lowered the binoculars and smiled. God was going to answer her prayer. Maybe it was her reward for deciding to get rid of those books, even though she knew God didn't work that way.

Esther was the best person Lizzie had ever known. They hadn't had a chance to play matchmaker in a long while. Who better to set on the path to romance than her beloved sister? It would be wonderful to watch Esther fall in love. And Dr. Stoltzfus might be just the right person. Lizzie had never heard her sister say a man was handsome until now—except for her beloved husband. There hadn't been any eligible Amish widowers their age in a long time. At least none that would lead to anything romantic.

For a moment Lizzie wondered if this was a silly idea, to play matchmaker at their ages. She decided it wasn't silly at all, and her heart smiled as she lay on the bed, resting her arms behind her head. God would continue to answer her prayers. Lizzie was hoping Esther and the doctor would fall in love. Even though he wasn't Amish, at their age, they could provide each other companionship, go out to supper together, roast marshmallows on a cold night. Esther had put up with her fair share of Lizzie's shenanigans. Her sister deserved another true love in her life.

Lizzie sat up on her elbows and looked up again. *Lord, could you make him be a Christian?*

She didn't want to get too far ahead of herself, but she dozed off feeling content that she was back in the matchmaking role she enjoyed. Only this time, Esther was on the other side of the playing field.

2

———— ✕ ————

Benjamin Stoltzfus stood on the front porch of the cottage he had recently rented. It was smaller than he'd thought it would be. Even though his house in Pennsylvania had become too much to manage, his new temporary home was a bit confining.

He waved when his granddaughter came up the driveway in her little red car. Ben had tried to buy her a newer and larger vehicle, but Mindy wouldn't hear of it. She said she liked the gas mileage and was comfortable in her automobile. Ben worried about her having an accident in such a small car.

"What in the world do you have in those bags?" He stuffed his hands into the pockets of his blue jeans. His granddaughter had already loaded him up with groceries, refusing to let him pay her.

"Just a few things you need." His only living relative

smiled at him. She'd been one of the reasons he had moved to Montgomery. The biggest reason.

Plastic bags hung from both wrists as she made her way up the porch steps. "I brought you a couple of scented candles to help with the musty smell inside, some extra ice trays, and a heating pad for when your back acts up."

"You are a sweetheart." Ben remembered telling his granddaughter how the refrigerator ran on propane and didn't have an ice maker. "The extra ice trays will come in handy, and the candles will be nice." He took the bags from her, smiling. "But unless the heating pad runs on batteries, I'm afraid it won't do me much good. I appreciate the thought, though."

Mindy stomped a foot. "Ugh. That's right. No electricity." She shook her head, then followed him inside. "I still don't understand why you rented a place with no electricity."

Ben had his reasons, but he wasn't ready to share them with his granddaughter yet. He set the bags on the couch and took a quick peek at the items before he reached into his back pocket for his wallet. "I'm not accepting these unless you allow me to pay you."

"Grandpa . . ." She rolled her beautiful green eyes. With her tall build and long, wavy brown hair, she looked so much like her grandmother it startled Ben sometimes. He and Elsa had lost their son, Jimmy, much too young, when Mindy was only four years old. After Nina, his daughter-in-law, had remarried, they'd moved too far away to really get to know his granddaughter, and Nina discouraged visits.

His daughter-in-law had moved on with her life, and it was either too painful for her to be around Jimmy's father, or she just chose to embrace her new life exclusive of the past.

Ben and Mindy had exchanged birthday and holiday cards for years. As much as he longed to be a part of her life, he wanted to do things at her pace. It wasn't until Mindy got older that she really reached out to him, and they began to email on a regular basis. They also talked on the phone when her schedule allowed it, although Ben went to bed early most nights.

His granddaughter was lovely on the outside and equally as beautiful on the inside. Ben was thrilled to be near her.

"I'm serious, Mindy. I have plenty of money, and I don't want you spending your hard-earned cash on me." He roughly estimated what she might have spent, then took two twenties from his wallet, pushing them toward her.

She sighed but took the cash. "I have plenty of money, too, and I enjoy doing things for you."

Ben smiled. He'd only been here a week. She'd likely tire of watching over him. He also doubted that their idea of plenty of money was the same. Ben had more money than he'd spend in his lifetime, especially at his age and in his condition. Mindy worked at a local nursing home, mostly answering the phone, but she also took classes at a community college nearby, hoping to get a nursing degree. Based on things she'd said, such as citing her dislike of anything bloody, Ben wasn't sure her heart was in the right place for a career in the medical field. But there was a shortage of nurses, and Ben would support any decision she made regarding her future.

"I enjoy your visits. You don't have to bring me things." He pointed to the worn couch in the room, a far cry from the sofa he'd had back home—something Elsa had picked out about a year before she passed. Benjamin had left all that behind. Everything but his memories, which he clung to daily, always lifting his spirits. He'd been a blessed man to have shared fifty-two years with such a wonderful woman. "Sit."

Mindy sat in the corner of the couch, which sank slightly as if someone had spent a lot of time sitting in that spot. His granddaughter also had on blue jeans, but they were a lighter color than Ben's, and they had holes in them. It had concerned him at first, but Mindy insisted that was the style for people her age. She'd just turned twenty-two. No husband, no boyfriend. She said work and school kept her too busy for much of a social life. And the girl was too busy to be fussing over Ben. As much as he wanted to spend time with her, she deserved a circle of friends her own age too.

"Do you have any dirty clothes you want me to take to wash?"

"Thank you for offering, but laundry service is included with my rent since there isn't a washer and dryer here. One of the landladies will pick up the clothes and deliver them back to me." It felt odd to have strangers handling his laundry, but his only other choice would have been to drive to a washateria, and he wasn't supposed to drive.

Mindy shifted her weight on the couch.

Ben grinned. "It's not the most comfortable sofa in the world, but I can live with it."

"Will the landladies let you replace it?" Mindy moved her weight again. "I can actually feel a spring poking me."

"Move to your right a little."

She did, squirming around until she got comfortable.

"I'm okay with the couch." He sat down in a rocking chair across from her in the small room. "I like this spot the best anyway. I can see the pond from here." He nodded toward the window to his left. "That pond is supposedly full of fish. It's been years since I threw a line in the water."

Mindy groaned. "Well, you're going to have to find things to do, for sure." She shook her head again. "There's no TV or anything in here."

"Hon, I told you before, I wasn't much of a television watcher at home. Too much bad news all the time."

"But there are so many good movies you could watch if you had electricity, you know, to kill the time." She slouched into the couch and crossed one leg over the other as she smoothed a few wrinkles from her blue blouse.

Ben chuckled. "'Kill the time'? I have plenty to do to keep me busy."

Mindy lowered her brows. "Like what?"

"Believe it or not, I like to be alone with my thoughts. The weather is perfect for walks, and as I mentioned, maybe some fishing." In truth, Ben hadn't been out of the cottage much at all. It hadn't been intentional. He'd just been tired since he arrived a week ago.

He frowned. "By the way, why don't you have a coat on today?"

She laughed. "Grandpa, it's only in the upper forties. I love this weather."

He shrugged as he pulled his jacket snug, then eyed the small fireplace, which probably needed another log. "If you say so," he said, opting to cart more wood in later.

"So, what are your landladies like? Two older women, right?" Mindy lifted a curious eyebrow.

Ben nodded. "I only met one of them. Her name is Esther. She looks to be around my age. Her sister's name is Lizzie, but I haven't met her yet."

Mindy hoped her grandfather would become friendly with the women. Maybe they would invite him to the inn for an occasional meal. Her grandfather was a tall and solid man. Not fat, just solid. But she worried he didn't eat enough vegetables and food that was good for him. In his emails before he moved, he had mentioned stepping out to get a burger a lot of the time. Or Taco Bell. That seemed to be a favorite also. She didn't think he'd cooked a meal since he'd moved here. Based on her last inventory of the kitchen, he'd gone through a loaf of bread in only a few days. Lots of sandwiches, she supposed. Mindy's schedule was so crazy it was hard to squeeze in a home-cooked meal for herself, but she needed to carve out some time to prepare her grandfather some healthy foods that he could just warm up.

"You said you played dominoes with some men back home. Maybe you'll find a group here." She nodded toward the window with a view of the inn. "Maybe the landladies like to play cards or something?"

Her grandfather placed his elbows on his knees, then rested his chin on his hands. "Mindy . . . you know I love you, but you don't need to worry about me, hon."

But Mindy did worry about him. She spoke to her mother and stepfather occasionally, but she wasn't close to either of them. She had loved her grandfather from afar for years. Now was their time to be together, and she wanted him around for a lot longer. If she ever found time to date and get married, she wanted him to live long enough to be there, maybe even get to know his great-grandchildren.

"Well, I do . . . worry about you, that it is," she said, resigned to tell the truth.

"I know you do." He grinned, flashing his pearly white teeth, all of them his. Mindy figured dentists must all have good teeth. "But don't," he added.

She cocked an ear toward the window. "Is that a lawn mower I hear?" She stood and walked to the window. "I thought mowing season was over." She eyed the guy on the tractor in the distance, unable to see him very well. He was Amish. She could make out the hat.

Her grandfather scratched his head. "I saw a lad on a riding lawn mower when I was moving in. It was early

20

evening, and you had already gone home. I didn't realize those type of mowers were allowed."

"From what I'm told, it depends on the bishop and the rules in the district. That goes for mowers, tractors, and other equipment that seems to fall in a gray area." She leaned closer to the window to have a better look. "I guess he's mulching the leaves. They're everywhere this time of year. Although, I don't have many trees in my yard, so the man who mows hasn't been there since the first of October."

She went back to her spot on the couch, inching around until she was able to avoid the spring.

"What are you doing here at four o'clock on a Wednesday anyway? Even though I'm thrilled to see you anytime, shouldn't you be at work or school?"

"I took a day off." She shrugged. "I haven't taken vacation in a while."

"I hope it wasn't so you could go shopping for me." He winked at her.

"No. I just wanted to sleep in and have some time to myself." It was partly true. Between school and work, sleeping had become a luxury. But she'd also had a bad day at work yesterday. Even though her job was mostly to answer the phone, she also assisted the nurses from time to time. They knew she was taking classes to move her career in that direction. She'd observed an older and experienced nurse struggling to put in an IV that a patient had removed. The small woman had dementia and cried hysterically every time Patricia, the nurse, tried to reinsert it. The scene went on for a long while, and Mindy had found it upsetting. The crying, the blood . . .

And later in the afternoon, a patient she was fairly close to had passed away. Mindy had cried all the way home. Sometimes she wondered if she had chosen the right career path, but nursing was so important, and there was a shortage. She was hoping she would get used to the unpleasantness of the job as her schooling progressed.

Her grandfather still had his chin resting in his hands, his elbows on his knees. He slowly straightened, yawning. "Sorry. I'm afraid I'm not sleeping very well. This is an old house, and it creaks at night. I enjoy sleeping with the windows open, but last night the coyotes were howling up a storm. They were a long way off, but you know how loud they can get."

She nodded, then stood up and walked to where he was sitting. "They can get loud. I hear them at my house sometimes too." After kissing him on the forehead, she said, "I'm going to go. You should take a nap."

"A little late for that, don't you think?" He lifted himself from the chair, towering over her. Mindy was five eight, but her grandfather was an easy six foot three, maybe four.

"Never too late for a nap." She smiled, thinking she might take a quick snooze herself when she got home.

They were almost to the door when they heard a loud crash outside. Mindy pulled the door open, then pushed the screen wide. "What happened?" She rushed down the porch steps to where the Amish guy sat on his lawn mower, his brown eyes wide as he stared at the dent in the side of her car.

———•———

Gabriel's heart thumped in his chest as he eyed the dent in the side of the little red car. Then he turned his attention to the woman running toward him.

"What happened?" she asked again.

He started explaining in Pennsylvania Dutch, then collected himself. "Sorry. I'm so sorry. It was a huge branch, and I didn't see it. I ran over it, and it shot from the mower and crashed right into your car." He couldn't believe what a large dent the branch had caused. "I will pay to get it repaired."

All thoughts of the car vanished when the woman locked eyes with his. Gorgeous green eyes that held his captive until he forced himself to blink. "Sorry," he said again as he cleared his throat.

"I'm sure we can get it taken care of, son. It was an accident." The older man walked up to the woman and stood beside her. "Don't worry about it. I'll take care of it."

Gabriel shook his head as he looked down. "*Nee*. It's *mei* fault, and I want to pay for it."

He pushed the rim of his straw hat up and found the woman's eyes again, but she was staring at her car.

"That's honorable, but we can talk about it later." The older man extended his hand to Gabriel. "I'm Benjamin Stoltzfus." He pointed over his shoulder with his other hand.

"I've rented the cottage for the next six months. Moved in a week ago. I reckon we will be seeing each other from time to time if you are a regular worker here."

Gabriel appreciated a firm handshake like this man had. "Stoltzfus? Are you related to—"

"No, I'm afraid not. I know Stoltzfus is a common Amish name, but my only kin is standing next to me." He smiled at the gorgeous young woman next to him. "My granddaughter, Mindy."

Gabriel shook her hand when she tentatively moved it in his direction. Surprisingly for such a dainty woman, her handshake was also firm. She was tall with long brown hair, but it was her twinkling green eyes that Gabriel kept getting lost in.

"*Ya*, I'm here two or three days a week helping Lizzie and Esther with mostly outside work, unless something breaks in the *haus* and I know how to fix it."

They all turned their attention to someone crossing the field in between all three houses, which reminded Gabriel of a baseball field. The inn was home base, the barn was first base, the cottage second, and the other house on the property was third base. He cringed when he saw it was Lizzie coming across the yard, arms swinging at her sides, and wished it was Esther stomping toward them instead. Although Esther didn't stomp. The older sister had a more refined stride. Lizzie looked like a miniature linebacker, and there was never any telling what might come out of her mouth.

"Good grief, Gabriel. What have you done?" Lizzie stared at the dent in Mindy's car, and Gabriel braced himself for a verbal lashing. Esther and Lizzie were two of the kindest people Gabriel knew, and everyone in the community loved the sisters. But Lizzie had a wild side, especially for someone her age. She spoke whatever was on her mind, and if there was a filter, he'd never seen it.

He could still recall Lizzie driving by in her buggy one day when he and some other boys had been outside the school during recess. A fight broke out, which didn't happen often, but when the young teacher struggled to break it up, Lizzie had brought her buggy to a halt, marched her tiny self to the boys, then yanked them both by the ears and separated them. She had also stopped English people on the street and told them, politely, that it was rude to take pictures of the Amish or anyone else without their permission. When she felt strongly about something, she didn't hold back. Gabriel hoped she would hold back right now.

He sighed as he looked at Lizzie, waiting for her to say more, but her eyes were on the big man. Benjamin Stoltzfus, he'd said when he introduced himself. Gabriel wished the earth would swallow him up before Lizzie embarrassed him in front of Mindy. But Lizzie inched around where he was still sitting on the mower and went directly to Mr. Stoltzfus.

Lizzie offered Mr. Stoltzfus her hand. "Hello. I'm Lizzie, one of the owners of the Peony Inn." She blinked her eyes several times at him, which caused Gabriel to grin. "What a pleasure to finally meet you."

Huh? So formal. This didn't sound like the Lizzie he knew.

"The pleasure is all mine." Mr. Stoltzfus smiled at her.

The handshake seemed to go on forever, and Gabriel and Mindy exchanged quick glances. She was grinning too. Lizzie appeared to be smitten with this man, and his granddaughter seemed to catch on, too, as Lizzie continued to smile, forgetting about the dent in the car.

"Would you like to join Esther and me for supper? It's nothing fancy. Pot roast with all the trimmings, buttered bread, chowchow, and apple pie." Lizzie flashed him a bright smile, batting her eyes at him again, which resulted in another glance in Gabriel's direction from Mindy, both of them grinning again like they were sharing a secret.

"I think that sounds heavenly." Mr. Stoltzfus smiled as well. His teeth were straight and white, and Gabriel remembered that Esther had said their new renter was a retired dentist. The man nodded toward Mindy. "This is my granddaughter, Mindy."

"Nice to meet you," Lizzie quipped before she turned her attention to Gabriel and scowled.

"I told them I'll pay for it." Gabriel's heart flipped. He wasn't sure if it was because Mindy was staring at him or if it was fear of what Lizzie might say. Maybe a little of both.

Lizzie waved a careless hand at Gabriel and Mindy. "You two can come for supper, too, if you want." She pinched her lips together and stared at Gabriel as if she was daring him to accept the invitation.

"Uh, I can't, Lizzie. I told *mei bruder* I'd have supper with his family tonight. But *danki*."

"Yeah, I can't, either, Miss Lizzie, but thank you for inviting me. You go ahead, Grandpa." Mindy smiled before she put a hand on her grandfather's arm. "Enjoy the meal, and I'll talk to you soon."

"Shall we?" Lizzie politely motioned for Mr. Stoltzfus to walk with her toward the inn. Gabriel wondered what had gotten hold of Lizzie to make her so polite. He was pretty sure he knew, but he waited until Mindy's grandfather and Lizzie were out of earshot before he turned to Mindy and said, "Did I just imagine it, or did those two seem to take a liking to each other?"

She smiled, and Gabriel's heart did the flip thing again. It was definitely Mindy that brought it on. "Well . . . I couldn't tell if it was one sided or not." She laughed. "I mean, it was hard not to notice Miss Lizzie batting her eyes. I'm not sure if Grandpa was just being polite or not."

"Or was just hungry." Gabriel laughed, and so did Mindy.

"Yeah, right. Either way, I'm happy he's going to have a home-cooked meal. I feel bad that I haven't had time to cook for him."

"Trust me when I say that Lizzie was acting out of character. I love both the sisters, but Lizzie usually shoots from the hip, and the things that come out of her mouth can sometimes be a little shocking, especially for an Amish woman her age."

Gabriel forced himself to look at the dent in Mindy's car

again. "I really am sorry about this." He gestured. "I have an *Englisch* friend who works at a body shop in Bedford. If it's okay with you, I'll ask him to come out here and have a look at it."

"That's so nice of you, but I can drive it to his shop. He'd probably have to repair it there anyway." She held the palm of her hand up when he opened his mouth to speak. "As for the cost, I'm going to leave that to you and Grandpa. He seemed firm about paying for it."

Gabriel shook his head. "*Nee.* I won't allow him to pay for it."

"You could, uh . . . maybe ride with me to your friend's place, though?" She blushed when she asked. "Or not. I'm sure I can find it."

"*Ya*, sure, I can go with you. When?"

"Tomorrow and Friday, I work and have classes in the evening. I could go now." She smiled, her cheeks still flushed. Maybe it was from the crisp breeze. Gabriel didn't think so.

"*Ya*, sure. Now is *gut.*" Spending time with Mindy had suddenly become his number one priority in life. She looked about his age, early twenties. No ring on her finger. She wasn't Amish, but his brain wasn't willing to process any complications that might bring forth. He just wanted to get to know her.

"Do you have to finish mowing?" She glanced around, then let out a small gasp. "Oh. Wait. You said you had plans to eat with your brother tonight, right?"

He shrugged. "I'm done with yard work today. I think I

broke a blade on the mower when I hit that big limb. And I can eat with Matthew, *mei bruder*, and his family anytime. I usually just drop in unannounced around suppertime. Mary Kate insists that I have an open invitation, and she always cooks enough for a dozen people even though they only have one *kind* that's barely old enough to eat real food. I didn't feel like hanging out at the inn." He scratched his chin. "I'd never tell *mei mamm*, but Mary Kate's cooking is some of the best I've ever had." He lowered his hand and chuckled. "Matthew married well in that department."

Mindy smiled. "Well, okay, then. I guess let's go. Maybe we can get something to eat after we go by your friend's shop? I don't want you to starve on my account."

"*Ya, ya.* Sounds great. It's a date." Gabriel chastised himself the moment the words slipped from his lips. He had no business accusing Lizzie of not having a filter when she spoke since he himself seemed to be suffering from the same affliction.

She playfully batted her eyes at him. "It's a date."

Gabriel's heart did the flippy thing again as he hopped off the riding lawn mower and walked with her to the car.

To go on his impromptu date.

3

———— ⋈ ————

E sther spent most of the meal wondering if Lizzie was having a stroke. It would be an understatement to say that Lizzie's behavior was "off." Someone else seemed to be inhabiting her sister's body. And words and movements. Along with everything else that made Lizzie who she was. Esther watched in bewilderment. One thing was clear: Lizzie was smitten with the handsome and charming Dr. Stoltzfus. But as much as Esther wanted Lizzie to have companionship, the good doctor was not seeing the real Lizzie.

"I can't thank you ladies enough for this fine meal." Dr. Stoltzfus flashed his pearly white teeth as he glanced back and forth between Esther and Lizzie. His full head of gray hair was combed to one side, he appeared freshly shaved, and his sapphire-blue eyes matched the jacket he was wearing atop a white shirt. He wasn't boisterous, but he had a deep voice.

Esther dabbed her mouth with her napkin, then cleared her throat. "Lizzie did most of the cooking." She decided to play along, and it was true. Lizzie had prepared the meal, but not without a fuss earlier in the day.

"I love to cook. It gives me great pleasure to please others." Lizzie smiled as she tucked her chin, then cut her eyes in Esther's direction, a warning not to correct the statement.

Esther almost choked on the bite of bread she'd just put into her mouth. She took a quick drink of tea and forced away a grin of amusement. It was true that Lizzie took pleasure in pleasing others, but it wasn't due to her love of cooking. At least not recently. Esther could remember Lizzie preparing meals when they were young girls, then later for her husband and others. But one day, not long ago, she'd stomped a foot in the kitchen, her black apron covered in flour, and said she was tired of cooking. Maybe it was the pressure of preparing meals for large groups when the inn was full, or she'd just baked one too many loaves of bread and was done.

"Do you have a favorite food, Dr. Stoltzfus?" Lizzie glowed like a young girl as she posed the question, her eyes twinkling. "Do you enjoy cooking? What about baking? It's untraditional for men to cook in our district, but *mei* husband, Reuben, enjoyed baking cookies." She smiled. "Do you have any hobbies since you've been retired?"

Lizzie had agreed with Esther prior to the meal that they shouldn't bombard their new tenant with intrusive questions. Lizzie had apparently forgotten the pact.

The bushy gray eyebrows above Dr. Stoltzfus's blue eyes rose slightly as he tipped his head to one side and kept his eyes on Lizzie. "Uh . . . yes, I do enjoy cooking, but I've found that it's hard to cook for one person. Most recipes are for more than one person, and often—at least in my experience—cutting the recipe doesn't always lend the best results. I confess to eating a lot of sandwiches lately, which makes me appreciate this meal even more." He held Lizzie's gaze, the hint of a smile on his face.

"I couldn't agree more about recipes. And we are happy to have you here." Lizzie's features became more animated as she grinned, batted her eyes, and twisted the string on her prayer covering. Even if her sister's behavior was uncharacteristic in current times, she reminded Esther of a young Lizzie during her running-around period—flirty, grinning, blushing—which warmed Esther's heart as she recalled their husbands courting them so long ago. Maybe it was okay that Lizzie had gone against their agreement not to question Dr. Stoltzfus. Especially since the man was smiling and couldn't keep his eyes off Esther's sister. "What about hobbies?" Lizzie added.

His smile broadened as he gave a small shrug. "Hmm . . . I suppose reading is a hobby."

"I love to read!" Lizzie pressed both hands to her chest. "What else?"

Esther slowly took a bite of bread as her eyes bounced back and forth between Lizzie and the doctor, unwilling to miss anything.

"When I was a younger man, I enjoyed woodworking. I had a workshop in our backyard and made the occasional piece of furniture. Small items like end tables." He paused, sighing. "I used to love to fish but rarely made time or had easy access to it."

Lizzie gasped. "There are a lot of fish in our pond. And I like fishing too."

Even though the dentist was still smiling, Esther scowled a little. Lizzie was going to need to ask forgiveness for some of these small lies she was telling. Esther couldn't remember the last time Lizzie had fished at the pond.

"Well, maybe you can escort me to the pond when you have time and show me the best spots to throw in a line."

Esther pushed past her thoughts about Lizzie's little lies. She'd roll back around to that later. Right now, she basked in the knowledge that playing matchmaker between her sister and Dr. Stoltzfus had been a good idea. Although, she worried if their new renter would still be smitten when he got to know the real Lizzie.

"I can show you the best spots." Lizzie pointed her fork at him. "And I don't need a man to put on my live bait. I do that on *mei* own." She lowered the utensil. "I also clean my catch. I'm a low-maintenance fishing partner."

Ah, here we go . . . the real Lizzie emerging. Esther pressed her lips together and tried not to smile.

Lizzie stopped chewing the bite in her mouth and swallowed as her eyes widened. "Uh . . . I mean, I might need some help." She was trying to regress back into the more polished Lizzie, but when Dr. Stoltzfus laughed aloud, Esther wasn't sure it was working.

"Oh no. You said you can do it all. I'm holding you to that." He winked at Lizzie.

Esther wasn't sure she'd ever seen her sister blush the way she was now. And she'd certainly never seen her speechless. There'd been plenty of playful banter going on even though Lizzie had slipped up and shown her true self.

Dr. Stoltzfus finally pulled his eyes from Lizzie and placed his napkin across his plate, a sure indication he was through with the meal, but Lizzie almost knocked over her glass of tea as she bolted upright from the chair.

"You can't leave. We have dessert!"

Esther hoped Lizzie didn't try to hog-tie him to the chair.

The doctor lifted an eyebrow, glanced at Esther, then back at Lizzie. "Uh, of course . . . I wouldn't want to miss dessert."

Lizzie shuffled to the counter and returned with an apple pie that Esther had made that morning. She'd already decided that if Lizzie took credit for the pie, she wasn't going to correct her. It was rather fun watching Lizzie being flirty, however uncharacteristic it was. She remembered Lizzie playing hard to get at the beginning of her relationship with her husband. That didn't seem to be the case with Dr. Stoltzfus.

Lizzie went to the cabinet to retrieve three plates. *What am I doing?* With her back to Dr. Stoltzfus and her sister, she squeezed her eyes closed and reminded herself that the plan was to make sure Esther and Dr. Stoltzfus fell madly in love. Esther was good to everyone, poised, well spoken, and more of a doctor's type. But Lizzie had never been this rattled by a man. Maybe in the early days of her marriage to Reuben, but she'd played hard to get back then, not thrown herself at the man.

She took a deep breath, blew it out slowly, then turned around and walked back to the table, resolved to get control of whatever infatuation had latched on to her. They'd chosen the small kitchen table as opposed to the larger setup in the dining room.

"Esther made the pie." Lizzie needed to get her head on straight and keep on task with the plan. "Esther makes the best pies in our community."

Esther cut into the pie, then handed the doctor a plate. "*Ach*, I wouldn't say that."

Lizzie tapped a finger to her chin as she thought of ways to boost Esther's qualities. Lizzie's sister was the best woman she'd ever known, and any man would be lucky to have her love him. With that in mind, she decided Esther would be able to sell herself on her own, so she opted to stay quiet and quit acting like a flirty teenager.

But when the silence grew awkward, Lizzie couldn't stand it anymore. "Esther, tell Dr. Stoltzfus about the quilt you made, how it was featured in a magazine."

Esther kept her eyes down as she picked at her slice of pie. "Now, Lizzie, I'm sure Dr. Stoltzfus doesn't want to hear about that." She looked up, her face red. "Besides, the bishop wasn't fond of that incident since the article they included with the photo was less than flattering about our lifestyle." She smiled a little. "Speaking of lifestyles, I must ask . . . Do you have relatives who are Amish? I mean, with a name like Stoltzfus."

Lizzie was curious about that, too, and glad Esther asked the question. Lizzie had rambled on enough with her line of questioning.

"No one to speak of," he said without looking up. "This pie is definitely one of the best I've ever had." He smiled at Esther.

"I told you," Lizzie said, struggling not to gaze longingly into the doctor's radiant blue eyes the way the heroines in her romance novels would do. She needed to tone down her infatuation with this man about a hundred notches. Even though, at the end of the day, it wouldn't matter what she did. Esther was more suited for romance with a man like Dr. Stoltzfus—someone well spoken, smart, and with a calm demeanor. If Dr. Stoltzfus was in the market for love late in life, Esther was the best fit for him and the most deserving for a second chance at romance.

Lizzie decided right then and there that she was done trying to impress this man, even though she felt suddenly tongue-tied and unsure of what to say.

"How are your accommodations at the cottage? Is there anything you need?" Esther briefly looked at Dr. Stoltzfus before she took a bite of pie that she shouldn't be having.

Lizzie was tempted to remind her there were sugar-free cookies in the jar on the counter, but she didn't want to embarrass her sister or offer up information that Esther might not want to share.

"Everything is fine." A baffled expression settled across his features. "But there are a few things that give me pause." He chuckled. "It's an older home, so I shouldn't be surprised that there are bumps in the night. It's probably the foundation shifting." Grinning broader, his eyes fixed on Esther. "Someone who believes in such things might think the place was haunted."

Lizzie stopped breathing. *I knew it.* But she'd thought Gus was only haunting her. She bit her lip so hard she feared it might bleed. If she agreed with the man, he might get spooked and want to move out. She drew in a deep breath and forbade herself to confirm that the cottage was haunted, pressing her lips shut so no words of warning escaped.

Esther glared at Lizzie for a couple of seconds, a warning not to say anything, before she looked at Dr. Stoltzfus. "It is an older house. If it bothers you, the other *haus* on the property is newer and bigger."

He nodded. "I considered asking you about that place, but I didn't know if you had plans to rent it to someone else."

"We did," Esther said. "When you inquired about a rental, someone had put a deposit on the guesthouse, but the deal fell through when the man's job transferred him to Illinois. So, it's available if you would be interested in moving."

Lizzie slowly released the breath she was holding, hoping

Dr. Stoltzfus would move into the other house. At some point Esther would be unavailable, and Lizzie might have to enter the cottage to retrieve or return his laundry. Just the thought caused her to shiver.

The doctor wiped his mouth, placed his napkin across his dessert plate, and rubbed his clean-shaven chin. "I think I'll stay where I'm at for now, but I appreciate the offer, and I might reconsider if you don't rent it out soon."

Esther smiled. "It's yours if you want it, but the rent is slightly higher."

Lizzie grumbled under her breath, wishing Esther hadn't said that. It might be a deterrent. Then she surmised that since the man was a retired dentist, he probably didn't have money worries.

Dr. Stoltzfus stood. "I want to thank you again for a wonderful meal. I best be going and get this tired old body to bed." He grinned at Lizzie. "I'll be looking forward to our fishing trip."

Lizzie gulped and forced a smile, wondering how she'd wiggle out of that trip. Her temptation to tell him there was nothing tired or old looking about him hung on the tip of her tongue, but she stayed quiet and took in his tall stance, full head of shimmery gray hair, and straight white teeth. Then she reminded herself again that the man was perfect for Esther.

"We were happy to have you." Esther stood and followed him through the living room, looking over her shoulder to see if Lizzie was coming.

"Good night, Dr. Stoltzfus!" Lizzie yelled without moving from her seat in the kitchen.

He turned, gave a quick wave, and then moved out of sight. Esther looked over her shoulder and scowled at Lizzie as Dr. Stoltzfus opened the front door. Lizzie was sure she had a talking-to coming.

Esther told the doctor bye again, closed the door, then padded back into the kitchen. She slapped her hands to her hips. "Lizzie . . ."

Lizzie sank down in her chair and scowled.

"Sit up. You're not a child who is about to get scolded. But I am wondering what is going on with you."

Lizzie did as Esther instructed, straightened in her chair, and raised her chin. "I don't know what you're talking about."

Esther grunted. "Of course you do. You acted like a silly schoolgirl most of the evening, then did an about-face, and the Lizzie I know was back. It was like flipping on a switch."

Lizzie knew Esther was right, but she couldn't tell her sister she had to give up her infatuation because she didn't want to stand in the way of any spark that might develop between Esther and Dr. Stoltzfus. "I was just trying to be normal."

Esther burst out laughing. "Normal?" She shook her head and began clearing the table.

"Maybe that wasn't the right word. I was trying to be nice." Lizzie thought further about her plan. "I didn't want to blow it for you since the man clearly took a liking to you.

I mean, I was trying to be extra nice, that's all." She sighed. Even if a spark hadn't ignited, it would once Dr. Stoltzfus got to know Esther.

Lizzie's sister spun around with a dish in her hand. "What in the world are you talking about? How could you say he took a liking to me? That's nonsense."

Lizzie stood and began gathering chowchow and jams from the table. "Didn't you see him constantly looking at you? Smitten, I'd say." She wanted to boost Esther's confidence in hopes that she'd spend more time getting to know him. As the doctor got to know Lizzie's sister, a friendly companionship would evolve, and Esther could bask in the euphoria of love.

"If the man took a fancy to anyone, it was you, Lizzie. Although he was probably confused when you went from batting your eyes at him to talking about worms and cleaning fish."

Lizzie shrugged. "*Ya*, okay. I might have been a little infatuated at first by his good looks, but he's clearly your type, not mine. He's smart, like you. He's polished and professional. Maybe even a little stuffy."

After Esther dipped the plate in soapy water, she turned to lean against the counter and chuckled. "Stuffy? I didn't think he was stuffy at all. And I hope you aren't saying I'm stuffy." She shook her head. "It doesn't matter anyway. He's only going to be here for six months." She sighed. "I can't believe we are even having this conversation. We're a couple of old widows. And did you forget that the man is not Amish?"

"We're as old as we feel." Lizzie stashed the items she was holding in the refrigerator. "And at our age does it really matter if he's Amish or not? He looks like a nice Christian man."

"Well, I feel old. And you cannot tell if someone is a nice Christian just by looking at him or her."

"I can," Lizzie spouted.

———◆———

Esther wasn't in the mood to get into a debate with Lizzie. Maybe it didn't matter as much as it should whether the man was Amish or not, but Esther would be hoping he was a good Christian man, and she hoped Lizzie hadn't blown any chance for a close companionship with Dr. Stoltzfus. The man probably thought she had multiple personalities. But now that Lizzie had returned to her normal self, maybe she'd try to spend more time with the doctor . . . as herself. Esther was going to put every matchmaking effort she had in her toolbox to good use. She loved Lizzie so much, and she wanted her to have a companion to lean on someday when Esther was gone. And there had been chemistry between Lizzie and Dr. Stoltzfus. Lizzie was mistaken to think the man had eyes for Esther.

"You mentioned he would only be here for six months. But you don't know that," Lizzie said. "He might be here to stay."

Esther recalled her first conversation with their new

tenant. He had told her on the telephone that he was moving here to be close to his granddaughter. "Maybe. I think he wants to be near his granddaughter, but I'm sure he won't be making his permanent residence in that cottage. He even said it's too small for him. After he finds a permanent home, I suspect we won't see much of him." She realized her thought process was probably correct. She would only have six months to put her matchmaking talents to good use.

"I think you should go fishing with him, like you discussed." She scowled at Lizzie. "Even though you lied about it, along with a few other things."

Lizzie pushed her lips into a pout. "I know. I just wanted him to like us, so he'd come around more. Uh, so you could get to know him better. And I'm not going fishing with him. I told you, he's your type."

Esther sighed. "You are wrong about any thoughts he might have about me, and when you say your prayers, you best ask *Gott* for forgiveness." She paused. "And you should go fishing with him. It's the polite thing to do."

Lizzie grumbled something unintelligible under her breath.

Esther wasn't going to push it. Lizzie's desire to have Dr. Stoltzfus come around more might be misdirected, but if he did, he would get to know Lizzie better, and that was Esther's ultimate goal. She would do what she could to encourage a friendship between Dr. Stoltzfus and Lizzie.

Ben walked to the cottage with a full belly and a light-heartedness he hadn't felt in a long time. The Amish sisters amused him, especially the little one, Lizzie. She'd been trying so hard to impress him that it was impossible not to see through her antics. He had been flattered at first, but then she seemed to turn into someone else right before his eyes. Getting up in age could do that to a person. His mood swings ebbed and flowed sometimes too. But she seemed spunky, and he looked forward to getting to know her better. Esther struck him as the logical and more grounded of the two women, based on his first impression. He also would enjoy getting to know her and learning more about their lifestyle.

Right now, it was his thoughts that ebbed and flowed. He wondered if he had made a mistake by coming here, despite the nice time he'd just had with his landladies. Prior to the move, all he could think about was getting to know his granddaughter, but would he eventually become a burden on her?

He walked into the small cottage, which was warm and cozy, then shook his head as he sat on the couch, careful to avoid the spring. He was not going to allow himself to become a burden to Mindy. He would exercise and eat right, do his best to stay healthy. Maybe Lizzie and Esther would invite him over for another fine meal from time to time.

Mindy's car was gone when he got back, so Ben assumed she and the boy had come up with a plan to get her car repaired, which Ben aimed to pay for. He couldn't take his money with him when he died, and he was sure he was in a better position to take care of the repairs than his granddaughter or the nice Amish kid who clearly felt awful about what had happened.

It was only a few minutes later when Ben headed to bed. Tonight, he'd have pleasant memories of the evening and his new friends whom he hoped to know better. Particularly the spunky one.

———◆———

Mindy followed Gabriel's directions to the buffet at Stoll's Lakeview Restaurant. "Wow. I'm not usually a fan of buffets, but this looks amazing." She'd noticed it was mostly Amish women tending to the buffet, and it was a young Amish girl who had seated them at a table with a view of the lake, gleaming in the evening light.

"*Ya*, the food here is *gut*." Gabriel began filling his plate, and Mindy hoped the food was as good as it smelled and looked.

When they arrived back at their table, Mindy chuckled. "I wasn't sure all that food was going to stay on your plate without spilling over the sides." Gabriel had about five times the amount Mindy had on her plate.

He laughed. "*Ya*, no problem with *mei* appetite."

Mindy lowered her head when he did. She'd been around the Amish enough to know that they prayed silently before meals, and it was something Mindy always did too.

After she took her first bite of chicken smothered in a delicious white gravy, she closed her eyes, sighed, and savored the taste. "Well . . ." She grinned. "Bad me for not coming here sooner. Like I said, I have this thing about buffets. I avoid them, but not visiting this place for the past three years was a mistake." She nodded toward the window. "And the view of the lake is great too."

"I *lieb* buffets." Gabriel laughed. "I enjoy *gut* food, but it's also about the quantity with me, the all-you-can-eat part."

"I see that." Mindy watched him lift up a spoonful of mashed potatoes smothered in the delicious gravy. She took an opportunity to study him briefly. Even with a long-sleeved blue shirt on, she could see he was muscular. Gabriel was tall and carried himself well, she'd noticed earlier. And he laughed a lot, a quality Mindy found appealing. His dark hair was cut in a typical Amish style, except his bangs were longer than most other men and swept to the side on his forehead. She wondered if that was intentional or if he was overdue for a haircut. His straw hat sat on the chair next to him.

"That was nice of your friend to loan me a car while he worked on mine. Benefits of small-town living, I suppose." She took a drink of her tea and watched as he finished chewing.

"Speaking of small-town living . . ." He paused, tipped his head to one side. "You said you've been here three years. What made you come to Montgomery?"

She smiled across the table at him, appreciative that he was staring right at her, not eating, and apparently interested in what she had to say. Her last boyfriend, which had been two years ago, hadn't seemed to listen to her or really care what she had to say. He had a way of shifting the conversation back to himself.

"My dad died when I was four. He had cancer." She watched his reaction, the way his expression fell, but she kept going. "My mom remarried a couple of years later, and that put some distance between us when I was growing up. I don't think it was intentional on her part. She was newly in love, and I get that, but her life was moving on, and I felt a little lost at the time."

He hung his head, his food abandoned. "*Ach*, I'm so sorry."

His sincerity touched her so much, she reached across the table and placed her hand on his. "I'm okay about the situation with my mom. I really am. I mean, we talk and all, but we've just never had the mother-daughter relationship I imagined."

She eased her fingers away. "I don't remember much about my father, but Grandpa said he was a great kid who grew into a wonderful man." She forced a smile and waved a dismissive hand, knowing that talking about her father might bring on tears. If he was anything like her grandfather, Mindy would have liked to have known him. Maybe they would have been close, unlike her and her mother.

"Anyway, as an adult, I began communicating with

my grandfather more, and he said he was familiar with Montgomery, Indiana. He said my father had wanted to move here before he died, but it only took one visit here for my mother to know she didn't want any part of it. I was super intrigued by that since I remember so little about my dad. Grandpa told me about the Amish in the area and how different they were here in Indiana."

"'Different'?" Gabriel had set his fork on his plate and was still giving her his full attention.

"I mean, like the clothes are different, the buggies are black instead of gray, like in Pennsylvania . . . stuff like that."

He nodded.

"It sounded like a quaint town, and before we knew it, we were planning to meet here for a vacation. And this city girl fell in love with the area. My mom about flipped when I said I was going to move here, saying I would hate small-town country living, but she was wrong. In the week that Grandpa and I were here, I landed a job in Bedford. Grandpa and I drove all around, sightseeing, and we ran across an old farmhouse that didn't look lived in, so we inquired about it. It was affordable, I had a job . . ." She shrugged. "So, I moved here. And no regrets."

Gabriel smiled. "*Gott* had a plan. I believe that when things fall into place easily, it was meant to be."

Mindy had always believed that too. "I totally agree."

Gabriel was still staring at her when she took a bite of chicken. "Where did you move from?" he asked.

"Oh . . . I guess I could have mentioned that." She blotted

her mouth with her napkin. "I grew up in Pennsylvania, but only until I was about six. After my mom remarried, my stepfather accepted a job in Houston. It put a lot of physical distance between me and my grandparents, but my mom also seemed to just want to put her entire past behind her and go to a new place." Right or wrong, Mindy hadn't nurtured a relationship with her mother. It took two to have a relationship, and her mother was preoccupied with two other younger children who were Mindy's stepfather's kids.

"Wasn't it hard to leave a place where you have lived for so long?" Gabriel was back to eating, but he kept his eyes on her, gleaming with genuine interest.

"I was terrified. I was nineteen, and I didn't have any other family. I don't have brothers and sisters, and my parents didn't have siblings either. Kind of crazy, I guess. My grandpa had planned to visit when I got settled, but my grandma got sick, and he took care of her until she eventually passed. But after he sold his house and got his affairs in order, he decided to move here. It took him about a year, though." She sighed. "My mom came to visit once after I moved in, took one look at my farmhouse—which I love—and thought I'd made the worst mistake of my life. But I wasn't deterred. Someday I'd like to have a horse, maybe even a couple of chickens. A small farm of my own."

"Country living isn't for everyone, I reckon. But I believe *Gott* helps us achieve the life we were meant to live." He smiled. "I hope you get your horse and chickens."

"Someday," she said again.

"I'm guessing you had a lot of friends in Houston? That must have been hard."

Mindy thought back to her old life. The parties, late nights out, the guys . . . "Yes, I guess you could say that I had quite a few friends. But I felt like I wanted to slow down. Life was moving too fast for me, I think." She chose not to tell him that she'd felt like she was on a path pebbled with self-destruction if she didn't make some changes. She'd never been in any trouble, managed to stay away from drugs, and had barely touched alcohol. But the temptation was always there, and she saw what that lifestyle did to people.

"Well, you picked a *gut* place if you're looking for *slooow*." He stretched out the word, and she laughed.

"I guess a slower life appeals to me. The few Amish people I've gotten to know a little bit seem at peace somehow. Maybe I'm misreading them, but it seems like slower is better. And there's no competition for anyone to be better than another person. I mean, there's no competition regarding clothes, fashion, houses, et cetera. It seems like there would be a certain freedom living that sort of life."

He chuckled. "Some folks might find it boring, but I think you're right overall. We mostly work hard, but tending the land is fulfilling, and the harvest is my favorite time of year, when the fruits of our labor are abundant. I'm not sure 'slower' is the right word, but I understand what you mean. What sort of work do you do?"

"I work at a nursing home in Bedford, and I'm taking classes to get a nursing degree."

He smiled. "Honorable work. Isn't that a long drive, though?"

"About forty minutes, so not too bad. It's nothing like the traffic where I lived in Texas. But . . ."

Gabriel set his fork down on his empty plate and wiped his mouth with his napkin, an eyebrow raised.

"Sometimes I wonder if I've chosen the right career path. I knew I didn't like the sight of blood, but I thought I'd get past that." She ran her finger around the edge of her tea glass. "But I also don't like seeing people in pain. I think that's why I originally chose nursing—to help people who were suffering—but it makes my heart hurt more than I can handle sometimes."

Gabriel nodded. "That makes sense."

"And as for friends, I confess, when Grandpa couldn't visit except a couple of times when I first moved here, I felt sort of alone, at least until I got to know some people." She paused. "I totally understood he wanted to take care of my grandma, as it should have been. But I was thrilled when he said he wanted to move here. I told him I had an extra bedroom, but he was insistent on having his own place, that he didn't want to interfere with my life." She did manage a chuckle this time. "I don't really have a life between work and school. I think Grandpa will eventually buy a place, but he didn't want to rush into something."

He gazed into her eyes as if he was processing everything she'd said. Maybe she was too citified for him or had shared too much. Then his eyes twinkled as his cheeks dimpled. "I hope you don't take this the wrong way, but I'm kind of glad I dented your car."

She smiled as she felt herself blush. "And why is that?"

"We might not have met otherwise."

Mindy was pretty sure they would have been introduced at some point since he worked for the two sisters who ran the inn. But she decided to run with the compliment, raised her glass, and as they tapped the rims, she said, "Then here's to you messing up my car."

Gabriel was quick to pick up the check when the waitress delivered it. "It's the least I can do," he said, grinning. He pointed to the other side of the restaurant where the restrooms were. "I'll be right back."

She nodded, knowing she still had to take him back to the inn to retrieve his horse and buggy, then he had to drive the buggy home. She had to get in her car and do the same. She wished she was the one driving the buggy home, with the wind in her hair, the smell of freshly plowed fields, and that sense of freedom she often dreamed about . . .

After she'd mapped out the rest of her time that evening, she lost herself in thought, searching her memories. There was one thing she'd omitted from her story. It was true that she didn't remember much about her father, but one foggy memory floated around like a restless cloud in her mind. She couldn't quite process it, but she knew it had something to do with a horse and buggy. A gray buggy.

4

Gabriel decided to stop by Matthew's house on his way home. Mindy had thanked him for the meal, he'd apologized for the tenth time about her car, then they had exchanged phone numbers. Gabriel was supposed to only use the phone for business or emergencies. Calling her would become an emergency if he didn't stop thinking about her so much.

"Whoa." He pulled his horse to a stop in front of his brother's house. He had four brothers and two sisters, but he was closest to Matthew, who was twenty-five, two years older than Gabriel, and the only one who had married and moved out. He enjoyed being at their house. Mary Kate was great, and the baby, Lillian, had stolen his heart early on.

"We missed you for supper." Mary Kate opened the

door with Lillian on her hip. The child reached for Gabriel right away, the way she always did. "You're usually here earlier on Wednesdays."

"*Ya*, I had a bit of a mishap earlier." He lifted Lillian up in the air until she giggled as they moved through the living room to the kitchen. Matthew was clearing the dishes. Gabriel liked that his brother did that, and he had always thought he would be that kind of husband—one who helped around the house. Their father was a good man, but he couldn't recall him ever helping in the kitchen.

"What kind of mishap?" Mary Kate draped a kitchen towel over her shoulder and reached for Lillian as Gabriel raided the cookie jar.

"*Ya*, what happened?" his brother asked as he carried plates to the sink.

Gabriel bit into the chocolate-chip cookie even though he was full from supper. Mary Kate's cookies were the best. "I was mowing the lawn at the Peony Inn, and I hit a huge branch. The mower shot it into someone's car. It left a big dent. Not to mention what it did to the lawn mower blade."

"But everyone is okay, *ya*?" Mary Kate steered Lillian away from the cookie jar she was pointing at. "She's already had two," she said to Gabriel, who was chomping down on his second one already.

"*Ya, ya*. No one was hurt. Only the car." He chuckled. "And the lawn mower, I guess."

"You two go chat. I can finish this." Mary Kate set the baby in her high chair and took a jar of jam from her husband.

Matthew kissed her on the cheek and whispered something in her ear that caused his sister-in-law to blush.

"Stop it, you two." Gabriel playfully rolled his eyes and went to the living room. He plopped onto the couch and waited for his brother.

Matthew added a log to the fire, then sat in a large tan recliner that was his spot. His brother never complained about anything and was generally a happy man, but it was an unspoken rule not to sit in his favorite chair. Gabriel did it sometimes just to get a rise out of him.

"I'm guessing the car belonged to a guest at the inn. How upset were they?" Matthew lifted the lever and reclined his socked feet.

Gabriel shook his head. "*Nee*, it was a woman visiting the man who rented the cottage."

"*Ya*, that's right. Someone moved into Gus's old place. Was the lady upset about the car?"

"*Nee*, she took it pretty *gut*. Her name is Mindy. She's the granddaughter of the older man who leased the cottage. We took her car to Harry's place, and he gave her a loaner. Her grandfather—Benjamin Stoltzfus—was insistent on paying for the damage, but I wouldn't feel right about that."

"Stoltzfus? That sounds Amish." Matthew crossed his ankles, tipping his head to one side.

"*Ya*, but he clearly isn't. He was dressed in *Englisch*

clothes. The girl—Mindy—is *Englisch* too. I took her to eat after we left her car at Harry's. I mean, I guess she took me, but I paid for it. I felt bad about what happened."

"It was an accident. And you're taking care of it."

Gabriel nodded, grinning. "*Ya*, and if I was going to smash anyone's car with a branch, I guess I'm glad it was Mindy's."

Matthew frowned as he locked eyes with Gabriel. "Be careful, *mei bruder*."

Gabriel knew where this was going. He'd watched two of his older brothers get involved with outsiders, and it had been a heartbreaking disaster both times. "Don't worry." He smiled. "*Ya*, she's gorgeous, and she's a nice woman, but I'd never pursue her outside of friendship."

It was the first time he could recall lying to Matthew. Pursuing more than friendship with Mindy was all he could think about. Her flowing brown hair, her full lips, and her long legs. He liked that she was tall. And their conversation had flowed naturally, nothing forced.

"*Ya, gut* you realize that." His brother scowled, probably remembering their brothers' ordeals. "Is her last name Stoltzfus too?"

Gabriel rubbed his chin. "I guess. I never asked, but her grandfather is from her father's side of the family, so I'm assuming it is."

"Hmm . . . Montgomery isn't a very big town. I wonder if we've met her."

Gabriel shook his head. "I doubt it. She works at a

nursing home in Bedford, and she also takes college classes. She sounds busy."

"*Gut.*" Matthew smirked at him. "The less time you spend with her, the better."

After they'd chatted about things, Gabriel stood, stretched his arms high above his head, and grinned. "*Ya.* You're right."

"*Mei* words are falling on deaf ears." His brother lowered the foot of the recliner, stood, and walked him to the door.

"*Nee*, I hear you." Gabriel looked over his shoulder and hollered, "Bye, Mary Kate! *Danki* for the cookies."

After he heard a faint response, he bid his brother farewell and headed home.

Throughout the rest of the evening, visions of his beautiful new friend swam around in his mind. He knew he should heed his brother's warnings, but later, when he climbed into bed, Mindy was all he could think about.

——◆——

Lizzie held her pillow over her face as if she could suffocate away her thoughts about Benjamin Stoltzfus. But when she'd held her breath as long as she could, his face was still in her mind. What was it about him that infatuated her so much? He was old but handsome. He was charming. And a dentist. He had a deep voice, but it was impossible not to hear the sincerity when he spoke.

"Argh," she whispered as she threw the pillow on the foot of her bed. The man would be a perfect companion for Esther, and Lizzie needed to keep her head in that game and not let her mind drift in other directions. Esther was far more deserving for a second chance at romantic love, and she wanted that for her sister. Maybe playing matchmaker between Dr. Stoltzfus and Esther would make up for some of the heartache Lizzie had caused Esther over the years. Never intentionally, but Lizzie was aware that sometimes she went overboard in all areas of her life, even if her intentions were meant to be good.

As she lay in bed, she heard Esther snoring in the room next to her, and she had to ask herself . . . What if she was the one to pass on before Esther? Her sister would feel like she'd lost a limb if Lizzie died. Even though Lizzie knew she was a pain in the behind sometimes. She was going to make sure that her sister and the dentist became close friends, maybe more. They were old, not dead yet. And it shouldn't be too hard. Everyone loved Esther. Lizzie just needed to squash this crush she had on the handsome dentist.

———— ◆ ————

Esther awoke startled and gasped. She glanced at the clock on her bedside table, surprised that the digital display read 2:30 a.m. Esther never woke in the middle of the night like this.

There were coyotes howling. Lots of them. They were closer than usual, and she said a quick prayer that the cows would be safe. The pigs, chickens, and horses were too close to the house for the coyotes to bother them, but they had lost two cows to coyotes despite the two donkeys they had roaming the back pasture in an effort to keep away the predators.

She yawned, but the sound of the critters howling had her on edge, and she couldn't go back to sleep. Esther allowed her thoughts to drift in another direction, which caused her to grin. Lizzie's behavior earlier had been so bizarre—first flirty and silly, then back to herself. It was clear to Esther that Lizzie had taken a fancy to Dr. Stoltzfus. And she was sure she'd seen a twinkle in his eyes when he looked at Lizzie. It might have been amusement on his part, but the spark was still there. And Esther was on to Lizzie's plan. Trying to convince her that Dr. Stoltzfus was smitten with her. She was wrong. Esther thought their new renter was a handsome fellow, and he seemed nice enough, but Esther didn't have a romantic bone in her body—at least not for herself. It would be lovely if Lizzie and Dr. Stoltzfus became chummy.

She rolled onto her side, knowing she needed sleep. There was a lot to do tomorrow before their six guests—a group of *Englisch* women who'd sounded about Esther's age when she spoke to one of them on the phone—arrived Friday afternoon. They were going on what they called "a girls' trip." Esther couldn't remember where they were traveling from or going to, but it seemed that staying at the Peony Inn was just a pit stop along the way. They were only staying for one night.

———◆———

Friday morning bustled with activity. Lizzie was mopping the kitchen floor since the cleaning service had canceled due to two sick employees. Esther had gone to the market for produce they needed to serve the six women due to arrive this afternoon. And a chirping smoke detector upstairs was getting on Lizzie's last nerve—definitely the next thing she would tackle.

A knock sounded at the door. She set the mop in its bucket, blew away strands of hair that had escaped her prayer covering, then marched to the front. She had overslept, had more than a plateful to handle this morning, and whoever was banging on the door best be prepared for her mood. "Coming!"

She turned the knob, flung open the door, and was about to tell her visitor she was busy, but the young girl she'd met a couple of days ago stood there, red in the face and breathing hard.

"Have you seen my grandfather?"

Lizzie looked over the girl's shoulder. The young woman must have run from the cottage. A strange car sat parked next to her grandfather's. Lizzie remembered her being in a red car before, the one that had gotten a dent in it.

"*Nee* . . . I mean no. I haven't seen him since he ate with us Wednesday night." Lizzie opened the door wider as she struggled to remember the girl's name. "Come in, come in. It's cold outside."

Mindy, that's her name.

Mindy's bottom lip trembled as she tucked her long brown hair behind her ears. She wore tan slacks, a white shirt, and a tan jacket that didn't look very warm. Fall had arrived in full force, and while pretty this time of year, Lizzie had to blow or sweep the porch of leaves several times per day.

Gabriel would take care of mulching the leaves. She hoped his mower still worked.

She refocused on the girl, wishing her thoughts wouldn't drift the way they did sometimes.

The young woman didn't cross the threshold as she shook her head. "Thank you, but I can't stay. I wanted to know if you have a spare key to the cottage. If so, can I please borrow it?"

"*Ya*, of course." Lizzie held up a finger. "Let me go get it." She scurried since the girl wouldn't come in and instead stood shivering on the porch and visibly upset about something.

She was back in less than a minute. "Here. What's wrong?" she asked as handed over the key and wished Mindy would come in. The wind was blowing through her tiny frame and filling the house with cold air.

"I've been trying to reach my grandfather. I tried all day

yesterday and until late in the night. I've been trying this morning too. I'm on my way to work, but I called and told them I'd be late so I could check on him. I knocked hard on the door several times, but no answer."

"*Ach*, hon." Lizzie touched the girl on the arm, a sudden ache in the pit of her stomach. "I'm sure he's fine, but you come back and let me know, *ya*?"

"Okay." Mindy chewed her bottom lip as she fumbled with the key in her hand. "Will you . . . uh . . . come with me?" She raised her eyebrows, pressing her lips tightly together.

"Huh?" Lizzie's heart pounded, and she clenched her dentures. Just the thought of going inside the haunted cottage sent a tingle up her spine. Dr. Stoltzfus was most likely napping and just hadn't heard the knocking.

"I'm sorry. It's just that I'm worried . . . um . . . about what I might find." Mindy blinked back tears as her eyes pleaded with Lizzie.

Lizzie swallowed hard and wished Esther were here. Not only would it be an opportunity for her sister to see Dr. Stoltzfus again, but if anything did happen to be wrong, Esther was better in a crisis. But the girl's concern for her grandfather was rubbing off on Lizzie.

"*Ya*, of course. Of course I'll go with you, hon." She grabbed her black cape off the rack by the door, then slipped into her black loafers, hoping she would be able to stay on the cottage porch and not have to go inside.

Mindy was still out of breath from her apparent sprint

to the inn, but she stayed in step with Lizzie as they quickly crossed the field.

"We've talked every day since he moved here, and I'm so worried." The girl shook her head. "If anything happened to him—"

"I'm sure he's fine." Lizzie spoke with confidence, but her insides churned. By the time they reached the cottage, her heart pounded like a bass drum in her chest. She slowly followed Mindy up the porch stairs, each step feeling heavier than the last.

The distressed girl shook as she knocked on the door. "Grandpa?" There was a tremor in her voice that tugged at Lizzie's heart, and when she began struggling with shaky hands to get the key in the lock, Lizzie edged closer to her.

"Here, hon. Let me get that. The lock is tricky." Lizzie pulled the door toward her slightly, knowing that was the only way the lock would click into place, then pushed the door open and stepped aside. "I'll wait here," she whispered just in case Gus's ghost could hear her from where she stood on the porch.

"No, please come with me."

Mindy was probably in her twenties, still a child in Lizzie's eyes, and she supposed this must be terrifying for her. Lizzie felt equally as scared to step into the cottage—her fear twofold—but when Mindy latched on to her arm, Lizzie told her feet to move.

All was quiet in the small living room. They could see

the empty kitchen from where they stood. All that was left in the small cottage were the bedroom and the bathroom. Lizzie dutifully followed Mindy to the former, where they found Benjamin Stoltzfus lying perfectly still in bed.

"Grandpa!" Mindy screamed, but the man didn't move, and Lizzie became light-headed. She wasn't sure if it was Gus's ghost or fear that their renter had died on them. She decided the latter possibility took precedence, which meant Lizzie would have to check to see if the man was breathing. She took a few steps closer while Mindy began to cry.

The doctor lay on the bed, his chest rising and falling.

"He's breathing," Lizzie said in a whisper as she bent over him.

"He must be unconscious." Mindy's voice cracked as she sniffled. "I should call 911."

"Wait a minute." Lizzie squinted as she leaned closer to Dr. Stoltzfus. She then yanked on both of his ears, pulling out the plugs nestled in each one.

Benjamin reacted immediately. In one swoop, he grabbed Lizzie around the waist, threw her on the bed on the other side of him, then jumped on top of her. Lizzie hollered at the top of her lungs, closed her eyes, and began swinging at him in every direction, making contact with his face at least twice.

"Grandpa! It's just Lizzie!" Mindy hovered behind him, attempting to pull him off Lizzie.

As his weight finally lifted, Lizzie rolled onto the floor with a thump. Of course she had to hit face down. When she sat up, she peered to the other side of the room, where the dentist stood with a dropped jaw. Mindy's eyes were wide as saucers.

"Are you okay?" The crazy dentist walked around the bed. "I thought you were a burglar. I'm so sorry." He offered her his hand, but Lizzie pushed him away and stood on her own. Handsome or not, this fellow was nuts.

Mindy picked up his cell phone on the side of the bed. Lizzie had no idea who the girl might be calling, nor did she care. All this was bound to stir up Gus's ghost, and she'd just been manhandled by a man in his underwear, which was unnerving in and of itself.

"Grandpa, your phone is dead." Mindy swiped at her eyes. "You scared me half to death."

"Sweetheart, I am so sorry." He gave a comforting look at his granddaughter, then started toward Lizzie again, his hand outstretched.

Lizzie took several quick steps backward. "Good grief. Put some clothes on over those undergarments." She covered her eyes with one hand, but she could still see him in his white underwear and T-shirt of the same color.

"I wasn't expecting company. And these are shorts, not underwear." He grinned when he said it.

Lizzie had had enough. Despite peeking between her fingers, she still ran into the bed frame, cried out, then darted for the door with Mindy and the dentist calling after her. She didn't look back or stop until she was back at the inn. She was glad to see Esther pulling her buggy onto the driveway.

Her sister stepped out carrying one bag, then gasped. "What in the world happened to you?"

Lizzie reached up and touched the top of her head. In the scuffle, she'd lost her prayer covering, and bobby pins held only some of her hair in place, leaving the rest of her gray strands blowing in the breeze.

"Lizzie, I think you have the beginnings of a black eye. Who did this to you? Were you assaulted?" Esther set the bag on the ground and moved closer to her sister. "*Ach*, Lizzie, honey. Let's get some ice on your eye and make sure you're not hurt anywhere else. What happened?" She latched on to both of Lizzie's arms.

Lizzie shook free and pointed over her shoulder to the cottage. "I'll tell you what happened. I was in bed with that crazy dentist, who jumped on top of me, then pushed me out of bed, which I think might have been an accident. I hit him a few times, though. He probably has a black eye too. I hope so. Crazy man." She clenched her fists at her side. "And all over a dead cell phone and a pair of stupid earplugs."

Esther's mouth hung open as she slowly pointed to the cottage. "Dr. Stoltzfus and his granddaughter are walking this way."

"Does he have clothes on?" Lizzie tried to shake the inappropriate image from her mind, but she suspected it would replay in her mind whether she wanted it to or not.

Esther bit her bottom lip, but Lizzie could tell she was trying not to laugh. "*Ya*, he has clothes on," she said, nodding.

Lizzie waved a hand in the air. "I'm going in. Tell them I'm fine."

She slammed the door behind her, went to the bathroom, and looked at herself in the mirror, then sighed. She didn't think she'd ever had a black eye before.

5

Ben couldn't believe what had just happened.

"Don't ever do that to me again, Grandpa," Mindy said as they closed the space between the cottage and the Peony Inn. "I was scared to death."

"I'm so sorry, Mindy. I really am. I didn't notice my phone was dead yesterday, and I should have mentioned that I sleep with earplugs." He ran a hand through his white hair, which needed a trim. Then he rubbed his stubbly chin. Since Lizzie seemed to think she'd caught him in his underwear, he'd thrown on a pair of slacks. He cringed when he thought about the way he'd tackled her, then how she fell off the bed.

They slowed their stride when they reached Esther standing by her buggy and holding a grocery bag. He'd already seen Lizzie sprint into the house.

"You look about as *gut* as Lizzie." Esther raised

an eyebrow as she studied his face, which already looked swollen.

"Yeah, your sister can pack a punch. Not that I blame her. I feel terrible about what happened. She startled me, and I lived in the city, where crime is rampant. I need to remember that I'm in a safer environment." He hung his head, then met Esther's eyes. "Is she okay?"

"I think so. I'll go check on her in a minute. I saw you walking this way, so I waited."

Esther appeared stoic, composed, levelheaded. Her sister was a quirky spitfire. Ben wondered how they shared the same genes.

"I guess this isn't a good time to talk to her and apologize again?" Ben grimaced.

"Probably not." Esther shifted the paper bag on her hip. He didn't know stores even used paper bags anymore, and this one was ripped at the corner with ears of corn, stalks of celery, and bananas peeking over the top of the bag.

"At least let me carry that bag in for you." He walked toward her and gently eased the bag from her arms. "It's as heavy as it looks."

"*Danki.* I mean thank you."

Mindy cleared her throat. "Grandpa, I've got to get to work." She pointed a finger at him. "Don't ever do this to me again. Go get your phone charged somewhere today." She leaned around the groceries in his arms and kissed his cheek.

"I'm sorry again." The day had barely begun and Ben already wished it was over.

"Miss Esther, please tell Miss Lizzie I'm sorry about what happened and I hope she isn't hurting too much."

"I will, Mindy. I'm sure she'll be fine."

Ben's granddaughter trotted back to her car.

"I feel terrible she's late for work and that she was worried," he said to Esther. "I feel even worse about Lizzie." He heard the shakiness in his voice. He was a big man with strong hands, and Lizzie was such a tiny woman. "I'm not going to feel better until I see her for myself."

"Well, let's at least get these groceries in the *haus* and some ice on your eye." Esther motioned for Ben to follow her.

They crossed through the living room, a comfortable space with white walls and tan furniture but enough color to make it cozy. Orange embers shimmied upward in the fireplace, and the aroma of something delicious hung in the air. *Homemade bread.*

When they entered the kitchen, Ben stopped abruptly. Lizzie was slouched down in a kitchen chair with a package of frozen peas on one eye and her other eye closed. Her lip was swollen too. She had a tan scarf covering her head.

"Is that wacky dentist back at the haunted cottage? I'm sure Gus caused all of that! And you can tell Dr. Stoltzfus that I'd prefer not to be around him for the remainder of his lease agreement." Lizzie huffed. "In addition to assaulting me, I saw the man half naked. How can I face him?" Her teeth clinked as she frowned, and Ben suspected she wore dentures.

Esther grinned as she glanced at Ben. "I guess you're going to have to face him since he's standing right here."

Silence. And no one moved. Then Lizzie slowly lowered the bag of peas from her eye and opened her other one. She studied Ben.

"It appears I have a pretty *gut* right hook. You look worse than me." She rolled her eyes before placing the bag of peas on her eye again.

Ben set the groceries on the table, sure he'd never felt so low in his life. "Lizzie, you can't imagine how bad I feel."

She jerked the peas off and glowered at him. More eye-rolling before she covered her bad eye. It hurt Ben to look at it.

"Sit down, Dr. Stoltzfus." Esther pulled out a chair for him, right next to Lizzie, who didn't seem to appreciate it when she scooched her chair over and away from him. "Put this on your eye," Esther said.

It was an ice pack, and he did as instructed while Esther unpacked her groceries.

No one said anything. When it became too awkward to bear, Ben asked, "What did you mean when you said Gus caused all of this? Who is Gus?"

Esther cleared her throat and said a quick prayer that Lizzie would be quiet. "He was our prior renter." She stashed celery in the refrigerator and continued to unpack her groceries.

Lizzie slammed her peas down on the table and huffed. Her sweet demeanor was no longer in play when it came to the dentist. She'd returned to full Lizzie mode, and Esther feared what might come out of her sister's mouth.

Before Lizzie said anything, she touched her swollen lip, then said, "Ouch. Even *mei* mouth hurts." She put the peas back on her eye.

Esther hoped the conversation wouldn't turn back to Gus.

Dr. Stoltzfus hung his head, visibly more concerned about Lizzie than about himself. He waited a few seconds before he spoke. "How could your prior renter have caused the problems at the cottage?"

Esther shook her head and kept her back to the black-eyed duo, knowing Lizzie would run with it.

"Gus caused the problems because he is a ghost in the cottage. I thought he was only haunting me, but you said you are hearing bumps in the night, so I guess you're a target too." Lizzie groaned. "But that doesn't completely excuse your irrational behavior."

Esther slowly wheeled around and leaned against the kitchen counter, turning her attention to their renter. "I have explained to Lizzie that there are no such things as ghosts and that the bishop would not approve of her thoughts about Gus. Nor would *Gott*." Shifting her gaze into a glare and focusing on her sister, she said, "That's enough of all that nonsense, Lizzie."

"Well . . ." Dr. Stoltzfus flipped the ice pack over and repositioned it on his face. "There have been some strange happenings over there."

Lizzie's bag of peas fell to the table as her jaw dropped. "See!" She pointed at their guest, then turned to Esther. "I told you so! What have you seen?" Lizzie put her elbows on the table, leaned forward, and cupped her chin with her hands.

Dr. Stoltzfus shrugged. "I haven't really *seen* anything. There's just a lot of unexplainable noises." He glanced at Esther. "As you confirmed, it's an old house, so the foundation is probably shifting." He chuckled. "There was a time when the can opener came on by itself. And a book fell off the mantel."

Lizzie's eyes were so wide, Esther feared they might pop out of their sockets. She scooted her chair as close as she could get to Dr. Stoltzfus and put a hand on his arm. "Don't let Gus know he scares you. Pretend you don't notice his shenanigans. Maybe he'll know he's not supposed to be here and cross over to the other side. That's what my book says you should do when dealing with these kinds of things."

Esther could feel the burn of embarrassment on her face. "Lizzie, you stop this nonsense right now. Gus isn't haunting you or the cottage." She was shocked that Dr. Stoltzfus seemed to be buying into this silliness. But then Esther noticed a glint in his eyes as he watched Lizzie carry on, along with the hint of a smile on his face.

Lizzie eased her hand away from the doctor but leaned close to his ear. "Easy for her to say, *ya?*"

Dr. Stoltzfus glanced past Lizzie at Esther, and while

Lizzie wasn't looking, he winked at Esther. She smiled. He must just be playing along with Lizzie. It had certainly won him some fast points. Lizzie was sitting right next to him and had even put her hand on his arm. If this was what it took to get Lizzie and Benjamin Stoltzfus to be good friends, then she was willing to take a step back and let this play out.

"Maybe you'd like to take a walk and compare notes?" Dr. Stoltzfus smiled at Lizzie. Esther had to admit, he was a flirty fellow, especially for a man his age. "Unless it's too cold for you?"

Lizzie shook her head. "*Nee*. Not too cold for me."

The sounds of voices outside stopped the conversation. "Oh no!" Esther brought a hand to her chest. "The ladies are here. I didn't even hear their van pull up. They aren't supposed to be here until this afternoon. We're not ready. I haven't even taken the sheets from the line." She moved her hand to her forehead.

"Let's take that walk," Lizzie said as she ignored the crisis.

"You will do no such thing," Esther snapped as she pointed at her sister. "You will help me get things together. I will explain to the women that I thought they were coming later and that we don't have their rooms ready. I'll suggest that maybe they visit some of the local shops."

Esther jumped as a herd of footsteps came up the porch steps, followed by a loud knock on the door. She glowered at Lizzie. "You go get the door. I'll set out cookies and tea."

But when Lizzie stood, Esther stepped in front of her. "*Nee*, never mind." She flinched at her sister's busted lip and swollen black eye. "You set out cookies and tea in the dining room. I'll get the door."

"You can't hide me forever," Lizzie said before she cackled.

"*Ach*, well, we need to hide you for now." Esther cupped Lizzie's elbow. "Get busy. Get the plates from the china cabinet in the dining room."

Lizzie cried out. "I'm hurt! Be careful!" She scampered out of the room.

Dr. Stoltzfus, who looked as bad as Lizzie, stood. "I should probably sneak out."

Esther's chest tightened. This wasn't the image she wanted to project to this nice group of women. "If you don't mind. You can go out the kitchen door just as I let the ladies into the living room through the front door."

Suddenly there came a flurry of footsteps, and all six women stood at the entrance to the kitchen. "I-I am so sorry," stammered one of them. "I'm Roberta Huffington. We spoke on the phone. One of our group feels light-headed, and when no one answered, we let ourselves in. We need a glass of water, please." The woman looked to be in her seventies, as Esther had presumed when she spoke to her on the phone.

"*Ya, ya*. Of course." Esther scrambled to the refrigerator and took out a bottled water just as Lizzie reentered the kitchen. When she turned around, all six women were staring at Lizzie and Dr. Stoltzfus as if waiting for an explanation.

Esther handed the bottle of water to Roberta, not even offering her a glass with ice. She needed to intercept the conversation before it got started. "Excuse *mei* sister's appearance"—she swallowed hard—"and our friend. They had an accident."

"*Ya.*" Lizzie nodded to Dr. Stoltzfus. "He pushed me out of bed."

Esther was a passive person who had led a mostly passive life, but right now she could have strangled Lizzie. All six women had varying degrees of shock on their faces, from dropped jaws to rapid eye blinking, and one of them even clutched the doorframe as if she might fall.

"It's not how it sounds." Esther tried to laugh, but it came out more like a trio of coughs.

"Let's go talk somewhere else about the ghost in the cottage." Lizzie took Dr. Stoltzfus's hand, and they exited out the kitchen door.

The doctor looked over his shoulder at Esther and shrugged, then winked at her again. Was he toying with Lizzie, and the wink was to signal that? Or was he toying with Esther?

She twisted to face her six guests, who stood huddled in the living room around one of the women, who was drinking the water.

"Can I get you anything else?" Esther asked. "I was just getting ready to put some cookies on the table in the dining room." She pointed to her right. "It's right through that door."

No one moved.

———◆———

Lizzie had no plans to default from her mission to fix up Esther and Dr. Stoltzfus, but she was thrilled that he believed the cottage was haunted too. She was even willing to overlook his crazy behavior to discuss it. Esther would be okay for a little while. This was important.

"I really am sorry about what happened." Dr. Stoltzfus was a giant walking next to her toward the cottage. She'd forgotten her cape, and her face was tight, cold, and tingly from the pack of peas she'd left on the kitchen table.

She took a sharp turn to her left, and Dr. Stoltzfus followed. "Where are we going?" he asked.

Lizzie pointed to the vacant house on the property. "I'm not going back in that cottage. We can talk inside the other house."

She briefly thought about how inappropriate it would be to spend time alone with the dentist, but it would be worth the indiscretion to avoid Gus and the cottage. She figured that rule only applied to younger people anyway.

After they went up the porch steps, Lizzie lifted the mat and produced a key. Inside, she waved an arm around the fully furnished place. "This one doesn't have electricity, either, but there's more room, and to my knowledge, it isn't haunted."

Dr. Stoltzfus rubbed his chin. "Hmm . . . It does have a lot more room."

"And you wouldn't have to worry about Gus." She put a hand on her hip, which was a little sore, and said, "Why would you want to live in a house without electricity anyway? You're not Amish. Aren't there places you could rent that would be better suited for you?" She didn't want the doctor leaving, but curiosity trumped her reasoning. "And Stoltzfus is an Amish name. You sure you don't have kin here?"

The doctor went from room to room in the two-bedroom home, then returned and sat on the couch. "I don't have kin here. Just Mindy."

Lizzie sat at the opposite end of the couch and scratched her cheek. She didn't want to push him away with too many questions, but there was a story here. Lizzie could feel it.

Refocusing her thoughts, she decided it would make her life a lot easier if Dr. Stoltzfus moved into this house. Her refusal to go inside the cottage irritated Esther, and rightfully so due to the laundry arrangement, but Lizzie couldn't be expected to deal with Gus. Her sister was being unreasonable when it came to that.

"Do you want to move into this house or not?" Lizzie crossed one leg over the other and placed her hands on her knee.

"I'd like to think about it." He flinched a little when he

touched his lip, which Lizzie noticed had a small cut, matching the one on her lip. *No kissing, for sure.* She felt her face reddening at the thought and reminded herself again that this man was Esther's type. Maybe she needed to get rid of her romance books along with her ghost and murder books. The doctor wasn't a murderer. She knew all she needed to know about hauntings. And perhaps her romance books were causing her to have thoughts that an old woman her age shouldn't have.

Dr. Stoltzfus grinned, but only on one side, which made him look a bit ridiculous, but Lizzie could only imagine what she must look like. "So, why do you think this Gus fellow is haunting you?"

Lizzie sighed. "I guess you could say that Gus and I had a love-hate relationship. The man was grumpy and belligerent." She cringed, worried Gus might somehow hear her. Even if he couldn't, the Lord could. "But he softened prior to his death." She shook her head. "Gus took every opportunity to harass me, was always critical, and just generally mean sometimes." Again, she thought about what God would think and the ways Gus truly did change toward the end. "But I thought me and Gus had made our peace before he died." She rolled her eyes. "Clearly, I was wrong."

"Lizzie . . ." Dr. Stoltzfus raised the eyebrow above his good eye. "I'm sure there is a logical explanation for anything you might mistake as a haunting."

She huffed. "I thought you believed me."

He held up a hand, his lopsided grin returning. "I'm not saying I don't believe you, but it's worth entertaining reasonable explanations. Maybe the batteries on the can opener are about to fizzle, and it's shorting out. The foundation is unlevel, thus the creaks. And that's probably what caused a book to slide off the fireplace mantel. It's not level and shifted when the house did."

Lizzie frowned, which hurt. "You sound like Esther."

"I'm just presenting other options for you to consider."

She boldly met his eyes, disappointed he wasn't more onboard about Gus, but she decided to make the most of this time. She patted the spot on the couch between them. "No loose springs on this one." She waved an arm around the room. "Lots more room." He still hadn't said why he'd chosen a house without electricity, but Lizzie didn't want to veer from the opportunity at hand.

"What if I can prove to you that the cottage isn't haunted?" He stared at her so intensely that it made Lizzie squirm.

"That's not possible. It *is* haunted, whether you believe it or not. But either way, this house would be a better fit for you." *I could bring you clean towels or launder your clothes. I could avoid that haunted cottage. Esther would be happy.* The laundering was an arrangement they'd made with him in the rental agreement since there wasn't a washer and dryer in the cottage or in this house either. Gus had used the washateria in town. Mostly he just wore dirty clothes and smelled all the time.

The doctor nodded, and Lizzie smiled on the inside since it hurt too much to show her enthusiasm. She stood as a wave of relief washed over her. "Great. I'll let Esther know you're moving. We can arrange for some folks to help you."

He stood, still with the intense look on his face, his eyes locked on her bruised-up face, which left her feeling self-conscious as she grabbed the ends of her scarf and attempted to tie them under her chin. Her shaky hands were failing her.

Dr. Stoltzfus took two slow steps toward her. "Let me help you." He eased the two ends from her hands and gently made a loose knot beneath her chin. "You're shaking."

"Of course I am. It's cold in here." Lizzie knew her shaking wasn't just from the cool air in the house. It was the feel of the doctor's hands on hers, and she reminded herself that she was a woman in her seventies, not a hormonal teenager or young adult like in her books. Books that were all going away. Esther was right. The bishop and God wouldn't approve of her reading choices that seemed to have an unsettling effect on her.

Stick to the plan.

"If you let me cook supper for you tomorrow night, I'll consider moving into this house." He folded his arms across his chest.

Lizzie lifted her eyes to his and stared at him, hoping to get a glimpse into his motivations. The offer surprised her. Was he serious? "*Ya*, okay," she finally said. She put a finger to her chin. "Can you even cook?"

He chuckled. "Yes. I know how to cook. Some people think I'm quite good at it."

She sighed, willing to sacrifice a night with the doctor to get him to move into this house that wasn't haunted. It would also give her a chance to talk up Esther.

She nodded toward the kitchen that wasn't visible from the living room in this house. "The kitchen is stocked with pots and pans, along with anything else you might need to prepare a meal. What time do you want me here tomorrow?" Her heart was beating too fast. She casually brought a hand to her chest, hoping to calm herself and keep on course with her plan.

The lopsided grin returned. "Here? No, no. Not here. I will prepare supper for you at the cottage." He paused. "I'll prove to you that the place isn't haunted."

Lizzie froze. There was no way she was going to voluntarily spend more time in that place. This morning had been an exception that would never happen again.

And yet . . . The more she thought about it, the more her plan evolved.

"Fine." She raised her chin. "What time?"

"Five o'clock tomorrow evening at the cottage. Do you have any allergies?" He half smiled again.

"I try to avoid sugar as much as possible." It wasn't true. Lizzie loved all things sugary. Her laundry list of lies was growing, and she'd have to remember to ask for forgiveness. But she wouldn't be the one showing up at the cottage.

6

———— ✂ ————

Esther thanked all the ladies for choosing the Peony Inn as she ushered them out the door. She was sure they wouldn't be coming back, whether they had specifically chosen this inn or if it had just been a pit stop like she'd assumed. She'd overheard one of the women say, "I thought the Amish were passive. Did you see the black eyes that both that man and woman had? It just seems bizarre, him throwing her out of bed and them beating each other up, married or not."

Esther had tried to explain, but she couldn't help but laugh now at her efforts, which had clearly failed. She'd told Lizzie to sleep in, that she would handle breakfast for their guests on her own. Lizzie hadn't argued. But the women were still packed before the meal and left immediately afterward Saturday morning.

Lizzie came into the kitchen yawning and with a slight limp. "The older we get, the harder we fall," she said as she made her way to the percolator. "Sorry I didn't help this morning."

"That's okay. Your appearance seemed a little off-putting to our guests. And I thought you might need the sleep. Aside from your face, I see you're limping."

"My hip is a little sore, but I'm not sure if it's from falling off the bed or falling off the step stool yesterday when I was changing the batteries in the smoke detector upstairs." She sat down at the table, and Esther decided the dishes could wait and joined her sister.

"How did it go with Dr. Stoltzfus yesterday? Is he really buying into all your haunted nonsense?" Esther grimaced. "He doesn't seem like the type of man who would believe any of that."

"I'm not sure, but he's thinking about moving into the other house. Then I wouldn't have to worry about going to that cottage again, and I could help you cart his laundry back and forth." Lizzie paused, grinning. "By the way, he invited you for supper tonight at the cottage. You're supposed to be there at five. Apparently, the man can cook."

Esther stiffened. "What? Why?" She'd hoped maybe the dentist and Lizzie would enjoy their time together the day before and possibly start spending more time with each other. "Why didn't he ask you? You were the one with him?"

Lizzie placed her hands firmly on the table. "The man is smitten with you, that's why."

"*Ach*, well . . . I'm not going." Esther was flattered, but she had to get out of this.

"Why not? We don't have any guests tonight. What's wrong with letting someone cook for you? You deserve a break." Lizzie raised an eyebrow but flinched.

Esther's heart rate spiked. She had to admit, the thought of spending time with Dr. Stoltzfus was appealing, but she refused to get derailed from her plan. "I just don't understand." Still, she recalled Dr. Stoltzfus winking at her. Could he really have a romantic interest in her? She quickly dismissed the thought. There had definitely been a spark between Dr. Stoltzfus and Lizzie during supper.

Lizzie sighed. "Esther, just go have supper with the man tonight." She stood, rubbed the back of her neck, and said, "I'm going back to bed."

Maybe Esther could use the time to tell Dr. Stoltzfus Lizzie's good qualities. Despite her quirkiness, Lizzie was the most giving person she knew. Sometimes her efforts were misplaced, but she had the biggest heart of anyone Esther had ever known.

Esther would go to supper and try to sell Dr. Stoltzfus on the Lizzie he really didn't know yet.

———◆———

Mindy thanked Gabriel and his friend for handling the repairs on her car so quickly. His friend gave a quick wave before heading back to work, leaving Mindy and Gabriel standing by the car.

"I can't even tell there was a dent." She held out her

hand again, flashing the cash her grandfather had insisted she take earlier that morning when she'd stopped to check on him. "Are you sure you don't want this money? My grandpa said he isn't taking it back."

Gabriel shook his head. "*Nee*, I wouldn't hear of it."

Mindy groaned. "Well, I don't feel right about keeping it. I'll get it back to him somehow, but we can at least use it to go eat lunch somewhere . . . if you're free." She held her breath, hoping he would say yes. She hadn't been able to stop thinking about him.

"Lunch sounds *gut*." He smiled, and Mindy let out the breath she'd been holding.

They spent the short drive to the restaurant talking about the weather. Gabriel mentioned how the sun was shining, not a cloud in the sky, a perfect day to do something outside. Mindy wondered if he was working up to something, a way for them to spend the day together.

They chose the same restaurant as before with the lake view. "Who would have ever thought I'd love this place with a buffet," she repeated as Gabriel opened the door.

Then they were ushered to the same table as before.

"What are the chances?" she asked as she sat down.

Gabriel grinned and shrugged. "Meant to be, I guess."

She wasn't sure how to take that, but after they filled their plates and sat down, he got an inquisitive look in his eyes. He waited until he was done chewing a chunk of roast before he spoke.

"*Mei bruder* asked me about your last name. I'm

assuming it's Stoltzfus since you said your grandfather is on your *daed*'s side of the family. Stoltzfus is definitely an Amish name. Are your relatives Amish?"

Mindy was surprised he hadn't asked this before. She'd been questioned at least a hundred times about her name since she'd moved here. "If they are, they must be so far down the line that no one knows about it." In her dream world, she was secretly Amish and enjoying all the peacefulness that went along with the role.

"Hmm . . ." Gabriel picked up a slice of bread and began slathering butter on it. "I just wondered."

They were about halfway through the meal when she told Gabriel about the bed incident with her grandfather and Lizzie.

He laughed so hard, Mindy thought he might spew food. "I would have loved to have seen that." He flinched. "But it's too bad they both have black eyes and busted lips."

"Oh, there's more. Do you want to hear a fun fact I just learned this morning?"

"*Ya*, sure," he said through a mouthful and a grin.

"Grandpa told me that he is having Lizzie over for supper tonight." She smirked as she waited for his reaction.

"You mean, like a date?" His eyes widened.

"Apparently, Lizzie thinks a man named Gus is haunting the cottage, and Grandpa wants to prove that such a thing isn't going on. But yeah . . . I think it's kind of a date too." She leaned back in her chair and smiled. "I think it's sweet at their age."

"It's sweet at any age." Gabriel winked at her and sent her heart fluttering. This was their second time to go to lunch, but she wondered if he would ask her out. But where could it go even if they did fall for each other? She didn't want to think about that right now.

"Although . . ." Gabriel paused, tipped his head to one side. "I'm a little surprised that Lizzie is the one he asked out. You can probably tell from the short time you've been around her, she's a bit kooky. I guess 'eccentric' is a better word. Since he's a dentist and all, I would have thought Esther to be more his type—kind of conservative. Maybe it's all about proving that the cottage isn't haunted, and there's nothing more to it than that. What was your grandma like?"

"Remember, I wasn't around them when I was growing up, so I don't really know. But based on the little time I've spent around both women, and based on what you've said, I agree that Esther seems to be more his type." She laughed aloud. "It's funny that we're even talking about this. I can't see Grandpa having a romance with either one of them."

"Maybe all three of them will just be *gut* friends." He playfully pointed his fork at her. "But I want a full report after this little date your grandpa has with Lizzie."

She nodded and smiled on the inside, since that meant they'd potentially see each other again. "I'm sure he's not one to kiss and tell, but . . ." She laughed again. "After what happened in the cottage before, I'm a little surprised that Lizzie was his choice for companionship and that she agreed to the supper date. You're probably right that it's just to convince her the place isn't haunted."

"I guess we'll see."

They ate quietly for a few minutes. If Gabriel had been talking up the weather earlier in an effort to spend more time with her, the conversation hadn't moved in that direction. Maybe he had simply been making small talk. Or maybe he needed a nudge.

"You were right—it is a gorgeous day outside. I noticed when we crossed the parking lot that there are no clouds in the sky, and although there's a crisp breeze, the sun is shining so brightly that it makes the cool air tolerable." She gazed beyond the lake outside the window. "This is my favorite time of year, when all the fall foliage gets so vibrant."

"*Ya*, it's pretty, but like I said before, I think *mei* favorite time of year is right before we harvest the corn. The stalks are tall, green, and everything is so lush. And there's a satisfaction that our hard work paid off."

Their conversation wasn't moving in the direction she'd hoped. It had basically just drifted into talking about the weather again, without any follow-up about things to do outside. She tried to think up something fun to do as a suggestion, but maybe she had read him wrong and he had no interest in spending time with her. Maybe he was just seeing her car repairs through to completion, then that would be it.

———◆———

Gabriel was desperate not to have this time with Mindy end after lunch, but his brother's warnings kept ringing in his ears. Getting involved with an English woman, outside of friendship, would be disastrous. Gabriel knew he would have a hard time not pushing the boundaries with Mindy. He liked her. She was gorgeous and easy to talk to. But he was thinking about her way too much, and he barely knew her.

"Have you ever been to Lark Ranch?" she asked as her mouth curled upward.

He wondered if this was a hint. "*Ya*, I have. Have you?"

"Yeah, I went the first fall after I moved here. The rides and the pumpkin patch are awesome, but the corn maze was a blast. That whole place can make anyone feel like a kid again. I'd love to go back sometime."

That sounded like a hint to Gabriel, and he was tempted to suggest they go, but then he remembered something. "I'm pretty sure they're only open in September and October. Even though it's beautiful outside today, most of the time, I think it's too cold in November." *Saved.* If she would have asked, he would have gone.

"Yeah, you're right." She dug around in her purse, took out a pair of black sunglasses, and eased them onto her head, pushing back her wavy brown hair. As she thrust a hand back into her purse, she pulled out her wallet. "This is

Grandpa's treat, but I've got to find a way to get him what's left of his money."

Maybe she wasn't hinting, or maybe she was and thought he didn't want to spend time with her. He should not hang out with her, but there was a desperation inside him fueling his need to get to know her better. When she stood, so did he, quickly enough that he almost tipped his chair backward. He had between now and the short drive to his house to come up with something or to heed his brother's warning and walk away.

She paid at the register, which made Gabriel feel weird. He was used to paying if he took any woman out to eat, even one of his sisters or his mother.

"Another great meal," she said when they reached the parking lot. She dropped her sunglasses down on her nose.

"*Ya, ya.*" Gabriel considered asking her if she wanted to go sit by the lake, but even with the bright sunlight, the wind across the water was chilly.

He got into her red car, and within a minute, she was heading out of the parking lot. This was for the best. He needed to say goodbye. He might see her from time to time visiting her grandfather, but no more lunches or anything else that could be considered a date.

"Would you like to come to my house for supper tonight?" She briefly glanced at him. "I mean, it wouldn't be anything fancy, maybe just—"

"*Ya.* Yes. I would like that very much. What time?" He

couldn't have sounded any more enthusiastic if he had tried, and clearly all logic had fled from his mind.

"Five o'clock?"

He nodded as his stomach swirled with anticipation. "What should I bring?"

"Just you and your appetite. I'll text you directions."

Gabriel smiled. "I'll be there."

———◆———

Ben had just finished setting out two plates on the small bar that divided the living room from the kitchen when Lizzie knocked on the door. The house smelled of baked pork chops, he had a nice fire going in the fireplace, and he was looking froward to getting to know more about Lizzie. She amused him, and he would convince her that the cottage wasn't haunted, just old and shifty.

He opened the door . . . and blinked. "Esther." He raised the brow over his good eye. The other one was stuck in place above his swollen socket.

"*Danki*—I mean thank you—for inviting me for supper." She smiled. Esther was a large woman, almost as tall as Ben. She had kind eyes and was soft-spoken.

Ben scratched his chin, confused. Then realized that Lizzie really was afraid to come to the cottage. She'd sent Esther instead.

"I didn't think to ask Lizzie if I should bring anything when she said you invited me for supper," she said, blushing. "I apologize for that. I don't usually arrive empty-handed."

Ben took a step back and widened the door so she could come in. At first he felt a tinge of disappointment that Lizzie had sent her sister in her place, but he decided to roll with it. It would be nice to get to know his other landlady, to be friendly with both women.

"No worries. I would have told you not to bring anything. I hope you like pork chops, scalloped potatoes, and carrots. I'm afraid I didn't prepare a dessert." He intentionally hadn't prepared a follow-up to the main course since Lizzie had said she didn't care for sugary food.

"*Ya,* I like all of that, and this is a treat, having someone cook for me." She slipped out of her black cape, and Ben hung it on a rack by the door. Esther wore a dark-blue dress covered with a black apron. She was an attractive woman, like Lizzie, even though their outward appearances seemed as far apart as their demeanor. "And no worries about dessert. I'm diabetic," she said, blushing.

Lizzie would know that about her sister. She'd had this planned from the moment she agreed to his invitation.

"I'm happy to have you. It's been a long time since I've had someone over for supper." He knew the Amish referred to *lunch* as *dinner,* and *supper* was the common term for the evening meal. He motioned to the two stools in front of the bar. "Please, take a seat. Either one is fine."

Esther sat and folded her hands atop the counter, glancing around the room, then refocusing on Ben. "Your granddaughter seems lovely. What does she do? Does she work? Go to school?"

"Both." Ben took the towel he had slung over his shoulder and laid it on the counter behind him. "She works at a nursing home in Bedford and takes classes at the community college."

Esther nodded. "So, she lives in Bedford?"

Ben shook his head. "No, she lives in Montgomery on seven acres with a farmhouse she is renting. She hopes to buy it someday. And since she is my only living relative, I wanted to be near her." He waved an arm around the cottage. "Thus, my move to Montgomery."

"Why here, in a small cottage with no electricity?" Esther eased her hands into her lap.

He took her plate and began to fill it, offering a weak smile. "Simplicity of life. I don't need much."

She chuckled. "You might feel differently in the summer if you're still here. It gets mighty hot in July and August, should you decide to renew your lease."

"I'm not afraid of a little warm weather." It was a moot point, but a subject he wasn't prepared to discuss.

"This looks delicious," Esther said when Ben placed a plate of food in front of her.

He began to load his own plate. "Hopefully it will be."

In a moment Ben sat on the other stool, and when he bowed his head, Esther did too. He had a lot to thank the Lord for, and he knew the Amish prayed silently.

When he lifted his head, Esther was staring at him.

"I must look a mess." He reached up and gingerly touched his swollen eye.

She grinned. "You look about like Lizzie. I wish I could have seen the events that unfolded."

"Looking back, I guess it is rather funny, but I do feel bad about Lizzie." He thought again how Lizzie had opted out of his invitation. She really was afraid the cottage was haunted. Or was there more to it than that?

"You probably don't share your sister's belief that this place is haunted?" He motioned around the room.

She wagged her head as she finished chewing. "*Nee*, of course not. Lizzie is . . ."

———◆———

Esther paused midsentence, reminding herself to talk up Lizzie and not highlight her quirks, however endearing some of her character traits might be. "Lizzie is superstitious, like some of our people tend to be, but she's the kindest person I've ever known. We were very close growing up, even throughout our long marriages. After our husbands died, we became even closer, and living together in our childhood home is a blessing. We are the keepers of each other's lives, a living diary of sorts." She paused. "I can't imagine living without Lizzie."

"I imagine there is never a dull moment with her around." Ben smiled. His tender expression reminded her of a kind and gentle grizzly bear, and more so now than when he'd moved in all clean-shaven. He appeared to be growing a beard. Or perhaps he chose not to shave because his face hurt. Esther didn't see any visible bruises other than his eye and slightly swollen lip, but it wasn't her place to ask.

"You are correct," she said. "Life is never dull with Lizzie around. I know she can be a bit quirky sometimes, but she has a huge heart, and she loves deeply."

Dr. Stoltzfus nodded.

"Lizzie moans and groans about cooking sometimes, but she is a master chef in the kitchen. And when I was diagnosed with diabetes, she went out of her way to adjust recipes and come up with new ones even though I told her that wasn't necessary. I would have prepared *mei* own food so she didn't have to adjust to *mei* dietary needs, but she wouldn't hear of it." She smiled. "She's so *gut* at it that most of our guests at the inn have no idea how healthy the food really is."

Dr. Stoltzfus nodded again. "I try to watch my sugar too. I'm not diabetic, but I'm in a gray zone, as the doctor put it. I don't always do a good job avoiding sugar, and I cheat a lot, but I tried to prepare a meal that wouldn't offset anyone's glucose too much."

Esther brought a hand to her heart. "That's so thoughtful of you, but I cheat also." She pointed to her plate. "The meal is wonderful."

They were quiet as they ate, then Esther said, "If you'd like, I can introduce you to some men in the area. I think some of them play dominoes, if that interests you. Others meet for coffee once or twice a week at a local café."

He shook his head. "Don't worry yourself with that. I left a big and bustling city. I'm happy to live a quiet life secluded from most of the population." Chuckling, he added, "Not that I'm exactly a recluse. I enjoy good company." He winked at her. Again.

Esther put her hand in her lap atop her napkin when it began to shake. She wasn't sure if it was the early Parkinson's disease the doctor had mentioned, but her hands had been trembling more lately. So far, she'd kept her diagnosis from Lizzie. Eventually, her shaking would become obvious.

She cleared her throat. "I enjoy entertaining people at the inn, but I also like to have quiet downtime as well."

"It sounds like you have good balance in your life. I believe that's key to good health and longevity." He pointed to her plate. "Another pork chop?"

Esther considered it. The meal was good enough that she was tempted to ask Dr. Stoltzfus for his pork-chop recipe. "I best not, but thank you."

As he wiped his mouth with his napkin, then put it on his plate, Esther studied him. He was a handsome man, as she'd noticed when she first met him. *Under different circumstances, perhaps . . .* She took a deep breath and reminded herself to stay on task.

"I was thinking about possibly moving into the other house on the property since it's available." Dr. Stoltzfus collected their dishes and put them in the sink, then pointed to the percolator on the stove. After Esther nodded, he poured them each a cup of coffee. He remained standing on the other side of the counter and set her steaming beverage in front of her. "But I've decided not to." Glancing around, he smiled. "There isn't much upkeep here, it's cozy, and I don't think it's worth the effort."

"Don't forget it comes with its own ghost." Esther grinned.

Dr. Stoltzfus laughed. "Yes, according to your sister, I am sharing space with a deceased fellow named Gus."

Hearing his name and dining where Gus used to live brought back memories for Esther. Gus had been a handful, but in the end, he'd made his peace with God and those who loved him, including Lizzie. "*Ya*, Gus was a different kind of person. But I don't believe in ghosts, Dr. Stoltzfus."

"Please, call me Ben. We're neighbors." He smiled as he wound his way around the kitchen counter. "Let's move to the sitting area, but I'd suggest you sit on the far left of the couch or in the rocking chair. Avoid that spot." He pointed to the right side of the couch.

Esther sat exactly where he told her not to. "*Ach, nee.*" She shifted her weight around the spring poking her. "Dr. Stoltzfus—I mean Ben—we will get you a new couch. I'm sorry. I knew it was worn, but I had no idea you could feel the spring sticking out."

He shook his head. "No need. Mindy knows to avoid that spot, and so do I." He pointed a finger at her and chuckled. "I was trying to spare you, but you don't follow instructions very well."

Esther felt herself blushing as she grinned. "I suppose I don't sometimes."

"Take the rocking chair." He offered her his hand, and she was glad for the extra help getting up. She sat in the rocking chair as Ben lowered himself onto the good side of the couch.

Esther glanced around the small cottage, everything visible but the bedroom and bathroom.

"Something on your mind?" he asked.

She tipped her head to one side and sighed. "I just don't understand why you are living here. I would think you missed electricity and modern conveniences, especially television."

Dr. Stoltzfus—Ben—looked around the room before he locked eyes with her. "Mindy had the same concerns, but I like the simplicity of it all." He scratched his chin. "When I was married, and before Elsa became too sick for us to get out of the house, we led busy lives. Looking back, probably too busy. Elsa was mostly a stay-at-home wife, but that was still a full-time job. She had a huge heart and volunteered for a lot of important charities, and she ran our household, cooked all the meals, did most of the parenting of our son, and taking care of me wasn't always a picnic." His expression sobered. "I worked a lot of hours."

He paused again, regret seemingly evident as he lowered his eyes. "Anyway . . ." After a few moments, he met Esther's curious gaze. "We attended a lot of events, both charity and social. We were always doing something, it seemed like. But on the rare occasions when it was just us, I was the happiest. Elsa laughed a lot, but I treasured the sound of her laughing the most when we were alone. Sometimes I think I hear it. Her. But to answer your question more directly, I prefer to close my eyes and hear her as opposed to a television. And I like that I don't have any place that I must be and that I've simplified everything."

His sincerity as he talked about his wife caused a knot to form in Esther's throat. "She sounds lovely. How long were you married, if you don't mind me asking?"

"Fifty-two wonderful years." He smiled. "I was a blessed man."

"I was also married for fifty-two years to Joe." She paused as she recalled their lives together. "And I understand what you're saying. We have *Englisch* friends, and I've watched them hustle and bustle around until they seemed to work themselves into early graves. I'd like to think that Joe and I worked hard, but I believe having a simple life is healthy for the soul. And laughter is always *gut*."

"I absolutely agree." He chuckled. "You know how bad I feel about what happened to Lizzie, but does it make me a horrible person to say that I laugh every time the scene plays out in my head?"

"*Nee*, it doesn't." Esther giggled herself. "Luckily, no one was seriously hurt, but I smile every time I picture Lizzie's behavior."

"She's one of a kind, isn't she?" Ben's eyes twinkled, which solidified Esther's plan.

"*Ya*, she is. The best person I know. Quirky, fun, mischievous, hardworking, and with the biggest heart of anyone I know."

Ben stared intently into Esther's eyes. "I can see that about her. And I hope I'll be seeing lots of you and Lizzie."

"I hope so too," she said as she smiled back at him. Esther had set the groundwork for him and Lizzie.

They talked for a while longer—about grief, the ways life changes, and their faith journeys. Esther was happy Ben was a Christian, and she was convinced he was the man for Lizzie even if he wasn't Amish. They would make wonderful companions with a dose of romance sprinkled in.

7

———— ✄ ————

Mindy had the table set when Gabriel knocked on the door right at five o'clock. She had been questioning her bold invitation all afternoon. It was unlike her to act hastily, especially when an attraction had nowhere to go. Amish men didn't date non-Amish women, and whatever infatuation she had going on, she needed to harness it.

Eventually.

"Right on time," she said when she opened the door. Gabriel handed her an arrangement of yellow roses that couldn't have been cheap. *Yellow equals friendship*, she told herself. "Thank you. These are gorgeous."

"It smells *gut* in here." He sniffed the air. "Fried chicken?"

She carried the flowers to the kitchen and motioned for him to follow her. "I guess it's hard to mask the smell of frying food. I hope that's okay." She opened a cabinet and took out a vase, then began filling it with water.

"*Ya*, of course." He nodded to the kitchen table. The old farmhouse didn't have a dining room, but the kitchen was big enough to hold a table and six chairs. "Pretty place settings."

"Thanks. Those dishes were the first thing I bought when I moved here, although I'm mostly a paper plate kind of girl." She arranged the flowers and set the vase in the middle of the table. "Thank you again for these. Everything is ready if you want to take a seat."

After they bowed their heads and prayed silently, Mindy passed her guest the platter with the fried chicken. She'd also prepared glazed carrots, mashed potatoes, and a salad. "I talked to my grandfather earlier."

"Was he excited about his date with Lizzie?" Gabriel grinned. "I'm still surprised that he invited her for supper instead of Esther."

"Well, I don't know either woman very well, but Grandpa probably thinks Lizzie is funny, and I think that means something to him. He used to say that my grandma made him laugh a lot and that laughter keeps a person young." She giggled. "I must admit, I laugh every time I think about the whole incident in the bedroom with Grandpa jumping on Lizzie, her rolling out of bed, and ultimately her reaction when she thought he was in his underwear. The whole scene played out like a scripted movie—a comedy."

Gabriel laughed. "*Ya*, I would have liked to see that. But

honestly, both sisters are good as gold and have kind hearts. I've seen them give so much of themselves to the community, both of them. They can have a full house at the inn, but they still manage to take meals to shut-ins, and they are the first to arrive at a barn raising with tons of food. And I think I mentioned that they have a history of playing matchmaker. They're pretty *gut* at it too."

"I wonder how it feels to be on the other end of that matchmaking. I mean, I wonder if Esther is trying to fix up Lizzie and my grandpa." She paused, chewed on her lip for a moment. "I have to confess that I was hoping Grandpa would make friends with the sisters, but I never—even once—thought about him in a romantic relationship with either one of them." She shrugged. "I think this is probably a friendly supper, a get-to-know-your-neighbor type thing."

"Maybe," Gabriel said after he wiped his mouth and reached for another chicken wing. "But just because they're old . . . I don't think that automatically rules out romance."

Mindy shook her head. "I just don't see it. They are probably having a nice meal, getting to know each other, and talking about things retired people talk about, even though Lizzie isn't really retired. I'm sure running the inn is a lot of work."

"Is that a tiny bit of cynicism I hear?" He grinned, and Mindy thought she might be blushing. "They might be sitting on the couch making out as we speak."

Mindy burst out laughing. "No! First of all, I don't see Grandpa playing kissy-kissy with anyone. And besides, wouldn't that be considered wrong for an Amish woman to allow that?"

Gabriel shrugged. "Define *wrong*. In some Amish communities, me being here alone with you would be wrong, especially since we are of courting age. In other areas, we would be considered old enough to act responsibly. Every district is different. Most folks would probably overlook your grandpa and Lizzie being alone because they would assume, like you are, that there wouldn't be anything romantic going on." He shrugged again. "But you're probably right. I don't see romance developing between your grandpa and Lizzie. They seem way too different to me. I'm surprised Lizzie even accepted the invite, especially since she thinks the cottage is haunted."

"I'll ask Grandpa tomorrow how it went with him and Lizzie."

"I'm going to want all the details. Maybe you can call me tomorrow once you find out."

Mindy avoided looking at him, sure she would get lost in his gorgeous brown eyes. "Sure, but . . ." She finally looked at him. "He's not Amish. A relationship wouldn't be allowed, right?" She knew the answer.

"Right. Most of the time when one of our people gets involved with an outsider, it's a disaster, and people get hurt." He kept his eyes locked with hers. "Although, in some cases things have worked out."

Mindy wasn't sure if they were still talking about her grandpa and Lizzie or themselves. A change of subject was in order. "I'd ask you if you wanted to watch a movie, but that's not allowed, either, right?"

He smiled. "I'm still in my *rumschpringe*, our running-around time. I haven't been baptized yet, so I can break a few rules. I'd love to stay and watch a movie after I help you clean things up."

She did a quick calculation, knowing the running-around period started at sixteen. "Playing that running-around thing for all it's worth, huh?"

Gabriel laughed. "*Ya*, I guess you could say that."

Mindy recalled her grandfather's words about laughter keeping a person young. She wasn't old, but the sound of Gabriel's laughter echoing throughout the house was a feeling she wished she could bottle to have around when she was older.

"Go make yourself comfortable in the living room. The remote is on the coffee table. You can find something to watch while I clean the kitchen. I don't need any help."

"*Nee*, I ate. I'll help clean up." He stood, lifted both their plates, and carried them to the sink.

Mindy followed and stood beside him. "Wow. You're different than the other Amish men I've dated." The comment was supposed to be funny, but she cringed inside at the use of the word *date* again.

Gabriel grinned. "And exactly how many Amish men have you dated?"

Should she say that he was the first? That would categorize what they were doing. She batted her eyes playfully at him, mostly hoping to hide her embarrassment. "Only a few," she said.

As they stood side by side, his arm brushing up against hers, he said, "And how did those work out?"

She slowly turned to face him, and he did the same, their eyes locked again. "I've never dated an Amish guy."

"I've never dated anyone who wasn't Amish."

She had to ask. "Is this a date?"

He laughed, which made her laugh. "I don't know. You invited me, remember?"

She playfully slapped him on the arm. "Let's don't try to define it."

Gabriel gave a quick nod. "I agree. Do you think your grandpa and Lizzie are having this same conversation?"

Mindy chuckled. "I seriously doubt it. But from what I've seen from Lizzie, I guess they could be talking about anything."

———◆———

Lizzie paced the floor of her bedroom, occasionally walking to the window to stare at the cottage. It was nine o'clock at night. What in the world could Esther and the dentist be doing for that long? She wanted to be glad about the possibility that they were becoming friendly, but her stomach churned like butter in the making. What were they talking about? Did they have anything in common? Would Dr. Stoltzfus be mad or glad that Lizzie had dumped him and sent Esther?

She tucked her long gray hair behind her ears and continued retracing her steps back and forth across her bedroom, her white nightgown dragging on the floor. Esther had made it for her, but they'd never gotten around to taking the hem up a couple of inches.

Esther, Esther, Esther . . . She said her sister's name repeatedly in her mind. She was the most important person in Lizzie's life, and Lizzie wanted her to have a second chance at love. That thought hadn't changed. But Esther spending time with Dr. Stoltzfus was having a strange effect on Lizzie, something akin to jealousy, which should be outrageously funny. But it wasn't.

A door closing in the distance caught her attention, and she shuffled to the window just in time to see Esther and the dentist standing on the porch. As Dr. Stoltzfus put a hand on Esther's arm, Lizzie gasped. Was the doctor going to kiss her? Of course not. That would be highly inappropriate, and Esther would never allow such a thing on a first date. A first date that had been meant for Lizzie.

She chuckled. *It's not even a date, just supper.*

Esther was almost as tall as Dr. Stoltzfus, and as her sister edged closer to the man, Lizzie's one good eye widened. *Don't do it, Esther. What's wrong with you?*

Lizzie gasped when Esther leaned even closer to him. Then it happened. She kissed him on the cheek, and as Lizzie slapped her hands to her forehead, she lost her balance and almost fell over. What kind of lovesick old-age horror had she created by pushing Esther into the arms of a man they barely knew?

A dirty old man who clearly has dishonorable intentions.
Or maybe it was Esther who had lost all sense of decency.
She's the one who kissed him!

———◆———

Esther crossed through the field between the cottage and
the inn feeling full, emotionally fulfilled, and a little lighter
on her feet this evening. Who would have thought that she
and Ben would have been so comfortable talking about their
feelings. He was a deep man with strong and genuine convictions, and Esther liked him very much.

She opened the door, closing it behind her, only to find
Lizzie standing in the middle of the living room with her
hands clamped to her hips, tapping one bare foot, with
a scowl that would have scared anyone who didn't know
her well.

"*Wie bischt.* What is wrong with you?" Esther disrobed
and hung her cape and bonnet on the rack.

Lizzie scooted toward Esther and glared at her as she
wagged a finger a few inches from her face, enough that
Esther had to lean back a little. "I saw what you did." Lizzie
stilled her finger but kept it pointed at Esther. "You kissed
that man!"

She lowered her hand and began pacing the living room,
all the while shaking her head. "Your behavior is inappropriate, and I am shocked to *mei* core! We are old women, not
hormonal teenagers. Kissing shouldn't even be considered at

our age." She slapped her forehead, then yelped when she caught part of her swollen eye. "What do you have to say for yourself?"

Lizzie finally came to a standstill in the middle of the room. Esther's jaw had dropped, and she was too stunned to say anything. When she finally collected her thoughts, she answered, "You're jealous."

Lizzie jumped up and down, her long gray hair bouncing all the way down to her waist. "You have lost your mind!"

Esther had seen Lizzie display some bizarre behavior, so not much surprised her, but this was enough to render her speechless. She forced her mouth closed, stared at her sister, and waited until Lizzie landed on both feet and stood still for a few seconds before she spoke.

"Not that I owe you an explanation, but Ben and I—"

Lizzie clenched her fists at her side. "Ben? He's *Ben* now? What happened to Dr. Stoltzfus?"

"If you will hush and let me finish . . . *Dr. Stoltzfus* and I talked about why he was living in the cottage. He enjoys our simpler way of life. We also got into a deep discussion about our long marriages, then we talked about the grief we felt after we had lost our spouses. His grief is much fresher since his wife hasn't been gone as long. We talked about the different stages of grief. The innocent kiss on the cheek was a thank-you for the great meal and wonderful conversation we had. So stop acting ridiculous."

Esther had been surprised by the kiss, but she hadn't meant it as anything more than a friendly gesture after Ben had told her how much he enjoyed her company. Maybe it *had* been a bit too bold.

Lizzie rolled her eye that wasn't swollen and let out a loud breath. "Well, you have to live with yourself, Esther." She turned, stomped to her bedroom, and slammed the door.

Esther knew Lizzie well enough to know that she needed to sleep off this surprise shock with a hint of jealousy attached. Lizzie was the one who had encouraged Esther to go, making her reaction a bit confusing. But she decided to get ready for bed and drift off to sleep replaying the lovely evening she'd had.

———◆———

Ben walked to his bedroom, pleasantly surprised how well the evening had turned out. Lizzie might be the quirky, funny one, but Esther was intriguing in her own way. She had an ability to convey her emotions in an understandable way that Ben could relate to. A casual discussion had morphed into a deep and meaningful conversation. Although he was still miffed as to why Lizzie had sent her sister in her place. He had to believe the woman really thought this cottage was being haunted by that Gus fellow.

After slipping into his pajamas and sitting on the edge of his bed, he pulled open the drawer of his nightstand and retrieved his Sunday-thru-Saturday pillbox. He slid his glasses on and took his Saturday-night pills—all eleven of them—then put the container back into the drawer with his pill bottles. On more than one occasion, he'd forgotten to take his medication since it wasn't in clear sight, but he didn't want to take a chance that Mindy might see all the prescriptions that were keeping him alive. She'd find out soon enough, and he didn't want to worry her any more than necessary.

While he fluffed his pillow, he glanced down at his blue-and-white striped pajamas. He preferred the shorts and T-shirts he'd worn to bed the last eight years of his married life. As she'd gotten older, the Lab he and Elsa had owned for thirteen years hadn't been able to make it through the night without going out around four in the morning. Ben had taken to wearing shorts so it was easier to take the dog out. It had become part of his routine. Unlike here, they'd had neighbors who might not appreciate Ben in his underwear. And Chloe had refused to go potty unless Ben went outside with her. She was an old gal but had lived a good life.

Ben hoped the same would be said about him at his funeral. He'd made his share of mistakes, but he loved the Lord and had done his best to please Him.

He laid his head back and closed his eyes. Sometimes he swore he could smell Elsa's perfume, and not in a haunted sort of way. It had been like that since she died, and it had a calming effect on him, the way her laughter did.

As he recalled his evening with Esther, and the lovely time he'd had, he still speculated why Lizzie had sent her sister for supper. Apparently Lizzie had told Esther Ben invited her. Did Lizzie dislike him that much that she didn't want to share a meal with him? He had truly thought he could convince her the cottage wasn't haunted.

The thought caused him to smile. She was a funny one, that Lizzie, and Ben liked her spunkiness. He hoped to be good friends with both the sisters, especially since he didn't know anyone here but Mindy. Friends back home had promised to visit, but most of them were in their seventies, like Ben, and travel could be a challenge for some of them. Mostly, they were set in their ways.

He thought again about Esther's suggestion to socialize with some of the men in the area, but he was mostly content staying home.

Ben was exactly where he was meant to be. He rubbed the whiskers on his face and knew he would have a full beard soon, good Lord willing. He planned to go out the way he was supposed to have lived—as an Amish man.

8

━━━━━━━━━━ ⋈ ━━━━━━━━━━

Mindy laughed aloud at the movie every time Gabriel did, whether the show was funny or not. Something about his laugh made her chuckle too. She wasn't a big TV fan and preferred to dive into a good book in the evenings, but seeing Gabriel's reactions was worth the wait to see who ended up with whom in her latest romance novel.

"I've never heard anyone laugh so much at a movie that isn't really a comedy." Mindy reached into the bowl of popcorn between them on the couch. She'd barely put a few kernels in her mouth when Gabriel laughed again, causing her to cover her mouth to keep from spewing the popcorn everywhere. "Stop it!" she said. "Now you're just trying to make me laugh."

"*Ya*, well . . . You laugh cute."

She kept her hand over her mouth until she'd chewed and swallowed the popcorn, then left it there.

Gabriel put on a straight face and stared at her. "Stop," she grumbled through her hand.

"What? I'm not laughing." He attempted to hold his solemn expression, but within seconds he broke into chuckles again.

It had been that way all night. Playful, fun, and comfortable. Gabriel was either the happiest guy on the planet, or he also enjoyed the sound of his own laughter, which was intoxicating and contagious. Mindy loved the escapism his mood exerted—escape from work worries, concerns about her grandfather, and her schoolwork that was piling up. Gabriel was a fun person, and it didn't hurt that he was incredibly good looking.

And Amish, she reminded herself.

When the movie ended, Mindy stifled a yawn.

"I saw that," he said, grinning. "I should go and let you get some sleep. I don't know where the time went. It's almost eleven." He slowly stood, and so did Mindy.

She finally allowed herself to yawn. "Yeah, I'm never up this late. But tomorrow is Sunday, and I'll sleep in and catch the eleven o'clock church service."

"Our church service starts at eight in the morning, so there will be no sleeping in for me, and I'll be tired." He playfully shoved her. "Thanks to you."

Mindy grinned as they got in step toward the front door.

"Yeah, I had you tied to the couch and forced you to watch a movie and make me laugh all night."

He picked up his hat from where he'd set it on a chair. "*Ya*, it's crazy. I had no idea I was such a funny guy." Then he laughed again. Mindy too. "Seriously, though, I had a great time, and *danki*—I mean thank you—for supper. And the entertainment."

She pointed to herself. "*Me?* I don't think I was the entertainment." She turned her finger to him. "That was all you, buddy."

"I meant the movie." He tried to frown, but he couldn't hold it, and a smile spread across his face. "I had a great time," he said again.

"Me too." Mindy felt the sting of reality setting in. They got along great, and if she was reading Gabriel correctly, he was just as into her as she was him. But it had nowhere to go.

He'd been holding his straw hat at his side, and as he put it on, he tapped the rim and tried to imitate one of the cowboys in the movie. "I'll be seeing ya, sweetheart."

Mindy burst out laughing and threw her arms around him . . . and all her caution flew out the window. He embraced her back, and they stayed like that for a few seconds before he eased away.

"Bye, Mindy." He tapped the rim of his hat before he went out the door toward his buggy.

"Bye," she said in a whisper, but he didn't turn around. Reality had clearly set in for Gabriel too.

Esther scurried around the house, upset with herself for oversleeping and not preparing breakfast. Her stomach would growl all through church service.

She knocked on Lizzie's door. "Lizzie, are you up? We both overslept. Chop-chop. We're going to be late for worship service. It's at the Bylers' *haus*, so we need to get a move on."

"I'm not going," her sister said from behind the closed door.

Esther huffed. "*Ach*, Lizzie, if this is about last night, you are being ridiculous." She turned the knob only to find the door locked. "Open the door." She rattled the knob.

"*Nee*. Don't come in. I'm probably contagious." Lizzie faked a cough. At least it sounded that way to Esther.

"You're not sick." Esther shook her head. Lizzie had been known to fake illness in the past when she didn't want to go somewhere.

More coughing.

Esther shook her head. "Fine. I'm leaving." She stood quietly outside the door for a minute or so.

"I know you're still outside *mei* door."

Esther sighed. "I assumed you would bounce out of bed once I left, because I know there is nothing wrong with you."

Lizzie coughed even louder than before, then groaned, which made Esther wonder if she might truly be sick. She doubted it. This was typical Lizzie behavior.

"Open the door, Lizzie. Right now." Esther shifted her weight when her knee locked up. "I mean it."

"I'm fine. I told you I'm probably contagious. I'd hate for you to get sick and then kiss Dr. Stoltzfus, whom you fondly refer to as Ben now, and get him sick too."

Esther grinned, deciding Lizzie wasn't sick. She'd never seen her sister jealous before. Things were moving in the right direction even if Lizzie's thought process was moving in the wrong direction.

"All right, fine. I'm going to worship service. I suggest you pray for *Gott* to forgive you for skipping church and faking illness."

Silence.

Esther finally left for worship service.

———◆———

Lizzie waited until she heard Esther's buggy heading down the driveway before she rolled out of bed and readied herself for the day. First thing she was going to do was give that dentist a piece of her mind. Whatever he had said to entice Esther to kiss him on the cheek should not be tolerated. Esther wasn't that type of woman.

She put on her shoes, slipped on her cape, then her bonnet, tying it under her chin. Then she just stood there.

What am I doing?

Fully dressed for the chilly weather, she sat on the couch and put her elbows on her knees, then her chin in her hands. This was exactly what she had hoped for Esther—that she and the dentist would become chummy and form a friendship. Now that her plan seemed to be in full play, though, Lizzie was struggling with her feelings. Out of nowhere that dentist had put a spell on them both. What were the chances of that happening?

She was still pondering her situation when there came a knock at the door. Lizzie dragged herself to the door and swung it open, only to find Benjamin Stoltzfus standing there in tan slacks, a crisp white shirt, and running shoes.

"Going somewhere?" he asked as he eyed Lizzie's outdoor attire.

"*Nee.*" She left the front door open but didn't invite him in. She removed her cape and bonnet, then hung them on the rack. "If you're looking for Esther, she went to worship service."

He folded his arms across his chest as he shivered. "I know. I saw her leave alone."

"Don't you own a coat?" Lizzie motioned for him to step over the threshold. "What do you want?"

His mouth dropped open. "Uh . . . I guess I'm wondering why I asked you for supper, but then you sent your sister and let her believe that I invited her. Which, by the way, I didn't have the heart to tell her I didn't."

"Well, everything worked out in the end, now, didn't it?" She raised her chin and tried to stow any hostility or jealousy.

"What's that supposed to mean?" Dr. Stoltzfus moseyed

to the fireplace, where smoldering embers still provided some warmth. After he'd stopped shivering, he said, "What things worked out in the end?"

"You and Esther. That's what I mean." Scooting around him, she added another log to the fire, then nervously poked at it, not about to look at him.

"Me and Esther? What are you talking about?"

Lizzie finally glanced his way—and he was grinning. "Wipe that smirk off your face. You know exactly what I mean. I saw Esther kiss you good night. She's a wonderful woman, and I wish you two the best." She cut her good eye at him. "Even if it was a bit inappropriate."

The dentist's eye wasn't as swollen as it had been, and it was starting to yellow around the edges like Lizzie's. He was able to raise both his eyebrows as he grinned. "Your sister kissed me on the cheek. It was a kind offer of thanks for the meal, and we had an enjoyable conversation." He chuckled. "Is that why you sent Esther for supper and didn't come yourself? You think I'm looking for someone to date at my age?"

Lizzie shrugged. She could feel her face turning red.

"You are the one I asked for supper, by the way."

"Stop grinning!" Lizzie stomped her foot.

He sat on the couch and laid his ankle over his knee, and if he hadn't already been injured—by his own doing—she might have tried to wipe that smug look off his face.

"Make yourself at home," she said as she stacked her hands at her waist.

"Thank you."

Lizzie huffed. "I didn't mean it. I was being sarcastic. Now, what do you want?"

He rubbed his scruffy chin with that wicked little smile still in place.

"You need to shave." Lizzie sat in the rocker across the room.

"You are a funny little Amish woman, aren't you?" The arrogant dentist's smile grew larger. "It's cute when you're all mad."

Lizzie bolted from the chair. "Don't you dare hit on me"—another term she'd learned from her romance books— "when you are actively pursuing *mei* sister."

"Hit on you? Pursuing your sister?" He shook his head as if he were trying to get water out of his ears. "I'm not hitting on *anyone*. I thought I was making new friends." He raised his palms. "I mean, at our age, I didn't think romance was on the table."

"It's not!" Lizzie blasted back at him. "Not with me, anyway."

"I dislike eating alone. I asked you to come over for a meal, and I thought I could convince you that the cottage isn't haunted by your old renter." He stood. "I should go."

"*Ya*, you should." She rose and followed him to the door.

She was about to close it when he spun around and said, "But you still amuse me, and laughter is good for the soul."

"Happy to help your soul." She slammed the door, took a deep breath, and went back to bed.

————— ♦ —————

Ben left with a bounce in his step. Apparently, Lizzie was jealous about the time he'd spent with Esther—and the kiss on the cheek. At his age, he couldn't help but be flattered, but he still didn't understand why Lizzie had sent Esther in her place. That seemed contradictory to Ben's interpretation of Lizzie's behavior just now.

Originally, Lizzie had had his full attention because she was so animated and full of personality. That's why he had chosen her to come for supper. He figured she would entertain him, and in return he could put her at ease about the house. But after spending time with Esther, he found the elder sister to be interesting and easy to talk to, albeit in a completely different way than he saw Lizzie.

Romance?

Back at the cottage, he laughed aloud as he sat on his couch—just to the right of the loose spring—and propped his feet up on the worn coffee table. Even if he was in the market for romance—and he hadn't thought he was— had Lizzie forgotten that he wasn't Amish? He rubbed his temples. It was all rather bizarre, but Ben felt his head had grown two sizes since he left the inn. He'd been hoping for friendship with both women. Perhaps they could keep an eye on Mindy after he had passed. But things had certainly taken a turn in an amusing away. He was sure he and Esther would be friends, but he was unclear about Lizzie. Maybe her attitude was how she'd gotten sideways with their old renter . . . Gus, they'd called him. Ben didn't find her off-putting at all. She was . . . entertaining.

———◆———

It was later in the afternoon when Mindy showed up, eager to hear about Ben's date with Lizzie. He filled her in on his evening with Esther, then on his morning with Lizzie. His granddaughter held her hand over her mouth, her eyes wide, while he detailed the events.

"Oh wow," she finally said before she giggled. "They're fighting over you, Grandpa."

He chuckled along with her. "I know it might seem that way, but I can't imagine that's true. It is funny, though."

"If you had to pick, which one would you choose?"

Ben shook his head. It was an unlikely option he had no plans to entertain. "I'm an old man, Mindy. I was married to your grandma for most of my life. Romance isn't in the cards for me."

"Aw, Grandpa, don't say that. You're never too old for love."

Ben agreed with her, but he couldn't tell her how unfair it would be for him to lead on any woman right now. "There are a lot of different kinds of love, child. I'm in the market for friendship, and that's all this old man has to offer."

She pointed to her chin. "Growing a beard?" she asked from where she was seated next to him on the couch.

"Yeah. What do you think?" He stroked the stubble on his chin.

"It works for you." She cringed. "How's your eye?"

He gingerly ran a finger over his injury. "Barely sore. Just ugly looking." He snickered. "Lizzie looks about the same."

Mindy grinned. "You like her. She's the one."

"I like both women." He slapped a hand to his leg, ready to change the subject. "Enough about all that. Did you know the other house on the property is available?"

"I suspected no one lived there. I never see a car, buggy, or any activity. Are you thinking about moving there?"

Ben shrugged. "I thought about it." He glanced around the small cottage. "And it's available if I want it. Lizzie sure wants me to move."

Mindy gave him a skeptical look. "And why is that?"

"She thinks this place is haunted. Apparently, she had a few run-ins with a man named Gus who used to live here, and she is convinced that he is haunting the place."

Mindy giggled. "That would explain her hesitancy when I asked her to come in with me to check on you. And maybe that's why she sent Esther to supper in her place. Although, based on the conversation you had with her, it sounds like Lizzie was jealous."

"I learned a long time ago that it's dangerous to speculate about what a woman is thinking." He grinned as he shook his head. "Getting back to my living arrangements, after thinking about it, I'm fine here. It's cozy and easy to take care of." He chuckled. "Haunted. Silly Lizzie."

"You even get a tender look on your face when you say her name." Mindy smiled.

He laughed again. "That's not true. Now . . . let's talk about you. You got your car back? Good as new?"

"Well, it was never new, but it looks great." She reached into her purse and took out an envelope. "I took Gabriel to lunch with some of this money, but you need to take this back. Gabriel wouldn't accept it."

Ben shook his head. If she had any idea how much money he had, she wouldn't even be asking. "I want you to have it." He tapped the purse in her lap. "Buy yourself a new bag."

"I like this one just fine." She pushed the money toward him.

"I'm not taking it." He swooshed her hand away. "Let's move on. What's happening in your life? School okay? Work?"

She scowled as she stuffed the money back into her purse, then chewed on her bottom lip and diverted her eyes from his. "I had a friend over for supper last night."

Ben waited for her to look at him. When she did, she grinned.

"Am I to presume this was a male friend?"

"Yep. It was Gabriel."

Ben's heart sank a little. "He's Amish."

"You're kidding." Mindy laughed as she dramatically brought a hand to her mouth.

Ben rolled his eyes. "Ha ha. You know what I mean. It isn't exactly a match made in heaven."

"We're just friends." She dramatically rolled her eyes back at him. "Kind of like you and your two new *Amish* friends."

"I'm an old man not looking for love." *At least I didn't think I was.* He tipped his head and cut his eyes at her. "Be careful."

"I know what you're saying." She leaned back against the couch and propped her feet up next to his. "I doubt we'll see each other again unless it's just in passing. I mean, we'll probably run into each other since he takes care of the property here at the inn."

"How is it that you're not dating a nice young man your age who isn't Amish, by the way?" Ben scratched above his eye, which was starting to itch, a good sign the small cut was healing.

"I've told you before. I'm busy with work and school."

"Not too busy for Gabriel, though?" He grinned at his granddaughter.

"Ha ha." She stood and swung her purse over her shoulder. "I gotta go. Church service ran longer than usual, and I still need to go to the grocery store. Do you need anything?"

Ben lifted himself from the couch, careful not to grimace when his back put up a fight. He had a slipped disk that needed surgery, but he couldn't see the point. At his age it would be a rough operation, and he didn't want to waste time going through a lengthy and painful recovery period. His little romp with Lizzie hadn't helped.

"Nope. I have everything I need," he said as they walked to the door.

"You should come to my church sometime. I think you'd like it." Mindy smiled.

"Maybe I will." It wouldn't hurt for him to attend with his granddaughter if it would make her happy. Ultimately, he wanted to be baptized into another religion, and that was something he needed to start working toward.

She kissed him on his cheek, a spot on his face that had become popular for such affection, then he watched as she left waving.

———◆———

Mindy carried her groceries inside the old farmhouse that still smelled the same as when she'd moved in. Some people might call it musty, but Mindy liked the way it smelled. Old. With a history. But today the aroma of fried chicken lingered in the air.

After she had her groceries put away, she sat at the kitchen table and stared at her phone. *Don't do it.* But Gabriel had said he wanted details about her dad and Lizzie's date. It was too great of a story not to share that it hadn't been a date with Lizzie at all.

She dialed his phone, which he'd said was for emergencies and calling drivers when necessary, but he answered on the first ring.

"Whoa, do I have a story about my grandfather's date last night," she said right away.

He laughed, and no matter the risks, Mindy was glad she'd called.

"I can't wait to hear about it."

She bit her bottom lip. "Um, do you want to hear about it over supper? I go back to work tomorrow, and I have classes after work every day but Wednesday . . . but nothing planned for this evening."

When had she become so bold? She held her breath when he seemed to be taking a while to answer.

"*Ya*, great. But I don't want you to have to cook again. Why don't I bring a pizza?"

She heard what sounded like excitement in his voice. "Sure. Five o'clock again?"

"*Ya*, see you then."

After they ended the call, Mindy was tempted to analyze the situation, but decided not to drum up trouble when there wasn't any. She was a grown woman inviting a man over for a meal.

But as she rushed to the bathroom to freshen up her makeup and hair, her stomach swirled with anticipation in a way she didn't recognize. Maybe getting close to Gabriel was a mistake, and she would get her heart broken, but she was living in the moment and would worry about it later.

9

———— ✄ ————

Gabriel sat on his bed with the phone in his lap, wondering what he would tell his parents. The day before, he'd told them that Mindy was cooking for him as a thank-you for getting her car repaired. His father had given him a questioning look; his mother hadn't said a word. A one-time supper wasn't cause for concern. Going to Mindy's house for the second evening in a row would bring on comments from someone, probably his mother.

"I won't be here for supper," he said about an hour later. It was four thirty, and he needed to get a move on so he'd have time to pick up the pizza, which thankfully was on the way to Mindy's house.

"If you keep eating so much at your *bruder*'s *haus*, I'm going to think Mary Kate is a better cook than me."

Lots of Sundays, Gabriel did eat at Matthew's house

for supper. And Mary Kate was a better cook than his mother. Not that his mom didn't prepare good meals, but it was more about quantity than quality since there were seven of them. Matthew was the only one of his siblings who had gotten married and moved out. Two of his brothers had girl-friends, but no engagements had been announced.

"Um, I'm not going to Matthew's house. Mindy, the woman I had supper with last night, invited me over again."

His mother stopped dead in her tracks in the middle of the living room, glanced at his father, who had looked above the newspaper he was reading, then looked back at Gabriel. "That's two suppers in a row with the *Englisch maedel*."

Gabriel was twenty-three years old, a grown man who was still in his *rumschpringe*. He didn't need his parents' permission to step out for supper, but he wanted to be respectful since he lived under their roof.

"*Mamm*, I know what you're going to say, but you don't have anything to worry about. We're friends. I'm old enough and wise enough to know there can't be any more to it."

His father seemed satisfied, lowering his eyes to the newspaper again. His mother narrowed her eyes. "Old enough and wise enough? I hope so. Sometimes the heart doesn't follow logic."

"Don't worry," he said as he took his hat from the rack. "I won't be late."

Gabriel arrived at Mindy's house at five fifteen. "Sorry, I'm late. The pizza wasn't ready, and I had to wait."

She stood in the doorway, looking beautiful in faded jeans, a pink T-shirt, and pink socks. Her hair spilled in wavy tresses past her shoulders. Momentarily, she took his breath away, and his mother's words rang in his head, echoed by his brother's earlier warning.

"No problem." She moved aside so he could come in. "The pizza smells heavenly."

"I didn't know what you like on it. I should have asked. I got pepperoni. Is that okay?"

"Perfect." She pointed to two paper plates on the coffee table and two cans of soda. "I thought maybe we'd be a little more casual tonight, if that's okay." She grinned, rolling her eyes. "Confession. I usually eat in here. It's warmer, and I like to bury myself in a good book."

Gabriel nodded and relaxed a little, surprised he was a bit nervous around her. It wouldn't last. They always fell into an easy conversation, but his temptation to tell her how beautiful she was stayed on the tip of his tongue.

After they'd prayed and each taken a slice of pizza, Mindy broke into an animated tale about how Esther had shown up at her grandfather's house instead of Lizzie. "It's so crazy, and he said he really enjoyed Esther's company, but I think he has a special fondness for Lizzie."

Gabriel laughed. "Really? I told you before that both women have huge hearts. Everyone in town loves them both, but Lizzie is . . . different." Chuckling, he tried to envision

Lizzie romantically linked to anyone, especially someone as seemingly reserved as Dr. Stoltzfus.

"Exactly. She's different. A bit quirky. But I think Grandpa likes her. Even during the whole crazy incident in the bedroom, I caught the way he was looking at her . . . once he got over the shock at what happened."

Gabriel chewed his pizza, shaking his head. "I can't wrap *mei* mind around them being any more than friends."

Mindy had her plate in her lap, as Gabriel did. She leaned back against the couch and propped her socked feet up on the coffee table the way they'd both done the previous night. Gabriel had dropped his shoes by the door as he'd walked in the night before, so he'd done the same this evening. Now his feet were next to hers, their shoulders touching.

"I think I told you that Esther and Lizzie are known matchmakers around here. If they see even a spark between two people, they consider it their job to nurture the relationship." He turned to her and grinned. "For example, if they knew I was having supper two nights in a row with you, they would make it their mission to play matchmaker."

"Why? I'm not Amish." She locked her eyes with his until he could feel his face turning red. Clearly, this wasn't a scenario she'd thought about and she held him firmly in the friendship arena.

Gabriel wanted to wiggle out of what he'd said, because her presumption that nothing could ever happen with them was correct. "It wouldn't matter to them. They've successfully matched up someone who isn't Amish with someone who is. Someone ends up converting, either to the *Englisch* life or the *Englisch* person gets baptized into the Amish faith. They've had some fails, but overall, they have a pretty high success rate."

———◆———

Mindy needed to tread carefully. Was Gabriel hinting that she might convert to Amish if their friendship grew into more? That thought had floated around in her mind like an untamed fantasy from time to time, but it wasn't anything she'd seriously entertained. Maybe she should have considered the implications before inviting Gabriel over for the second night in a row. Her heart was already in dangerous territory, but it was way too soon to picture herself in an Amish bonnet. She needed to change the subject.

"So . . . the sisters are known matchmakers?" She lifted her plate, twisted to face him, and tucked one leg underneath her. He nodded with a mouthful. "Why don't *we* play matchmaker?"

He stopped chewing. "Huh?"

If they couldn't be romantically involved, it might be fun to help her grandfather find love again. "I really sense that my grandpa likes Lizzie. Maybe we need to turn the tables and do a little matchmaking of our own."

Gabriel finally swallowed. "Are you suggesting that you and I try to get Lizzie and your grandpa to fall in *lieb*—I mean love?" He chuckled. "Lizzie is lovable in her own quirky way, but they're . . . old."

"Stop saying that." She playfully poked him in the chest. "I have an idea." It would be an excuse to spend time with Gabriel and to live vicariously through someone else's love story.

"I'm scared to hear it." He laughed, and she did too.

That wonderful laughter of his.

"Here's the plan . . ."

———◆———

Esther sat at the kitchen table eating a forbidden cookie long after her bedtime. Lizzie had barely spoken to her all day. She should have never gone to Ben's house for supper, but at the time, it had seemed harmless, a chance to get to know the man and make sure he was a good fit for Lizzie. She'd learned that Lizzie and their new neighbor were mostly opposites. But, as the old cliché went, opposites attracted, and there had clearly been a gleam in Ben's eyes at the mention of Lizzie.

Esther was determined to stick to her original plan. She herself had a stomach ulcer, diabetes, worn-out knees, back pain due to arthritis, and, unbeknownst to Lizzie, her recently diagnosed Parkinson's disease that she eventually wouldn't be able to hide. Despite her sister's unruly behavior the previous night and this morning, Esther didn't want Lizzie alone after she was gone.

"You shouldn't be having that cookie, especially so late at night. Your blood sugar is going to be all messed up in the morning," Lizzie said as she shuffled into the kitchen in the white nightgown Esther had made for her.

"We need to take up the hem in that gown." Esther was happy Lizzie was speaking to her.

Lizzie lifted the gown up until it rose above her ankles. "*Ya*, you're right. It shows how dirty the floor is."

Esther eyed the dark ring around the bottom of the garment. "It's because the cleaning service had to cancel, and we didn't have time to finish cleaning the floors. "I'll run the sweeper tomorrow."

Lizzie sat in a chair across from Esther, but she didn't reach for a cookie. Maybe because she didn't have her teeth in. Her gray hair stood in a tight bun atop her head as she slouched into the chair, sulking. "I'm sorry," she finally said. "I should be happy for you that Dr. Stoltzfus and you hit it off."

Esther shook her head. "*Nee*, you're wrong, Lizzie. Ben is a nice man, charming and handsome. I enjoyed our visit and supper. But even if I were so inclined—and I'm not—he isn't my type." She chuckled. "It's odd that we're having this conversation, don't you think, at our age?"

Lizzie cracked a smile, but her face quickly sobered. "The dentist is exactly your type. He's poised, polished like a shiny nickel, handsome, and the perfect man for you. I should have never reacted the way I did. But I was caught off guard. When I think about you being best friends with anyone besides me, it scares me."

Esther's heart melted as she reached a hand across the table. Lizzie slowly lifted hers and they clasped their worn fingers together, the wrinkles evidence of the miles they'd traveled together in this life. "You will always be *mei* best friend."

Lizzie squeezed her hand before she straightened in her chair. "I'm serious, though. You need to explore whatever is going on with you and Ben, as you now call him."

Esther shook her head again. "I have no desire for any type of romantic relationship with Ben Stoltzfus or any other man. But . . . you are constantly reading those romance books, and it is more fitting for you to pursue him in a romantic way if it suits you. He's clearly smitten with you."

———◆———

Lizzie was sure Ben Stoltzfus wasn't interested in seeing her after her behavior this morning, but it touched her that Esther was willing to give up any potential feelings or attraction she had for this man and pass him off to Lizzie.

"I don't want anything to do with that man. He came over this morning, and we didn't exactly get along well." Lizzie was digging herself into a hole that she didn't know how to get out of, but she had no intention of telling Esther that Ben had invited Lizzie for supper and not her. No matter the circumstances, Lizzie wasn't going to do anything to intentionally hurt Esther. And the more she'd thought about it, the only reason Ben had invited her to the cottage was to prove it wasn't haunted. He wouldn't have won that argument anyway.

"The two of you squabbled?" Esther's eyes widened. "What about?"

Lizzie hadn't thought this through. She knew how easily one lie could turn into another, then snowball. "He said he wasn't moving out of the cottage, and we argued about it." She sighed as she felt the snowball starting to roll. "I tried to tell him that since the other house was bigger, he'd be more comfortable." The snowball was now gaining speed, and Lizzie was shrinking into a person she didn't want to be.

No one likes a liar, especially me.

"That doesn't sound like squabbling." Esther's stance relaxed back into the chair. "And he did mention to me that he was more comfortable in the cottage, that he liked the coziness and wasn't up for moving."

Lizzie waved a hand dismissively, hoping to stop the buildup of more lies. "Anyway, the man doesn't interest me outside of anything but the fact that he's our renter." She pointed a finger at her sister. "But I won't be going in that cottage again, even if his granddaughter does think he's dead."

"*Ach*, that's fine. I'll collect his laundry and deliver it to him."

"Fine." Lizzie wondered why that bothered her so much. She knew. But once again, she thought about Esther having a second chance for love.

She stood, knowing she needed to go back to bed and tell God she was sorry for the lies, then try to explain to Him that they'd been necessary, which sounded stupid in her mind. God didn't condone lying, no matter what.

"I'm going back to bed." She waved a hand at Esther. "The good dentist is all yours." The words stung a little.

Esther laughed. "*Nee*, Lizzie. He's not. He's a man renting the cottage who has taken a liking to you."

Lizzie grunted. "You're wrong, but I don't want to argue."

Esther smiled. "Even if I were interested in Ben—and again, I'm not—I'd choose you over a man if it were someone you were fond of in a romantic way."

Lizzie walked around the table and hugged her sister. "I'd choose you too."

———◆———

The next morning Esther snatched her grocery list from the table, glad she hadn't forgotten it. "I'm off to the market, Lizzie," she said loudly. She'd meant to go much earlier in the day, but her knees hadn't wanted to cooperate until now. After slathering them with ointment that the doctor had prescribed when Esther's home remedies had failed her, the swelling in her knees had gone down.

"Okay!" Lizzie hollered from upstairs. "I'll have the room ready by the time you get back."

They'd had a last-minute reservation this morning.

Luckily, Lizzie had remembered to check the answering machine in the barn, the only place on the property that had electricity. It was on her list of things to do when she collected eggs, but sometimes she forgot.

The bishop allowed the machine since it was directly related to their business. Without use of the internet, it was the only way people could make reservations. It was still hard to believe there was a service like the internet where you could learn new things, read books, and buy anything a person could imagine—according to Lizzie, who had looked at it when she was in the library.

Esther took easy steps toward her buggy but slowed her stride when she saw an envelope pinned to the fence. She yanked it free, and sure enough, it had Lizzie's name on it. Esther had told Ruby Lunsford to stop buying scratch-off lottery tickets for Lizzie and explained that it went against their beliefs to gamble. Ruby, an English woman about Esther's age who lived nearby, had introduced Lizzie to the tickets. Lizzie wouldn't go into the convenience store to get them, to her credit, but she'd give Ruby money to purchase them for her.

One time Lizzie won ten dollars, jumped up on a kitchen chair, and lifted her arms almost to the ceiling. "I won, I won, I won!" she had screamed over and over. From that moment on, she was hooked. After Esther had scolded her, Lizzie was more discreet. Her sister had either missed the envelope this morning while collecting eggs or Ruby had been by recently and they hadn't heard her car pull in.

Esther marched back to the house as fast as her knees would allow, the envelope in one hand and her purse swinging from her elbow. Inside, she set her purse on the coffee table next to the envelope, cupped her hands on either side of her mouth, and took a deep breath. But she stopped herself from hollering for Lizzie upstairs. Things had been so tense between Esther and her sister, and then everything had returned to normal the night before. She didn't want to stir up Lizzie about anything.

She lowered her hands, picked up her purse, and left the envelope on the coffee table. Lizzie would know Esther had found it. Maybe she'd give up the habit on her own.

I doubt it.

Esther shook her head as she left the house again.

———◆———

Lizzie blew the long gray tresses that had slipped from beneath her prayer covering out of her face, then peeled off her rubber gloves. She'd been upstairs for over an hour, and her teeth were bothering her again this morning. She shuffled the bothersome dentures around in her mouth, which only made her think of their dentist neighbor.

"I didn't like him anyway," she said aloud as she came down the stairs, knowing Esther was gone. Then she gasped when she saw a white envelope with her name on it lying on the coffee table. "I told Ruby to put my lottery tickets in the *barn*. She doesn't listen. Or doesn't remember well," she continued aloud, thinking maybe she was the one with the problem since she was talking to herself.

She would get a lecture from Esther later, but adrenaline shot from head to toe as she considered that this batch might contain a winner. She ripped open the envelope. "Huh?"

There were usually five one-dollar tickets inside. Today the envelope contained a folded piece of white paper.

Oh no. It was probably a note from Ruby that she couldn't get the tickets for her anymore. *Esther must have gotten to her.*

Lizzie huffed as she unfolded the lined white paper, then read.

My Dearest Lizzie,

I am still trying to decide whether I would like to relocate to the larger house on the property. Can you meet me there today at eleven? I'd like to have another look at it.

Fondly,

Ben

Lizzie grunted. *I'll send Esther.* She was glad the dentist was reconsidering the larger house.

Then she looked at the clock on the wall and gulped. It was ten forty-five.

IO

---❈---

Ben sat in one of the rocking chairs on the front porch of the larger home. Lizzie was late. It was ten after eleven, but as he took in the view from this house, he realized it was far better than from the cottage. The elevation was higher; he could see part of the pond and two horses grazing in a pasture beside the inn. Fluffy clouds had parted to make way for the sun, and a cool breeze complemented the atmosphere. He liked it here. Not enough to move. But still . . .

Movement in the corner of his eye caught his attention. Lizzie was stomping across the field, her arms swinging.

"You're late," he said when she got within hearing distance, mostly to agitate her, but he couldn't help but smile when she scowled.

"It's not like I was given much notice." She padded up the porch steps, lifted the doormat, and retrieved the key.

Ben stood. "What?"

Lizzie sighed, shook her head. "Never mind." She opened the door and walked inside. Ben followed.

She pointed to the fireplace. "I forgot to mention last time that's gas," she said as she moved toward the kitchen.

Ben followed her. He almost ran into her when she stopped abruptly. Then they both stood with their mouths agape. He couldn't believe the effort Lizzie had gone to in an effort to impress him. The kitchen table was set for two, with a mixture of fresh flowers in a vase and two white plates etched with blue flowers waiting next to linen napkins. There was a pitcher of tea and two glasses filled with ice. But it was all the food that caught Ben's attention. A full display of rolled deli ham, turkey, roast beef, and salami lined a silver platter. Three types of bread sat on an elongated plate next to several condiments. Another dish held lettuce, sliced tomatoes, pickles, and olives. There was a plate of cookies—it looked like a mix of chocolate chip, peanut butter, and possibly oatmeal. And also an apple pie and two bags of chips.

Ben finally closed his mouth. "Wow. What a spread. But you shouldn't have."

Lizzie's eyes widened, one still a little swollen and yellow like Ben's. "I didn't! I assure you that I didn't do this." She glared at him. "And by the look on your face, you didn't either."

"Then who?" It was mattering less and less. His mouth watered at the lavish spread on the table. None of the food was fancy, but the presentation was lovely.

"*Ach*, I know who!" Lizzie balled her fists at her sides,

then reached inside her pocket and handed him a letter. It was short, and he quickly read it, then handed it back to her, laughing. "I didn't write that."

"I know that *now*." She crossed her arms and shook her head.

Ben reached into the back pocket of his gray slacks, lifting the light jacket he wore, and retrieved a note he had found taped to his front door. He handed it to Lizzie, who snatched it from his hand. As she read, Ben recalled the contents of the note.

My Dearest Ben,

I really believe you would like to live in the larger house on the property. Can you meet me at that house at eleven for another look?

Kindest Regards,

Lizzie

She waved the paper close enough to his face that he had to step back. "'My Dearest Ben'? Does that sound like something I'd say?" Her face was as red as the barn.

"Your letter was addressed to me the same way." He chuckled. "We've been set up. Who would send us each a letter, prepare this lovely meal, and . . ." He raised one shoulder and dropped it slowly. "I can't think of anyone. But you said you knew. Who?"

Lizzie knew exactly who the culprit was. Her matchmaking sister. This was just the kind of the thing she and Esther would have done to spark a romance between a couple. "*Mei* sister," she said. "Esther." This was overboard even by Esther's standards.

Ben grinned as he rubbed his chin. "Why would Esther do this?"

Lizzie stared at her feet for a few seconds, unsure how truthful to be with the dentist. Finally, she lifted her eyes to his. "She is trying to fix us up"—she waved a dismissive hand—"as in romantically."

Ben laughed. "Really? Interesting."

Lizzie's stomach growled. Maybe from hunger. Maybe fury. "What is so *interesting* about it?" She waved her hand again. "Never mind. It doesn't matter." She stared at him and pressed her lips firmly together before she spoke. "Do you want to move into this *haus* or not?"

"No. I don't." He was still grinning.

"Bye. I'm leaving." Lizzie spun around, but as she passed by Ben, he latched on to her arm.

"Wait, wait, wait."

Lizzie shrugged free of his hand on her arm. "Wait for what?"

"No matter Esther's intentions, you're not really going to pass up this lovely lunch, are you?" Ben's smile was more genuine this time, unlike his smirky grin.

Lizzie's stomach growled again, and this time she was certain it was from hunger. She wondered when Esther had been able to pull this off. She surmised it must have been before she left for the market when Lizzie was upstairs cleaning.

Ben didn't wait for her to answer. "Be right back." He walked to the living room, and Lizzie peeked around the corner as he walked to the fireplace, crouched, and ignited the gas logs. He glanced over his shoulder. "Hopefully, some of this warmth will make its way to the kitchen." He stood again. "Shall we eat?"

"At least you had the common sense to wear a jacket this time." She sighed again before she stepped back to the kitchen. Ben entered behind her. "I must admit, Esther did a nice job."

She shed her black cape and hung it over one of the four chairs that didn't have a place setting in front of it. After letting Esther's shenanigans sink in, she had to admit it warmed her heart that her sister would go to all this effort. "I guess we shouldn't let this go to waste."

Ben came around the corner of the table and nobly pulled out Lizzie's chair. "Madam," he said so formally that Lizzie couldn't help but chuckle.

After he was seated across from her, they bowed their heads in prayer, but only for a second or two. "Wait. If it's all right with you, I would like to offer the blessing aloud," he said.

"*Ya*, okay." Lizzie had hoped he was a man of faith, but she hadn't anticipated that he would reach his hand across the table. She hesitated, but finally let his massive hand hold hers, and he began.

"Dear heavenly Father, we thank You for this bountiful feast . . ." He paused, winked at Lizzie. "And we thank Esther too. Please bless my new friends with good health and happiness, and continue to shed Your goodness on them for all their lives. Help us to grow in our faith, to always hear Your good word, and may we stay on the right path to do Your work. It is with thanks and praise that we glorify You. Amen."

Lizzie eased her hand from his and swallowed hard. "That was nice, Dr. Stoltzfus," she said, keeping her eyes cast down, slightly taken aback by the sincerity of his words. She recalled her prayer in hopes that Dr. Stoltzfus was a Christian.

Thank you, Gott.

"I'd like it if you would call me Ben." He spoke quietly with a smile on his face, and Lizzie recalled how she'd made fun of Esther for using his first name.

"*Ya*, okay." She stood, lifted the tea pitcher, and filled their glasses while Ben reached for two slices of bread. It looked like grocery-store bread, not Esther's, which made sense. Her sister wouldn't have had time to do any baking this morning and have all this laid out too.

"I love this kind of lunch with an assortment of offerings." Ben put everything available on the massive sandwich he was building.

"You must like olives pretty well too." Lizzie smiled as the little round black olives spilled from his sandwich as he took a bite. She took some bread for herself and started making her own sandwich, nodding to her left. "Don't forget chips."

Ben took a large handful and dumped them on his plate. Lizzie had always thought people ate less as they got older. She and Esther didn't eat nearly as much as when they were younger. Esther probably ate more than Lizzie, but she was a larger woman. But neither of their appetites compared to Ben's.

They ate quietly, both admitting they were too full for dessert. Finally, Ben sat back with a contented sigh, swiping a few crumbs from his scruffy beard. Lizzie was tempted to tell him that he needed to shave but decided against it. It had been a pleasant lunch, and she didn't want to mess it up.

"You should take the pie and cookies home with you." Lizzie was sure Esther had desserts prepared at home for their guests' arrival soon.

"Are you sure? Because I won't argue." He winked at her, which should have felt unnerving, but something deep inside her stirred, a feeling she couldn't recall having had since she'd first met her husband.

This is silly. She did her best to stow the thought, but the wink repeated itself several times in her mind's eye.

"So, what are your plans today?" Ben dabbed at his mouth with the ivory-colored cotton napkin. *Nice touch, Esther.*

"We received a last-minute reservation for a room tonight. I'll help Esther get those folks settled, then I need to go to the Donation Spot. That's the actual name of it, kind of like a Goodwill drop-off place. I have some books to donate." She wanted all those murderous books out of her possession right away, but she was undecided about her romance novels.

"I'd offer to drive you, but I'd prefer to ride in your buggy, if you wouldn't mind me tagging along." He gave her a hopeful look. "It's chilly, but such a pretty day for a ride through the countryside."

"I haven't seen you drive that automobile since you arrived."

He shrugged. "I haven't needed to."

Lizzie opened her mouth to tell him no to going with her, but she hesitated, her mouth open, long enough for him to hold up his palm.

"I won't be any trouble," he said as he winked again.

Lizzie avoided his eyes, then mumbled, "Uh, okay, I reckon." This was Esther's man, but Lizzie was struggling to harness her feelings for Ben.

———————◆———————

Their guests, a young couple from New York, arrived much earlier than expected, and after Lizzie got them settled, they took off to go sightseeing. Lizzie wondered where Esther was. Her sneaky older sister should have been home before now, and she had some explaining to do.

She put another log on the fire, sat on the couch, and

recalled her lunch with Ben. It felt odd not to think of him as "Dr. Stoltzfus" or "the dentist." Soon they would be going to the Donation Spot together. Lizzie had mixed emotions about that. Ben was truly better suited to Esther, but Lizzie couldn't forget about the winking and the fact that he had originally asked her to supper, not Esther.

Of course, that could have been solely to convince her the cottage wasn't haunted.

He caused her stomach to swirl in a weird way. Sometimes she liked the sensation. Other times it was annoying because it made her feel like a teenager. She didn't have the time or desire for that type of nonsense when it came to herself.

When she heard Esther pull up the driveway, Lizzie waited inside. As she peeked out the window, she saw her sister carried only two bags.

"You'll never believe what happened on the way to the market." Esther swooshed by Lizzie in the living room, went straight to the kitchen, and began unpacking the groceries. She obviously didn't notice Lizzie's foul expression or irritated stance, so Lizzie followed her and resumed her position, pursing her lips with her arms crossed.

"I'm all ears," Lizzie said, followed by a sigh.

Esther looked over her shoulder and frowned. "I'm sorry if you're upset that I wasn't here to help you get our guests settled, but I was shook up, and then the police came, and . . ." Her voice was shaky, and her hands trembled more than usual.

Lizzie dropped her arms and went straight to her, putting a hand on her back, everything else flushed from her mind. "What happened? Are you all right?" Her chest tightened.

Esther nodded. "A car hit *mei* buggy from behind, and . . ." She wagged her head quickly. "*Ach*, Lizzie, I really am fine, but I was so nervous after it happened that I avoided every highway on the way home. I didn't have our phone, but the people who hit the buggy called 911 because they thought I was injured, which I wasn't. An ambulance came, too, and they made me lie down inside to take my vital signs. It just scared me, but I was cleared to go home. They were a very nice couple from Bedford, the ones who hit me, and they felt terrible. Anyway, I'm fine. Everyone made too much of a fuss."

Lizzie reached inside the other grocery bag to help Esther put things away, but she couldn't stop looking at the way her sister's hands shook. Maybe this wasn't the time to reprimand her for her little matchmaking mission.

"I'm just glad you are okay. The *Englisch* follow too close behind us in their fancy cars." Lizzie stashed some lettuce in the cooling bin of the refrigerator, biting her lip the entire time.

After the groceries were put away, they sat at the kitchen table. "Did the young couple make it here?" Esther asked. "I didn't see a car outside."

Lizzie nodded. "They arrived early. They're sightseeing right now. I told them supper was at six." She glanced at the clock on the wall. "But you'll have to handle it. I need to take some things to the Donation Spot at five, and I might not be back in time."

She was trying to give Esther time to fess up about what she'd done.

Esther sighed. "That's fine. I prepared most everything yesterday. I just need to heat it up."

They were quiet, and finally Lizzie couldn't stand it any longer. "Don't you have something to tell me?"

"As a matter of fact, I do." Esther straightened in her chair and glowered at her. "I thought you were going to stop having Ruby buy those lottery tickets for you. It's so wrong, Lizzie. You know that. But I spotted one of her envelopes pinned to the fence this morning. I'm assuming you found it on the coffee table and must not have won any money, or you'd be acting all crazy like last time."

Huh? Lizzie tipped her head to one side and scratched her cheek. "You know good and well that there weren't any lottery tickets in that envelope. Don't play dumb with me, Esther. Didn't you think Ben would tell me he didn't write the letter? And that he'd received a note taped to his door?"

Esther truly looked dumbfounded as her jaw dropped and her eyebrows knitted into a frown. "What are you talking about?"

Lizzie reached into the pocket of her apron and took out the envelope and note. She studied them for a moment and noticed for the first time that the penmanship didn't look like Esther's. She slid the note across the table. "That's what was in the envelope."

"And you think I wrote this? That's not even my handwriting."

Lizzie slinked down in the chair. "*Ya, ya*. I see that now. But I just assumed it was you, and when I got to the house, there was a lavish lunch spread out on the table. I figured you set it all out before you went to the market. And since Ben got a similar note, we were clearly set up." She frowned. "If it wasn't you, then who would do such a thing?"

"I'm sure I don't know." Esther's voice was indignant as she raised her chin.

Lizzie puffed her cheeks out, then blew the air out slowly. "I don't get it." She thought for a few seconds, then snapped her fingers. "Maybe you were trying to make up for your lengthy supper with Ben and the little kiss on the cheek. That's why you set us up. To level the playing field."

Esther maintained her indignant expression. "That is the most ridiculous thing I've ever heard. I told you, I was not involved in any matchmaking scheme. And there is no playing field. *Ach*, and now you are the one calling him Ben?"

"He asked me to." Lizzie feared the conversation might be headed in the wrong direction, and Esther had already had a bad day. How was she going to tell her that Ben was going with her on her errand shortly? She shouldn't have agreed to him riding along, but she hadn't had the strength to say no. She was going to need to toughen up and shed this infatuation she had with Ben Stoltzfus.

"And I don't have anything to make up for, by the way."

Esther huffed, something she rarely did. "Whoever set up your lunch must feel you and Ben are a perfect match." She stood from the table. "I'm going to lie down even if I only have a short time before I need to get supper ready . . . on *mei* own." She started to walk off.

Lizzie didn't like the sound of Esther's voice. Her sister hadn't seemed upset about handling supper at all until after Lizzie told her about her lunch with Ben. Lizzie decided to test the waters. She needed to know her sister's true feelings. "He asked if he could go with me to the Donation Spot in a little while."

Esther stopped in her tracks and didn't move for a couple of seconds, nor did she turn around. "Fine. Have a lovely time." She resumed her walk to the bedroom, slamming the door behind her. Something else she rarely did, if ever.

Esther had lost her composure. How much was due to the accident, and how much had to do with Ben? Or maybe Esther was just mad that Lizzie had accused her of playing matchmaker and she really hadn't. Whatever the reason, Esther's hands hadn't stopped shaking the entire time she sat at the table.

Lizzie slowly lifted herself up and was headed to the bathroom when she heard Esther crying in her room, a sound that tugged at Lizzie's heart so much that it made her chest hurt. She held her hand up to knock on the door but changed her mind and instead went to the front door, slipping into her shoes and grabbing her cape on the way out. If there was any chance this was about Ben, Lizzie was going to nip it, along with her own infatuation with Ben. The whole thing was starting to feel like a love—or infatuation—triangle, and Lizzie wasn't willing to risk her relationship with Esther.

When she got to the cottage, which gave her the creeps, she pounded on the door.

"I'm not going to the Donation Stop today. Esther was in an accident, and I don't want to leave her." Lizzie turned and trekked down the porch steps.

"Lizzie, wait." Ben was behind her in a flash. "Is she okay? What happened?"

As Lizzie spun around, she took in his worried expression and genuine concern. She wanted to run into his arms and cry. And she wanted to stay in those strong arms for a long time. "She's fine," she said, forcing herself to be strong and detached from this man. He was causing problems between her and Esther, and now someone else was involved. Lizzie would get to the bottom of the mystery, but for now, Esther was her only concern.

"Goodbye, Ben."

He called after her again, but she didn't look back.

When she returned to the inn, she didn't hear Esther crying. Maybe she was asleep, but Lizzie rapped lightly on the door. "Esther, can I come in?"

No answer. Lizzie gently turned the knob and pushed the door open. Esther was sitting on the edge of her bed and staring at her hands, which were still shaking.

"I thought you were going with Ben to the Donation

Spot." Her sister didn't look up, only sniffled. "I'm sorry for *mei* behavior. I just . . ."

Esther cared about this man. Therein lay the problem. So did Lizzie. But she loved her sister more than any attraction to a man. "I decided not to go today. I'm going to stay and help you make supper for our guests."

"Are you sure?" Esther asked as she met Lizzie's eyes. "I don't want you canceling your date because of me."

"That's exactly why I'm canceling our *outing*, not a date . . . because of you."

Esther frowned.

Lizzie smiled at her. "*Ach*, Esther, let's quit beating around the bush. As ridiculous as it sounds, we both fell for the same man." She let out a half chuckle. "At our age." She shook her head. "He's charming, but we don't really know him. He is causing problems between us, and I won't have that." She reached for her sister's hands and squeezed, but Esther's hands continued to shake.

"*Ach*, Lizzie, he is a charming man, and I admit I was flattered when he asked me to supper, but I sincerely believe he is interested in you, and I mean as more than a friend. I really want you to have a companion after I'm gone. I don't want you to be alone."

Lizzie still didn't have the heart to tell Esther that it was Lizzie whom Ben had invited to supper. As much as she wanted Esther to have a second chance for romance, Lizzie's own feelings for Ben were complicating things.

"I feel the same way. I don't want you to be alone after

I'm gone." Lizzie decided that maybe it was best for both of them to steer clear of Ben Stoltzfus. They both seemed to have each other's best interests at heart, but things were backfiring, and emotions seemed to be running high. "Let's just make a pact that we won't see Ben anymore outside of what is necessary. No buggy rides, no lunches or suppers, or anything else. He's a renter. Period."

"*Nee*, Lizzie. I don't think you should give up an opportunity to—"

"There's no opportunity there, and it's all a silly notion." She nudged Esther's shoulder, still holding her trembling hands. "Deal?"

Esther was quiet, nodded, then said, "Men certainly do cause trouble, don't they?" She smiled a little. "At any age."

Lizzie still wasn't sure about Esther's feelings for Ben one way or another or what had caused her to cry. But maybe when things settled down, and Lizzie put some distance between herself and Ben, then she could resume her plan for Esther. For now, she threw her arms around her. "*Ya*, they do. Even when they're old like Mr. Dentist over there." She eased away and nodded to Esther's hands. "Now, tell me what's going on with your shaky hands."

Esther looked away quickly, which caused alarms to ring in Lizzie's mind. "Esther, what's wrong? Are you sick?" *No, please, God, no.*

Esther looked right at her. "I'm perfectly fine, Lizzie. There is nothing wrong with *mei* hands. I think *mei* blood sugar is low, or I'm still distraught about the accident earlier.

I'm perfectly fine." She grimaced. "Other than bad knees, arthritis, and my diabetes."

"Okay. You can live with all of that." She stood. "Now let's go make supper for that nice couple, and we never have to socialize with Mr. Dentist again."

Esther nodded.

11

⊗

A WEEK LATER...

Gabriel sat next to Mindy on her couch. He'd vowed not to see her again. But she had sounded upset when she called. He had headed her way after helping his father and brothers repair the fence surrounding the south pasture, which took most of the day. She'd said she skipped school this evening.

"What do you mean our plan backfired?" He took off his hat and set it on the coffee table, forcing himself not to look at her lips. They'd talked on the phone twice, but he hadn't seen her since they set up the luncheon for her grandfather and Lizzie. She'd told him then that her grandfather hadn't mentioned anything about the lunch date, which seemed odd.

"Not only has Grandpa not questioned me about our

little setup, but he also hasn't even mentioned it. Maybe he doesn't have any idea or hasn't considered the possibility that I—or we—set things ups."

He scratched his head. "Well, we might have failed, but how did it backfire?"

"Grandpa said he hasn't seen Esther or Lizzie for the past week. He just sits in that cottage by himself all day long. I go when I can, but with school and work, I've only seen him twice this week. Thanksgiving is in three days, and when I suggested that he and I spend it together, he said he wasn't feeling up to it, and that's not like him at all—not to want to spend time with me, especially on a holiday. And he looks terrible. He still hasn't shaved, which is okay, but he looks like he's lost weight, and his face was pale. Do you think I should talk to Esther or Lizzie?"

Gabriel heard the worry in her voice. He wrapped an arm around her and held her close. It should have been awkward, but it felt as natural as breathing. The thought of being involved in any matchmaking between her grandfather and Esther or Lizzie had been mostly an excuse to spend time with Mindy, but it was getting too hard. Their friendship was blossoming, and he sensed her attraction to him as well. The next step could only cause them heartache, but he couldn't stand to see her so upset.

"Do you want me to talk to Esther and Lizzie?"

"No." Her voice trembled. "I will."

He held her tighter.

"I've missed your laughter." She raised her head and

locked eyes with him. Hers were moist, and her pain jabbed at his heart, but he couldn't think of anything to make her laugh.

"I've missed everything about you," he said, knowing he shouldn't have blurted it out but unable to stay quiet anymore.

Her face lit up, which wasn't the reaction he was expecting. It would be even harder to have this talk. "I've missed you."

Gabriel took his arm from around her and twisted to face her. "What are we doing?"

She chewed her bottom lip, then nodded at the empty plates that had held sandwiches earlier. "Eating?" She tried to smile, but Gabriel sensed she knew what was coming.

"If I keep coming here, there's going to come a time when I cup your cheeks, look into your gorgeous green eyes, and kiss you with all the passion that is building up inside me." He sighed. "There, I said it."

She gazed at him, expressionless.

"Say something." His heart pounded in his chest.

"I have those same feelings when I'm around you."

What should have been words he longed to hear sent him into a tailspin. He abruptly stood, ran a hand through his hair, and began pacing. "We can't be around each other. I feel like our friendship could lead to . . ." He stopped moving back and forth across the room and locked eyes with her. "Could lead to something more."

She leaned her head back against the couch and closed

her eyes. "I hear what you're saying. I've thought about that too."

He sat on the couch again, facing her after she lifted her head. "I know I've probably ridden the *rumschpringe* train longer than most men. I'm twenty-three. But I want to be sure that I find the right woman. You are someone I want to get to know better, and that scares me." He stared at her. "I have to marry an Amish woman. I'm committed to *mei* faith. And I know it's too soon to be having a talk like this, but I feel something for you, something undefinable that I haven't felt for another woman."

———◆———

Mindy blinked back tears. She'd known this moment was coming, and it was probably best that it had arrived sooner rather than later. Her random thoughts about practicing the Amish lifestyle had suddenly become more than frivolous fantasies. It was a potential reality that she wasn't ready to consider. *Surreal.*

"*Nee . . .*" Gabriel put a hand to his forehead as he scrunched up his face and squeezed his eyes closed. "Don't you dare cry. Please."

"I'm not." She quickly dabbed at her eyes with her fingers. "It just makes me sad that we can't even be friends. But I totally understand. Really. I do."

He slowly relaxed his face and opened his eyes. "I'm going to tell you something about me that you don't know."

Mindy waited. He was so serious that she was almost afraid to hear what he had to say.

"You know how, when I laugh, you say it makes you laugh?"

She nodded, managing a smile. "It's contagious."

"*Ya*, and when I see someone cry, especially a woman, it makes me cry!" He threw his arms up before slapping his hands to his legs. "And that isn't very manly, now, is it? So . . ." He pointed a finger at her. "No crying."

She tapped a finger to her chin. "I think I'd like to see what you look like when you cry." She pursed her lip into the most exaggerated pout she could manage, then sniffled, trying not to grin.

He closed his eyes. "I'm not looking."

Mindy held the expression, thinking she might burst out laughing even though there wasn't anything funny about the context of the conversation. It was just him, the way he was so animated and dramatic.

He opened one eye, which was moist. She covered her mouth with one hand as she lifted her eyebrows. "You really are going to cry, aren't you?" she said between her fingers.

"Nope." He grabbed her ribs and began to tickle her until they were rolling around on the couch giggling hysterically.

"Stop it! No fair." But that wonderful laughter soothed her soul, and when they finally caught their breath, they were lying side by side on her couch, barely fitting, and facing each other. The feel of him next to her and their ragged breathing sent her heart racing.

They weren't sixteen. They were grown adults, and Mindy knew how quickly this could lead to a place they had no business going. Gabriel had a look in his eyes that confirmed what she was feeling. She forced herself to sit up, tucked her hair behind her ears, and waited until he lifted himself to a sitting position.

"We can do this." She stared into his eyes. "Be friends. I've had male friends before. Haven't you had friends who were women? It doesn't mean we have to take things any further."

He grinned at her. "Really? You think we can just be friends?"

"Of course," she said as she sat taller and folded her hands in her lap. "We're adults." She shrugged, attempting to appear nonchalant.

He stared into her eyes, and twice he opened his mouth as if he were about to say something, but instead he cupped her cheeks with both hands and tenderly brushed away a strand of hair that had fallen across her face. "I'm going to do it. Now's the time to tell me to stop and to give me that friendship speech again."

Her heart thumped. "What speech?"

Gabriel kissed her with his eyes before his lips brushed against hers, and the heady sensation sent the pit of her stomach into a wild swirl that bypassed mere physical attraction. She quivered at the sweet tenderness of his mouth on hers, the dreamy intimacy she felt, and the way her emotions swirled and skidded. Logic tried to slip into her thoughts, but she quickly pushed it away. His lips were warm and sweet on hers, and she couldn't force herself to put an end to the emotional connection they had.

Gabriel gently eased away, putting an end to what they both knew couldn't be.

"I told myself I wasn't going to let that happen"—he kissed the tip of her nose—"but I would have imagined it in my mind for the rest of *mei* life."

Mindy knew she would replay the velvety warmth of his kisses over and over in her mind like a favorite song, one that made her heart sing, but she didn't know what to say.

He smiled before he reclaimed her lips, and she kissed him back as if it were the last time she would feel this delicious sensation. And it probably would be.

———◆———

Gabriel cupped the back of her neck and drew her closer to him. All his preconceived notions that he could control his attraction to this woman leaped from his mind, replaced by the passion building in every ounce of his being. He'd never made love to a woman. He believed in saving the sacrament for marriage, but she was testing his resolve through no fault of her own.

He breathed a labored sigh of relief and disappointment as she eased out of his embrace. Breathless, he gazed into her eyes, tempted to tell her how hard he was falling for her, but how would that help either of them? Instead, he recalled what she liked most about him and flashed her a big smile. "You sure are an aggressive *Englisch* woman."

Her jaw dropped before she said, *"Me?* I believe it was you who kissed me." Her own smile deepened into a snicker, which caused Gabriel to chuckle, which made her laugh more.

Finally, they caught their breath.

"What now?" she asked as she gazed into his eyes.

She wanted an answer as to where they went from here. Gabriel had no idea. He grinned as he shrugged, hoping to keep the mood light and avoid a conversation about what had just happened. Then he recalled the box of cinnamon rolls she said she'd picked up at the bakery earlier. "Uh . . . cinnamon rolls?"

She laughed as she stood up. "Sounds good to me."

Gabriel followed her to the kitchen. He suspected any serious conversation about their relationship was tabled for today. He hoped so, just wanting to bask in the pleasure of her company.

After two cinnamon rolls and a cup of coffee, he decided he should go home, although it went against what he wanted to do. He would have liked to stay, curled up with her on the couch. Anything to be close to her.

He stood and pushed in his chair. She did the same. *"Danki* . . ." He rolled his eyes. "I mean *thank you* for the sandwich, the cinnamon rolls, and I guess for seducing me. That was fun." He chuckled at how goofy he sounded, but when she giggled and poked him in the stomach, he had no regrets.

At the front door, her green eyes brimmed with passion. He could feel the connection between them, but Mindy's eyes also hinted at contemplation. She was probably wondering if he was going to kiss her good night and was speculating that it was a bad idea. They could either nip this right now, or . . .

He tenderly touched her cheek with one hand as he gazed into her eyes. "What am I going to do with you?"

She didn't smile, and her eyes gleamed with a sheen of purpose, as if she was deep in thought. Her smartest move would be to verbalize the obvious—that it would be best if they didn't see each other, at least for a while. The thought caused Gabriel's stomach to churn, but when she leaned closer to him, his lips descended toward hers. At the last moment, she rested her head against his chest and hugged him.

Here they were. Reality check. "I guess a hug it shall have to be," he said as he held the back of her neck, then planted a kiss on her forehead when she eased out of the embrace.

"Probably best, don't you think?" She lowered her eyes, but Gabriel gently lifted her chin until they were holding each other's gaze.

"*Ya*, probably." Even though mixed emotions swirled around him like a tornado, when her lips parted slightly, it was an invitation he couldn't resist. He kissed her with everything he had. Reason eventually forced him to put some distance between them, but he quickly pulled her in for a tight hug and clung to her. "What am I going to do with you?" he asked again, whispering the question in her ear.

Following a long pause, she said in a soft voice, "Keep me."

Gabriel didn't let go of her. She might see the moisture in his eyes. *I can't,* he thought. It was impossible. He'd never leave the only life he'd ever known. But instead of being truthful, he said, still in a whisper, "Okay."

———◆———

Mindy closed the door after they'd said their final goodbyes. She shuffled to her room and sat on the bed, covering her face with her hands and shaking her head. "'Keep me'?" she said aloud. What kind of a thing was that to say? She might as well have said, *"If you care enough about me, you'll consider having a relationship with me. I know it will alter your entire life, but I'm worth it."* It was possibly the most selfish thing she'd ever done.

She lay back on her bed as horse hooves clicked in the distance and threw her arms behind her, knowing deep down that she was going to have to end things with Gabriel before hearts were broken. Yet as a tear slipped down her cheek, she realized her heart already had a giant crack in it. They barely knew each other. Was it even possible to fall so hard for someone this quickly? She recalled her mother telling her that her father had proposed only a week after they'd met. They'd had a good marriage even though it was cut much too short. And her mother had definitely moved on.

Tomorrow was Tuesday, which meant work and school,

and she needed sleep, but she feared she would be up all night analyzing her situation with Gabriel. She put her fingers to her lips, closed her eyes, and tried to capture the memories of him kissing her, which should have been mesmerizing. Instead, another tear rolled down her cheek.

She startled when she heard her cell phone ringing in the kitchen where she'd left it. Gabriel hadn't had time to get home yet. Had something happened during his commute? She rushed to the kitchen, found her phone, and as she looked at the number, her stomach clenched.

"Grandpa, is everything okay?" It was after nine o'clock, and he was usually asleep by now. When he didn't respond, she said, "Grandpa!" Louder this time.

"Mindy . . ."

"Grandpa, are you okay?"

"I need you to come over. I'm sorry."

"Do I need to call an ambulance? What's wrong?" Her heart pumped against her chest much too fast. "Grandpa?"

"No ambulance. Please come quickly, hon. I'm sorry."

"On my way."

She prayed all the way to the cottage, a thread of hysteria swimming around with her speculations. She reminded herself that the last time she'd been this scared, her grandfather had been fine.

He didn't sound fine this evening.

12

———— ✗ ————

E sther awoke to Lizzie sitting on her bed and shaking her. "Esther, wake up."

Her foggy mind hadn't engaged, but she halfway sat up and rubbed her eyes. "What's wrong?"

"There's something going on at the cottage. I was reading, and I heard car tires squealing to a stop, and when I looked out the window, Ben's granddaughter was running toward the cottage."

Esther fumbled for matches and lit the lantern on the bedside table. "I guess we better go see what's wrong."

"The *maedel* has a key. I let her keep the one I used last time since we have another one." Lizzie stood, already dressed.

Esther put some drops in her eyes, dressed quickly, and wrapped a scarf around her head since she didn't want to take the time to pin up her hair and top it off with a prayer covering.

By the time they reached the cottage, Esther's knees felt like putty, like they might give out any second. She'd made the mistake of keeping up with Lizzie, but her worry had prompted her to stay in step with her sister.

"I hope he didn't just not answer the phone again and get his granddaughter all worked up." Lizzie shuffled her teeth around so much that Esther heard her grinding them. Shifting her dentures seemed worse when she was upset or nervous, and Esther had to admit that she was also worried about what they might find.

"If something happened to him, I'm going to feel terrible that we just cut him out of our lives a week ago." Esther trudged up the porch steps where Lizzie waited with her chin slightly raised.

"Let me know if everything is okay." Lizzie stood perfectly still, her prayer covering lopsided.

Esther scowled. "*Nee*, Lizzie. You are coming in with me."

"But what about Gus's ghost? I'm sure Ben is fine." Lizzie pouted.

Esther grabbed her sister by the arm, opened the door, and dragged her over the threshold. "I better not hear one more word about Gus and this cottage being haunted." She paused, slowing her steps when she realized Mindy must be in the bedroom. "Mindy! Ben!"

"Help me, please!" the girl shrieked.

Esther couldn't remember moving as fast as she was now, but Lizzie had sprinted past her. Inside the bedroom

Mindy was leaning over her grandfather. At least a dozen pill bottles were strewn across the bed, some of the bottles open, and quite a few pills on the floor.

"I would have called an ambulance, but he told me not to when he called me. I just called for one. He doesn't know what he took." She held up two of the bottles as her bottom lip quivered.

"Ben, can you hear me?" Lizzie yelled much too loud, but when Ben nodded, a wave of relief washed over Esther. "Can you breathe okay?"

He shook his head, and Esther watched the slow rise and fall of his chest. It reminded her of the last labored breaths her husband had taken toward the end.

"Let's see if we can prop him up, see if that helps him breathe better." Esther put an arm behind Ben, and Lizzie and Mindy assisted. His breathing seemed a little better once he wasn't lying flat.

Mindy looked at all the pill bottles everywhere. "What are all these pills for?" She directed the question at Esther and Lizzie.

"We don't know," Esther said as she kept her eye on Ben's breathing. She heard sirens in the distance. "Sounds like the ambulance is getting close."

"Are you in pain, Ben?" Lizzie yelled again, and Esther wanted to tell her that she didn't think Ben was hard of hearing. But he didn't respond, so maybe he didn't hear her after all. Or he was losing consciousness.

Esther touched his forehead when she saw sweat dripping

down his temples. "He's burning up. Hon, can you wet a cloth with cool water?" The man was sweating profusely.

Mindy was back in less than thirty seconds. "Here."

Esther pressed the washcloth to Ben's forehead just as she heard the paramedics arrive. They announced themselves just inside the door.

"In here, in the bedroom!" Mindy wouldn't leave her grandfather's side until the paramedics—a young man and woman who looked to be fifteen in Esther's eyes, although she knew they were older—asked them to step aside.

"He's lost so much weight in only a week," Lizzie whispered. "We are terrible people for not checking on him."

"*Ach*, well . . . We didn't know he was ill. He never mentioned anything." Esther brought a hand to her chest, hoping to calm her heart rate.

"The man eats like a horse." Lizzie shook her head, which caused her prayer covering to slip to the side even more. "How could he have lost so much weight?"

Esther hadn't realized how much she'd missed Ben until now, and seeing him in this state caused tears to well up in the corners of her eyes. She glanced at Lizzie, who never liked anyone to see her cry, but her eyes were moist as well. Poor Mindy was openly weeping.

After identifying Mindy as Ben's granddaughter, the young female paramedic began firing questions at the girl. "Is he diabetic? Does he have a pacemaker? What about allergies?"

"I don't know! I didn't even know anything was wrong

with him. He must have had all this medication in a drawer or somewhere else that wasn't out in the open. I've never seen all this."

The paramedics glanced at each other. It wasn't as if they were judging Mindy for not knowing, but maybe they were. The poor child was beside herself and as clueless as Esther and Lizzie.

Through half-opened eyes, Ben pointed to his bedside table, and the young man opened it up and took out a thick folder. He began flipping through it. "After we get his vitals, we need to call his oncologist. The number's here." He pointed to a page in the file.

"Oncologist. That's a cancer doctor," Lizzie whispered in Esther's ear.

"I know." Esther had a sinking feeling in her stomach.

"Blood pressure is normal. So is his heart rate," the young woman said after they had hooked up Ben to all kinds of medical devices. "Mr. Stoltzfus, I'm going to put this oxygen on you, and we're going to start an IV to get some fluids in you since I think you might be dehydrated."

"Is he going to be okay?" Mindy swiped at her eyes.

The male paramedic, a handsome fellow probably around Mindy's age, put a hand on her arm. "I think so. But we need to talk to his doctor to know how to proceed." He nodded to his partner, who had stepped away and was on the phone. "She's trying to find him now."

Mindy inched her way closer to the bed and squeezed her grandfather's hand. "Grandpa, you're going to be okay."

He nodded, which Esther took as a good sign. She and Lizzie stayed out of the way.

"Well, someone is more alert." The male paramedic smiled when Ben opened his eyes all the way. "I think you were dehydrated, sir. I already see a little color coming back in your face."

The young woman ended her call and walked to Mindy. "You said you're his granddaughter, right?"

She nodded, and the other paramedic cleared his throat as he moved closer to her. "Mindy Stoltzfus, right?" He had his head in the file again, scanning the pages.

"Yes. I'm Mindy Stoltzfus." She'd stopped crying now that her grandfather was becoming more alert.

"Your grandfather has several powers of attorney in this file. Did you know that you are the one he designated to make all his medical decisions? You are also in charge of his finances and where he will live if he can't make decisions for himself." He pushed the folder toward her. "It's all in here."

Mindy took the folder, but she didn't look at it. "What's wrong with him? You mentioned an oncologist." The girl was as pale as her grandfather had been moments ago.

"His doctor is going to meet us at the hospital to have him completely checked out, but since his vitals are okay, he's becoming more alert, and getting some color back, I think he will be fine. But due to his condition, he really does need a full evaluation."

"What is *wrong* with him?" Mindy asked through gritted teeth.

The man shook his head. "I'd be lying if I said I'd ever heard of the type of cancer he has. I'm sure his doctor can answer all your questions."

"Can I ride in the ambulance with him?" Mindy asked in a shaky voice. Both paramedics nodded.

Ben removed the oxygen, and all eyes turned to him as he struggled to speak. "I'm sorry, Mindy."

Esther put a shaky hand to her lips when they began to tremble, the same way Ben's were.

"Grandpa, don't you dare be sorry. I love you. We'll get through this together."

Esther and Lizzie exchanged looks. They'd been through this type of thing at least a hundred times—Lizzie more than Esther since Esther avoided hospitals if she could. At their age they'd seen many people travel on this journey.

Mindy was pale, trembling, and probably had no idea how to deal with the contents of that folder, the questions to ask. And how would she be able to take off work to tend to Ben?

"Should I call a driver?" Lizzie asked in a whisper.

Esther nodded. "It's *mei* understanding they are all each other has, and we don't want that child having to deal with everything herself." Her stomach clenched at the thought of going to the hospital. Just the smell reminded her of times past, when she'd had her own diagnosis, when she'd had to take care of her husband, and the many trips she'd made when Gus was ill. But it was the right thing to do, and she cared about Ben more than she'd let on to anyone.

"Hon, can I borrow your mobile phone? We'd like to follow the ambulance to the hospital if that's all right with you?"

Mindy eased her hand out of her grandfather's, located her phone in her purse, and handed it to Esther, who called a driver who worked late.

"I'm going to run back to the *haus* before the driver gets here and leave our guests a note in case they wake up or have an emergency before we return," Lizzie said. Esther was relieved she didn't have to make that trek home. "I'll grab our phone while I'm there."

"And *mei kapp*," Esther said as Lizzie swooshed by her.

Ben was becoming more alert, and Esther noticed the IV bag was half empty. When she looked his way, he was staring at her. He lowered the oxygen mask again. "I guess the cat is out of the bag," he said weakly but clearly.

Esther forced a smile. "*Ya*, I reckon it is." She twisted the ends of the scarf she'd haphazardly thrown atop her head as they'd rushed out the door.

Then he shifted his gaze to her trembling hands and said, "Maybe two cats."

Esther quickly stuffed her shaking hands in her apron pockets and pretended not to hear him.

Ben chastised himself for not reading the prescription bottles more carefully. He suspected he'd taken too much of something and not enough of another. He was in and out of sleep during the ambulance ride to the hospital, but he squeezed Mindy's hand occasionally to let her know he was okay. This was a terrible way for his granddaughter to find out he was ill.

Even though things felt out of whack and he was drowsy, he was alert enough to catch bits and pieces of the conversation between Mindy and the young man who was reading through his file in between checking Ben's vital signs.

"I googled it—the name of the cancer that I found in that folder," the man said. "But it's impossible to know much without talking to his doctor. I've never heard of it." He paused, and they were quiet. Ben was about to drift back to sleep when the sound of Mindy's voice jerked him back to semi-alert.

"Does it say what stage the cancer is?" Her voice was shaky, and Ben closed his eyes and prayed the paramedic wouldn't tell her.

"It says Stage 4, but listen . . ." The man's voice was soothing as he spoke. "Stage 4 doesn't always mean the worst. I've seen lots of people pull out of Stage 4 cancers, so don't let that alarm you."

"I would have known if he was getting chemo or radiation. He would have had some type of symptoms, needed rides, help with things." Mindy sniffled.

Ben's already damaged heart was crumbling. He'd had

his last round of radiation and chemo before he moved here. He shouldn't have moved to Montgomery. It was selfish, but he'd wanted to know his granddaughter, although not have her worried and burdened with his care. Maybe he hadn't thought things through well enough.

He must have fallen into a deeper sleep, because the next time he woke up, he was in a hospital room with monitors beeping, a blood pressure cuff on his arm, and a pulsometer on his finger. A doctor was chatting with Mindy.

"Ah, look who is awake." The man walked to the bed and patted his arm. He was a fellow who looked to be about Ben's age but obviously in better health. Ben had never met the guy. He'd chosen him as his doctor before he moved to Montgomery and had his medical records transferred to his office. When he'd told Mindy he was handling his affairs prior to the move, radiation and chemo had been part of that process.

"I'm Dr. Andrews," the man said.

"I took the wrong medication, didn't I? Did I take too much of something?" He glanced at Mindy. "Hi, sweetheart."

"Hi, Grandpa." She attempted to smile.

"Actually, you didn't take too much medicine. At least not that I can tell. I can only speculate that you got confused due to severe dehydration."

The doctor had kind eyes. Ben liked that. As someone in the medical field, he tried to show his patients compassion, and he appreciated others doing the same.

"I'm sorry we're meeting under these circumstances," the doctor continued, "but we're pumping you full of more liquids, and as long as your lab work is okay, you'll be free to go home." He pointed a finger at him. "Lots of fluids from now on. Call my office and set an appointment for us to chat. I've reviewed your file, so I'm up to speed on your condition."

Ben nodded, hoping Mindy didn't question the Stage 4 diagnosis.

"I've got a critical patient down the hall that I need to check on, but we'll talk soon." He turned to leave, and without saying a word to Ben, Mindy was on his heels and out the door.

———◆———

"Wait. Excuse me, Dr. Andrews. I know you're in a hurry, so I'll walk with you." She got into step with him. "I didn't even know my grandfather was sick, much less with cancer, and I'm his only relative. Can you please explain to me what is going on?"

Dr. Andrews slowed his stride and eventually stopped. He eased her to one side of the hallway. "He should have told you." The doctor's face pinched, and Mindy's heart ached as she prepared herself for what she presumed was coming.

"Your grandfather has a fairly rare type of cancer." He rattled off a super-long name that Mindy didn't think she would remember how to pronounce. "He had his last round of chemo and radiation before he moved here, which was part of a clinical trial. His former doctor briefed me, but it's my understanding that unless this trial is successful he only has a few months. I'm sorry, but don't lose hope."

Mindy thought back to a friend in high school who had been given only a few months to live, and she ended up living a few more years. "No offense, but doctors aren't God. That's not a set-in-stone amount of time even if the trial doesn't work. Right?"

"It is always our best guess." He touched her arm. "Let that soak in, and feel free to accompany your grandfather to his appointment. Two sets of ears are always better than one, and I'll be able to answer any other questions then."

He rushed down the hallway. Mindy just stood there, numb, not moving. She wasn't even crying. Was this what shock felt like?

"Hon?"

She recognized Lizzie's voice and spun around to see both sisters standing in front of her.

"We saw you talking to the doctor from where we were sitting and decided to come see if you are okay," Esther said. "Can we all go sit down?" She nodded to a seating area at the end of the corridor.

Mindy nodded and forced her feet to move in that direction. She sat in one of the six chairs against the wall. Esther and Lizzie took a seat on either side of her. She glanced back and forth between the sisters with a mixture of gratitude and of unjustified anger.

"I've only seen Grandpa twice in the past week because of school and work, and I don't feel good about that at all, but he said he hasn't seen either one of you for a week. I thought you were becoming friends."

Mindy struggled to keep any irritation out of her voice. It wasn't Lizzie and Esther's responsibility to check on her grandfather. "Lizzie, when Grandpa invited you to the cottage for supper, I was surprised to hear Esther showed up instead." She looked at Esther. "But it turned out fine. Grandpa said he had a lovely time. And Lizzie, Gabriel and I set up what I thought was a very nice surprise lunch date for you and Grandpa, even though he never mentioned it to me. In fairness, he probably didn't think I had time to organize it, but Gabriel helped me. Now I'm wondering if what we did caused you both to avoid my grandpa."

Lizzie dropped her face into her hands, and Mindy was wracked with guilt. Was Lizzie crying? She glanced at Esther, whose mouth hung open.

"The supper date was for your grandfather and *Lizzie*?" Esther blinked her eyes a few times as she directed the question at Mindy.

"Yes. Grandpa had mentioned how Lizzie amused him. I thought maybe they had struck up a, um . . . special friendship, so Gabriel and I played matchmakers." She paused and shrugged. "Like I hear the two of you have done many times. And I think Grandpa also wanted to convince Lizzie that the cottage wasn't haunted."

Lizzie still had her face in her hands, but she was silent,

no sniffing or sounds of crying. Mindy wondered if she knew her prayer covering was lopsided.

Esther leaned around Mindy. "Lizzie, look at me," she said in a snappy voice.

"I don't want to," Lizzie mumbled without looking up.

Esther turned her attention to Mindy. "I was under the impression that your grandfather invited *me* for supper." She lowered her head and sighed. "I'm very embarrassed now."

"Don't be." Mindy shrugged. "He said he had a great time with you. But Gabriel and I wanted him to have equal time with both of you, so we arranged the luncheon with Lizzie. I mostly wanted Grandpa to have friends nearby since I can't be there as often as I would like because of work and school."

Esther's face was as red as Mindy's fingernail polish. "Lizzie, how could you let me embarrass myself like that? Why did you send me in your place to have supper with Ben?"

At least they were on a first-name basis, Mindy thought as she watched Esther's nostrils flare. She opened her mouth, presumably to lash out at her sister even more, but when Lizzie didn't lift her head, she turned back to Mindy again.

"I'll deal with Lizzie later. What did the doctor say?" Esther pressed her lips together as her forehead crinkled.

It was Mindy's fault for not being more responsible, making sure he was getting enough liquids and eating enough. She should have paid more attention to his weight also. Her initial anger that the sisters hadn't visited him was unwarranted, a reaction to her own feelings of failure. And she'd panicked today, just like she had when she and Lizzie had gone to the cottage. It happened at work, too, if she was put into any type of situation where someone was in pain or there was uncertainty about what was happening to a patient. If blood was involved, sometimes her adrenaline pumped so hard and fast that she felt like she might pass out. She was questioning her career choice more and more.

Mindy took a deep breath. "He has a rare form of cancer. It has a long name that I'd never heard of." She chewed on her trembling bottom lip. "He only has a few months, according to the doctor, unless the clinical trial he is in works."

Esther lowered her head but then slowly turned to face her. "Doctors don't know everything. Only *Gott* knows when it is our time to join Him. And that sounds hopeful, about the clinical trial."

She had told the doctor the same thing, but it didn't stop tears from gathering in the corners of her eyes.

"Aw, hon." Esther put an arm around her. "I know we haven't known each other long, but Lizzie and I will help you take care of your grandfather, and I'm sorry for both of us that we hadn't been by to see him in a week. We had our reasons, but I wish we hadn't—"

"Just tell her!" Lizzie moved her hands from her tear-streaked face, straightened, then threw her arms in the air before slapping her palms to her knees. "We both have a crush on the same man, and we decided to put some distance between us and your grandfather to clear our heads."

A crush? Mindy's mouth dropped open, and even amid

the tragedy of the day, she had to cover her mouth with her hand to stifle a grin. When she glanced at Esther . . . Mortified didn't begin to describe the expression on the older woman's face. Her eyes were round as saucers.

"Lizzie, what is wrong with you?" Esther groaned as she glared at her sister, then, after taking a deep breath, looked at Mindy. "That is simply not true."

Esther was about to say something else when a nurse exited her grandfather's room and walked toward them. "Is one of you Lizzie?"

Lizzie straightened her tiny body, raised her chin, and gave a taut nod of her head. "That's me. I'm Lizzie." She ran her hands across her moist cheeks.

"Mr. Stoltzfus asked for you, if you'd like to go see him." She was an older woman, like the sisters. Mindy stood when Lizzie did.

"He asked to see Lizzie alone," the nurse said.

"Oh." Mindy scratched her cheek, then glanced at Esther, who was still seated. Esther lowered her head.

"You go, Esther," Lizzie said.

"He asked for you." Esther spoke firmly with an edge to her voice. Mindy wondered if Esther might have told a small fib. Maybe she did have what Lizzie referred to as "a crush" on Mindy's grandfather.

"He's probably not right in his head or he would have asked for you." Lizzie crossed her arms across her chest and grimaced.

"Stop it, Lizzie. Just go see the man." Esther shook her

head, attempted to smile, then looked at the nurse. "We've had a long night."

Mindy glanced back and forth between the sisters. She'd been right. Her grandpa was interested in Lizzie more than Esther. She watched as the two women went another round about if Lizzie should go see her grandpa, with Lizzie saying Esther should go and Esther stubbornly objecting. Despite Mindy's temptation to tell them to stop bickering, it was amusing and touching at the same time to see them like this.

It was also heartbreaking. If the clinical trial failed, her grandfather wouldn't be around long enough to have a romance with either woman.

13

Lizzie shuffled into Ben's room and made a mental note not to cry. But just seeing him lying in the hospital bed caused her bottom lip to tremble.

"You asked to see me?" She raised her chin and did her best to keep her emotions in check.

Ben grinned and patted the bed next to him. "We've been in bed together before. I promise I won't push you to the floor again."

His color had returned to his face, along with his unnerving charm.

Lizzie huffed, grabbed a chair, and dragged it to the side of his bed, then sat. "I see you are feeling better." She was glad her lip had stopped trembling. Ben probably deserved a good reprimanding for allowing his granddaughter to find out about his illness this way, but Lizzie didn't have the heart to say anything. She was relieved that Ben looked much better than when they'd been at the cottage.

"Lizzie, you know I just like to toy with you." His grin disappeared as tenderness brimmed in his eyes.

She hung her head and said a silent prayer that the knot in her throat would go away. She didn't want to be a babbling mess. When he didn't say anything, she lifted her eyes to his. "I'm sorry about your cancer."

"And I'm sorry I didn't tell Mindy or you and Esther." The smile returned. "Why do you think I paid the rent in advance? I didn't want you and Esther out any money in case I died before my lease was up."

Lizzie covered her face with her hands. "Don't say things like that." She couldn't stand for people to see her cry, and she'd already let her emotions get the best of her only moments ago. And Mindy would surely tell Ben about her outburst, announcing that she and her sister were both smitten with Ben. She cringed inwardly, but she needed to hold herself together.

"Look at me," he said softly as he lifted himself to a sitting position.

She slowly raised her eyes to his.

"Why did you send Esther for supper instead of coming yourself?" His expression had a hint of sadness in it, his head tipped slightly to one side as he waited for her to respond.

Lizzie wanted to lie, and if she stalled a little longer maybe something would come to her, but she'd already told a string of small fibs, and it was a growing habit she needed to break. After taking a deep breath, she said, "I was hoping you and Esther might fall for each other." She squeezed her eyes closed. Esther would want to kill her for being this honest. "She's the best person I know, she loves deeply, and I thought she would be a *gut* match for you."

He raised his eyebrows. "Even though I'm not Amish?"

"I know, I know. Maybe I didn't think it all the way through."

"Oh, I think you did." He grinned. "But what if I'm interested in someone else romantically?"

Lizzie's eyes widened. "You just got here! You've already met someone? You never even leave the *haus*. Who is it?"

He clicked his tongue, winked at her, then pointed a finger at her. "Here's looking at you, kid."

Lizzie stopped breathing. "Huh?"

Ben laughed. "I think that quote is from a movie, but . . . it's you I'd like to get to know. Esther is lovely and a wonderful conversationalist, but you make me feel . . . alive. And I need that feeling now more than ever." He chuckled. "You make me laugh. I always tell Mindy that laughter soothes the soul."

She smiled as she let that information soak in, but as soon as it did, her chest tightened. "Please don't tell Esther." With a hand to her heart, she locked eyes with him. "She's a better woman than I am, but if that is really how you feel, then I don't want her to know." Then she looked at Ben hooked up to all those medical gadgets. She felt tears coming on again.

He reached out his hand to her, and without hesitation, she held on tightly.

"I won't. And maybe it's selfish of me to tell you I like you a lot when I might not be around for too long, but—"

"Don't say that," she said, her voice trembling.

He shrugged. "A lot can happen in a few months. The clinical trial might work and turn things around." He winked again, and Lizzie grinned, needing to lighten an emotional load that was spiraling out of control.

She eased her hand from his and stood. "You wink a lot. Maybe you are just a dirty old man."

He chuckled. "Maybe I am."

"You'll probably outlive all of us."

He winked at her yet again. "Maybe I will."

Lizzie leaned down and kissed him on the forehead, lingering for longer than she had intended.

———◆———

Esther was too embarrassed to make small talk with Mindy. Just the thought of herself showing up at the cottage, thinking Ben had invited her, caused her stomach to twist into knots. She was ready to string Lizzie up by her toes, and her sister would get a good piece of her mind when they got home.

Her embarrassment was equally matched with the sadness she felt about Ben.

Mindy had done her best for the past few minutes to hold a conversation. Esther tried to stay focused on what she was saying about her job and classes at school, but she wondered if the girl had any idea how many times she mentioned Gabriel, even if just in passing while talking about things that didn't relate to him.

Under different circumstances, she and Lizzie would have jumped on the chance to play matchmaker between the two young people, even if one of them wasn't Amish. But Esther wasn't sure she had the strength for it, and those type of situations always had the potential to leave someone with a broken heart. She hadn't seen Mindy and Gabriel interacting, so there was no way to know if it was worth the effort.

Mindy stopped talking, and they both looked at Lizzie as she exited Ben's room. Esther could almost always tell what was on Lizzie's mind. Her sister was transparent, and her emotions showed in her expressions. Something had happened, but whatever it was, Esther was unable to decipher Lizzie's blank look. "Ben wants to see you," Lizzie said without making eye contact with Esther.

Esther didn't want to see Ben, but she lifted herself from the chair, letting her left knee hold most of her weight until she was fully standing. Today it was her left knee that felt the best. Tomorrow it might be the right. She hoped they didn't both go out at the same time.

Before she left for Ben's room, she gave Lizzie a stern look. She'd handle her sister later. For now, she had to face a dying man who had politely served her a supper that was meant for Lizzie. She wasn't sure if now was the time to bring it up or not.

"Hello, Esther." Ben was sitting up in bed, his hands folded atop the hospital blanket. "Thank you for coming."

Esther took a seat in the chair by his bed. "How are you feeling?"

"Physically? Much better. Mentally, not so good. I should have told Mindy I was sick." He averted his eyes from her.

"*Ya*, you should have. But she knows now, and she'll need time to process and accept the information."

"She's a strong girl, but I don't want to be a burden on her. When the time comes, I have money set aside for care-givers to come to the cottage, or in case I need to be moved to a . . . um . . . facility."

Esther swallowed hard, then cleared her throat. "Ben, winters are cold here. Sometimes we see below-freezing temperatures. Are you sure that being in a house without electricity is the best idea? We would certainly refund all the money you paid up front to rent the cottage." Her heart was splintering with tiny cracks in all directions. Sadness led the emotional destruction, and embarrassment was among the mix also. But now was a time to do what was best for his health. Considering this new information, maybe she also needed to give up on her plan to nudge Ben and Lizzie together. Lizzie could end up with a broken heart if Ben's experimental treatment didn't work.

"The fireplace keeps the place nice and toasty, and that battery-operated heater in the bedroom will come in handy." He tried to smile, and Esther could only imagine what must be going through his mind. She recalled the fact that everything happens on God's time frame—even for Ben. There were no guarantees for another day for anyone. Esther had a drawer full of pills and insulin syringes. She could be the one to go first.

"It will be more difficult when summer gets here without air-conditioning," she said before she put a hand to her forehead and winced. "I'm sorry. You don't know if . . ." Ben most likely wouldn't be here by summertime.

He smiled. "It's all right, Esther. Really. I feel fine right now, and I'm choosing to enjoy each day the Lord sees fit to give me. I'm upset with myself that I allowed myself to get dehydrated. I just hate this for Mindy."

"Don't beat yourself up about that, Ben. And Lizzie and I both want you to reach out to us for anything you need."

She recalled Lizzie's outburst, telling Mindy how they were both smitten with the same man. It was a stretch. They were more like two old ladies who fancied a man they didn't know well. Mindy would probably tell Ben what Lizzie said. Esther might as well get the other issue out in the open.

"There is something I want to tell you." She could feel her face turning red before she even spoke the words she dreaded. "I know that you invited Lizzie to your *haus* for supper and not me." She shook her head. "I'm not sure why she told me to go and allowed me to believe you invited me." In truth, she did know. Lizzie was afraid of leaving Esther without companionship, the same way Esther was scared to leave Lizzie.

"Esther, I don't want you to give that another thought." He shrugged. "I suppose that sometimes it's anyone's guess why Lizzie does things." They both chuckled. "But I had a wonderful time, and I enjoyed having supper with you."

Esther felt her blush spreading, deepening. "I had a nice evening as well." She paused. "This seems trivial to be discussing in light of . . . you know."

"It's important to me that you don't feel strange about coming for supper instead of Lizzie. I mean that. She probably didn't want to come for fear about her haunting issues. I thought I could put her mind at ease about that." He smiled. "And I've known I was sick for a long time. Mindy is probably not happy with me." He held up a finger. "But before they come back in here poking and prodding at me, I have two things to ask you."

"*Ya*, of course."

"Does Lizzie know about your Parkinson's disease?"

Esther's breath stuttered. He'd seen her hands shaking. Should she lie to him, the way she had been to Lizzie, always telling her sister her glucose was out of balance or giving her some other excuse?

"*Nee*, she doesn't." She hung her head in shame.

———◦———

Ben was touched by the way Esther and Lizzie tried to protect each other, however misdirected it might be. The moment he had the thought, he realized he had done the same thing to avoid hurting Mindy.

"It will eventually become impossible to hide it," Ben said as he eyed Esther's hands, tucked safely beneath the purse in her lap. Her bottom lip started to tremble. "Oh, Esther, please don't get upset." He reached out his hand to her, and to his surprise, she latched on. "I know a thing or two about Parkinson's. My wife had it."

Esther's eyes widened.

He gave her hand a squeeze before he eased away. "It's not what she died from, but she struggled with it. Are you on medication?"

She nodded. "*Ya*, I am. But please don't mention it to Lizzie. She worries about me so much as it is."

"It isn't my place to tell her. That's up to you." He shook his head. "I'm sure Mindy will give me a lecture about keeping my cancer from her. Don't let yourself get in too deep with Lizzie. Beneath that whimsical demeanor, I suspect there is a kind and loving woman."

She stared at Ben for several seconds. "She is the kindest and most loving person I know. And Lizzie has done some things that have absolutely astounded me, but setting me up for supper at your place when I wasn't invited—"

"We are letting that go, remember?" He smiled at her.

"*Ya*, I know. I'm sorry." She got a faraway look in her eyes for a few seconds before she looked back at him. "Lizzie is *mei* best friend. I'll tell her soon about *mei* Parkinson's."

"Okay. And did your doctor tell you that certain foods

can worsen the symptoms? Like eating too much sugar, for one thing." Ben recalled the days when Elsa's hands shook so badly that she couldn't feed herself.

"I'm diabetic, so I try to watch *mei* sugar. And yes, *mei* doctor gave me a list of foods that I should avoid or limit." She rubbed her forehead. "I don't know how we got so wrapped up in this conversation about me when you must have so much to think about."

Ben chuckled. "I've had several months to think about things. My affairs are in order, and I plan to accept each day as the blessing it is without regrets. I've lived a good life, Esther, and when the Lord calls me home, I'll be ready. And that brings me to the second thing I need to ask you."

She waited patiently, her hands still folded beneath her little black purse.

"Sometime soon, I would like to visit with your bishop. Do you think that would be possible? And if so, would you be willing to take me to see him?"

Esther tipped her head to one side. "Are you secretly Amish and haven't told anyone?" She grinned.

"It's a question I get asked often since my last name is Stoltzfus, but I have no family here, as I said before. Considering my condition, I would like to talk to a member of clergy, and based on what I know about your beliefs, I think the bishop is the best person for me to speak with. Would he be willing, do you think?"

She nodded. "Bishop Lantz is a wonderful and kind man. I'm sure he would be happy to see you."

Ben nodded. "Thank you. Now, I suppose you better send my granddaughter in here. I need to convince her that I am at peace with things and that I don't want her worrying."

Esther slowly stood and kept her hands hidden with her purse. She'd obviously practiced the maneuver a lot. "Drink lots of fluids," she said.

"I will."

Mindy walked into her grandfather's hospital room with an emotional backpack that was wearing her down, but she wanted to be strong for her grandpa.

"Don't yell at me," he said when she walked in, then sat in the chair by the bed. "I was going to tell you soon, after the holidays."

"That's not exactly soon. Unless you were going to tell me after Thanksgiving, which is in three days."

"I would have told you when the time is right. I'm sorry you found out like this. I try to drink plenty of water, but my stomach had been upset, and I guess I didn't stay hydrated." He paused as his expression sobered. "Mindy, you listen very carefully to me. I am at peace with what is happening. I don't want us to live with doom and gloom. We go on how we have been for as long as possible. When the time comes, I have made arrangements to have nursing care or be transferred somewhere if necessary."

She blinked back tears. "I will always take care of you.

But I'm not giving up. The clinical trial could turn things around."

He nodded. "You're right. But if our time is cut shorter than we'd like, the best thing you can do for me is to live your life. Don't waste a day. That is what will make me happy."

Mindy felt like her heart might break open and release all the emotions inside, but more than anything, she wanted to please her grandfather. "Well . . . I'll do my best." She tried to smile. "Lizzie probably overshared with me, but I have some things to tell you if you promise not to spill the beans. They're both such nice ladies. I don't want to betray their trust, but Lizzie never came out and said not to tell you some of the things she told me." She smiled for real this time. "Or maybe she *did* want me to tell you."

"I love a good secret. Let's hear it all."

Mindy was glad that, despite the beeping monitors and the fact that he was in a hospital bed, her grandfather seemed like his old self. She felt cheated at the possibility that they might not have a lot of time together. Selfishly, she also couldn't stop thinking about Gabriel. There'd been a certain finality when they were together. But for now, she would do her best to bring some light into the darkness for her grandfather.

"Lizzie said that she and Esther are both smitten with you. That's the word she used—'smitten.' That part she said in front of Esther, and I could tell Esther was so embarrassed."

Her grandfather burst out laughing. "Both of them? They barely know me."

"I guess you're a hot commodity around here, Grandpa." She shrugged, enjoying the sound of his laughter. Then she recalled something she wanted to ask him. "Have you ever noticed how Esther's hands shake sometimes? There's a patient at work whose hands shake like that, and she has Parkinson's disease. Do you think Esther has that? I know you said Grandma had it too."

Her grandfather lowered his gaze, fidgeting with his blanket. "Yes, I noticed it, and Esther admitted it to me. She also asked me not to tell Lizzie."

Mindy slouched down in the chair, crossed her legs, and sighed. "What is it with all of you? Everyone is keeping secrets. It only makes things worse. Please don't ever keep anything from me again, especially related to your health."

"I promise I won't." He tapped a finger to his chin. "However, I do believe you are guilty of keeping something from me."

She held her breath.

"Setting up a lovely lunch for Lizzie and me?" He smiled.

Mindy closed her eyes and playfully hung her head. "Guilty as charged." She glanced up, then lifted her head. "Did it go well? If you had to choose, it would be Lizzie, wouldn't it?"

Her grandfather chuckled. "Gentlemen never tell. But, hon, I'm a bit old for you to be playing matchmaker."

"But I was right, wasn't I? It's because she makes you

laugh, and I totally get that. Gabriel makes me laugh so hard sometimes that I feel like I'm going to bust. There is something about laughter that truly does soothe the soul, just like you said."

"Uh-oh." Her grandfather frowned. "Don't fall for that boy. He's Amish. Only around five percent of the Amish ever choose to leave the church, and they rarely get involved with outsiders. I read that somewhere."

"I know all of that. We're just friends." Even though she wanted it to be more. Again, she recalled the way they had told each other goodbye.

"If you know all that, then why were you trying to fix me up with Lizzie?" He raised an eyebrow.

"Because at your age, I thought it would be companionship. I mean, I thought you would be good friends, or . . ." She couldn't come out and say that she thought being physical was off the table at their age because she had no idea about such things. "I just wanted you to have friends your own age."

He chuckled. "I'm not five and don't need playdates."

Momentarily, she had forgotten about the cancer, but the reality kept forcing its way back into her mind. She pushed it away and tried to hang on to the sound of her grandpa's laughter. Her soul definitely needed soothing.

"That reminds me. Lizzie invited both of us for Thanksgiving. She said they don't have anyone booked at the inn. It would just be the two of them." She shrugged. "I told them you didn't want to do anything for the holiday."

She tried not to look as sad as she felt about spending Thanksgiving alone. As much as she appreciated Lizzie inviting them, she didn't want to go without her grandfather, knowing he was sitting alone at the cottage.

Her grandfather smiled. "I've changed my mind."

"Really? Are you sure? Do you think you'll feel up for it now?" Mindy pressed her palms together and smiled.

"When I told you before that I didn't feel up to it, I didn't. I was probably already getting dehydrated and didn't realize it. But I think it would be nice for you and me to spend Thanksgiving with Esther and Lizzie. It would be good for all of us."

Mindy stood. "Great. I'm going to go let them know."

"And tell them to go home. You're stuck with me since I need a ride home, but it could be early morning before I get sprung from this place."

She nodded before she left to let Lizzie and Esther know they would be there for the holiday.

———◆———

I still have it going on at my age.

Ben laughed at his arrogance. It was a thought he would never speak aloud to anyone. But if his speculations were correct, Esther had a soft spot for him. Still, he didn't believe she was smitten with him. They seemed to be on mutually friendly ground. If the two women were competing for his affection, as his granddaughter had said, it would make this last phase of his life entertaining, he suspected, no matter how challenging things got at the end. He truly did believe laughter was good for the soul, and he'd seen plenty of instances where a person's joyfulness had prolonged their life. Ben wanted to spend the last part of his life drenched in happiness, no matter how long he had left. He was still hopeful about the experimental chemo and radiation he'd had before the move, but God had blessed him with a wonderful life. He wasn't ready for it to end just yet, but he also didn't want to cause any problems for Mindy, Esther, or Lizzie. That would be one of his main objectives, along with not being a burden to anyone else.

14

———— ⊗ ————

Lizzie opened the oven to check on the turkey. "I'd say it needs another hour," she said before closing the door.

As usual, no response from Esther. Lizzie had checked on Ben for the past two days and had even gone inside the cottage briefly. As much as she enjoyed being in his company, she couldn't bring herself to stay for long. She was sure Gus was laughing from heaven during the times he wasn't haunting the cabin. Ben tried repeatedly to get her to stay longer, and it tugged at her heartstrings, but this was all a tricky situation.

Lizzie loved Thanksgiving, and she was glad Mindy and Ben would be joining them, but Esther had cast a cloud on the day. This was the third day her sister hadn't spoken to her after hollering at her for blurting out that she and Esther were smitten with Ben. In hindsight Lizzie realized her comment had been a bit over the top, but she'd been under duress at the time. Esther had also lambasted her about saying Ben had invited her for supper when he hadn't. She said she was too embarrassed to face the man.

Esther hadn't shirked her duties. As was tradition, Lizzie handled the turkey and side dishes while Esther prepared the dressing, which was a two-day ordeal. She had finished it a while ago and was slicing bread that they'd made early this morning.

"You have to talk to me at some point." Lizzie placed her hands firmly on her hips.

"*Nee*, I don't."

"Ha! You just did." Lizzie bounced up on her toes before she took a seat across from her sister.

"You lied to me, Lizzie, by telling me that Ben had invited me to supper. You know how I feel about lying." She set the knife down. "And what were you thinking when you told Mindy we had both taken a fancy to Ben? He probably thinks we're both crazy."

Lizzie recalled her conversation with Ben. He had made his feelings clear—that he was interested in her and not Esther. He was making a mistake, but Lizzie's own emotions wouldn't let her completely back away. She still didn't want Esther to know about the conversation, because she wasn't completely sure how Esther felt about Ben. Right now, Lizzie's sister was embarrassed. But how would she feel if she knew about Ben's feelings for Lizzie?

"*Ya*, I shouldn't have said that last part. But we can't be afraid to face him. We both like him, and I'm sure he's let it go by now. Otherwise, he wouldn't have accepted our invitation for Thanksgiving." Her stomach churned. "Esther, I can't stand it when we argue. It makes *mei* stomach hurt and *mei* heart too. I'm sorry for everything."

Esther frowned. "If you behave yourself today, I will forgive you."

Lizzie crossed her arms. "Esther, you're not always truthful with me either."

Her sister straightened in the chair and glared at her. "When have I lied to you?"

Lizzie wasn't sure this was the right time, but would there ever really be a right time? "Avoidance of the truth is lying too."

Esther returned to slicing the bread, shaking her head. "I don't know what you're talking about."

"*Ya*, you do."

Her sister set the knife down again and put her hands in her lap.

"Do you really think I don't know that you have Parkinson's disease? It's why you have your hands in your lap right now." When Esther lowered her head and didn't respond, Lizzie wished she hadn't said anything. "I want to be able to help you."

"I didn't want to worry you." Esther lifted her hands from her lap, both trembling more than before. She could barely slice the bread, and Lizzie was afraid she was going to cut a finger off, so she walked around to Esther's side of the kitchen table. "Let me finish the bread, and you can finish setting the table in the dining room."

Lizzie was ready for her sister to put up a fight, but Esther nodded, then slowly stood. "*Ya*, all right." She turned to face Lizzie before she entered the dining room. "I'm sorry I didn't tell you. I honestly didn't want you to worry."

Lizzie walked to her sister and best friend. Esther was right. She was worried sick and wondered how bad the disease would get for Esther. "I'm always going to worry about you." She held up a hand. "And before you say worry is a sin, I'm aware of that. The good Lord will keep us wrapped in His loving arms, but we are human, Esther, and I know you worry about me too. That's just a part of old age and *lieb*. And I *lieb* you more than anyone in the world." She wrapped her arms around Esther's waist and laid her head against her chest.

Esther held on to her tightly. "I want to tell you something, Lizzie, and I want you to really think about it."

Lizzie eased out of the embrace and looked up at her.

"Ben might go Home soon, and I will go . . . Both of us will likely pass before you. And leaving you alone without someone special in your life scares me. At our age I realize romance isn't the same as for young people. But if you find someone who holds your heart and lights up your life, you run toward it, not away from it." She smiled. "Otherwise, I'll haunt you just like Gus."

Lizzie blinked back tears.

"I need you to promise me, Lizzie, that if someone enters your life after I've left this one, embrace it. Promise me. No one needs to be alone, and since we have no children, it's come down to just the two of us." Esther smiled. "Two peas from the same pod."

Lizzie was tempted to tell her sister that she might have already found that person, however short-lived any romance with Ben might be, but she just couldn't.

"I promise." Lizzie would promise Esther anything if it would make her happy. "But I could get run over by a crazy *Englisch* driver or choke on *mei* food or slip and fall and crack *mei* head open and bleed out or—"

"Lizzie, stop it!" Esther covered her ears with her hands. "And please stop reading those books of yours."

"Okay, okay. But what I'm saying is you must make me the same promise, if I go first—that you will try to find companionship." She folded her hands in front of her. "That's only fair."

Esther nodded. "*Ya*, okay."

Lizzie knew that their destinies were in the hands of the Lord and that all things were on His time frame. But somehow, deep inside, she did feel like Esther would go first, and it terrified her.

———◆———

Ben couldn't remember the last time he wore a tie, and he'd chosen a bright-blue one since Elsa had always said it brought out the color in his eyes. And he had two lovely women to impress today. He laughed. It was humorous, but the thought was there just the same. Although he still had doubts that Esther harbored any potential feelings for him outside of friendship.

"Grandpa, it's me."

Ben left his bedroom dressed in black slacks, a crisp white shirt, his blue tie, and a black leather jacket. Mindy had her head peeking around the door before she stepped in.

"Wow. Look at you, all fancy." She glanced down at her own attire. "My jeans, boots, and sweater don't compare to my handsome grandfather."

"You look beautiful as always." He kissed her on the cheek. "I'm looking forward to this meal."

"I'm looking forward to watching the sisters dote on you." Mindy batted her eyes at him.

"I think you should forget that you ever heard Lizzie make that comment." Although Ben had hung on to it like gold, especially where Lizzie was concerned.

"We'll see." She pointed over her shoulder. "How are you feeling? Do you want to take my car to the inn or walk? It's chilly outside, but there're no clouds, and it's a beautiful day. But it doesn't matter to me."

"Let's walk, feel the breeze and the sun in our faces, shuffle through the leaves. Speaking of . . . I haven't seen Gabriel here to mulch the leaves." He rubbed his chin, concerned for his granddaughter to get involved with an Amish man. Ironic since she seemed to think it was okay to have a romance with an Amish woman . . . and at his age. "Have you seen him lately?"

Mindy wanted to appear nonchalant, so she shrugged. "No. I haven't seen him or talked to him." Not a moment had gone by that she hadn't thought about him, though, missed his laughter, their playfulness, his tenderness, the kisses. He obviously didn't feel the same way since he hadn't called her. Or he'd realized they were in dangerous territory and that it was better to cut things off before their hearts became any more involved. Maybe he realized Mindy wasn't strong enough to do it.

"Honey, it's probably for the best." Her grandfather gave her a sympathetic look.

"I know, and I'm fine with it. You ready to go?"

"I am."

Her grandfather closed the door behind him. He said he didn't lock it anymore. They both knew why without him explaining. *In case of a medical emergency.* But today her grandpa didn't look sick at all. There was color in his face, at least what she could see of it, and he just seemed in a jolly mood.

"Are you ever going to shave?" she asked him as they padded through the fallen leaves in hues of orange, yellow, and brown.

He rubbed his chin. "I don't know. The ladies seem to like this look."

Mindy laughed. "Well, I wouldn't want to do anything to put a damper on that."

She'd been praying daily that God would give her more

than a few months with her grandpa. Today was going to be a good day. She could feel it as she breathed in the smells of fall, along with a whiff of her grandpa's aftershave. There was only one thing missing: Gabriel.

———◆———

Gabriel was the last person to join his family at the table for the feast his mother and sisters had been working on for two days.

"We were about to eat without you," his mother said as she carried the turkey to the table.

"*Ya*, sorry." He forced a smile, happy to see that Matthew, Mary Kate, and Lillian were able to come. The baby had been sick the past couple days, and they'd been unsure if they would make it.

Gabriel had gotten up earlier than usual, completed his share of the chores, then taken off on his horse and run hard through the back pasture, the wind burning his face as he fought to shake off his feelings for Mindy. He hadn't called her. And he hadn't felt like laughing about much of anything.

He stayed quiet through most of the meal, lacking much of an appetite. He ate enough so that his mother and sisters wouldn't be offended, but his thoughts were somewhere else. No one seemed to notice since there were at least three different conversations going on at once. His two youngest brothers talked about a new Amish girl who had moved to town with her family, which only made him think about Mindy. His two sisters discussed a quilt they were working on, arguing slightly about the final touches. His father was busy eating double portions of everything on the table, seemingly uninterested in any of the conversations around him. His mother was quiet, and Gabriel caught her glancing his way several times.

When the meal was over and everyone had gushed about how wonderful the food was, his father and brothers—Matthew included—went out to the barn, probably to pass around a cigar. It was mostly forbidden but overlooked by his mother on holidays. Gabriel had declined the invitation. He just wanted to go upstairs and be alone.

As his sisters, Mary Kate, and his mother began clearing the dishes, Gabriel told them how good everything had been, then retreated upstairs. It was about fifteen minutes later when someone tapped on the door.

Gabriel was lying on his bed with his ankles crossed and his hands behind his head. His battery-operated heater hummed. "Come in."

His mother walked to the bed and sat, staring at him for a while before she spoke. "It's the *Englisch maedel*, isn't it? That's why you've been so mopey the past couple days, *ya*?"

He could lie, but she'd see through him. Mothers had a superpower when it came to lying. "*Ya*, I guess so. And *ya*, I know it's *mei* fault for caring about her, knowing we can't be together. I felt like we were heading down a path that was only going to hurt both of us. I think she felt it too." He sighed. "I think we knew that when we said goodbye the last time we saw each other, it was a real goodbye."

His mother hung her head for a few seconds. Gabriel waited, surprised she hadn't nodded in agreement. "Why do you think *Gott* put you in Mindy's life and vice versa?"

Gabriel frowned. His mother wasn't known for trick questions. "Just to be mean," he said, halfway meaning it.

His mother scowled, and Gabriel knew she was waiting for a better response—an adult response, not something a child would say. "I don't know, *Mamm*."

She slowly stood, clasped her hands in front of her, then said the words Gabriel would remember for the rest of his life. "Then go find out."

"What?" He grimaced as he ran a hand through his hair. Everyone knew it was an Amish mother's worst fear that one of her children would leave the nest, choose not to be baptized into the faith, and live among the English.

"You heard me. If you care about this *maedel* as much as it seems, then you owe it to yourself and her to find out why you are in each other's lives."

"How can you even say that? Our friendship has the potential to turn into something much more, and we might be hurt more than we are now." At least, he suspected Mindy might be hurting the same way he was.

She sat on the edge of the bed again and sighed. "I've always wanted you and your siblings to be baptized into the faith. You're right. All Amish mothers want that. But, even more so, we want our *kinner* to be happy." She paused.

"This is something I wouldn't admit to just anyone." She twisted her mouth back and forth. "Maybe not even your *daed*. But there are many ways to *lieb* the Lord. Ours is not the only religion. There are many Christian denominations with fine people who share many of our beliefs, and I believe you are grounded in your faith and have a solid foundation when it comes to *Gott*. Of course, I want you to raise your future *kinner* Amish and be a part of our community, but you aren't baptized. You wouldn't be shunned if you chose to leave someday. I guess that what I am telling you is that *mei lieb* for you will never change, no matter the choices you make, even if it wouldn't have been *mei* first choice for you. It is your journey. I can only walk alongside you for so long before you must trust your heart and make your own decisions."

Gabriel lowered his hands from behind his head and gazed into his mother's adoring eyes. She probably loved him more than anyone in the world.

"*Mamm*, I know you would still *lieb* me, no matter what choices I might make in the future. And *ya*, I'm a grown man, but what you think of me still matters. I appreciate everything you're saying, I really do. But the problem is . . . I also want to raise *mei kinner* Amish, to abide by the rules that have been set forth in the *Ordnung*, and to enjoy the fellowship of our community, the closeness. I don't want to give up all that. And you're asking me why *Gott* put me and Mindy in each other's lives? I have no idea."

His mother stood again and slowly walked to the

window, peering out with her back to him. "I love the way our area enjoys every season. Fall is ending, and we are entering into winter, a new season. But then there will be spring, summer, and fall again. It will repeat with *Gott*'s perfect timing, varying by days or weeks, but we will still be able to appreciate every season." She turned around and faced him, a slight smile on her lips. "It would be sad to let a season slip by if it had something to offer us, something unforeseen that only *Gott* ordains."

Gabriel was tempted to pinch himself, make sure he wasn't dreaming, because it felt like his mother was giving him permission to leave the only life he'd ever known to pursue a relationship with an outsider.

"You don't need *mei* permission to live your life the way you see fit." His mother took a step closer to him. "You don't need your father's or siblings' approval either. Your choices are between you and *Gott*."

Mind reading. Another superpower mothers possessed.

She leaned down and kissed him on the forehead, then slowly exited the room, leaving him alone with his thoughts, which were a mishmash of emotions. If she had hoped to ease his mind, make him feel better about exploring his options, she had done just the opposite. He was more convinced than ever that he needed to avoid Mindy. His heart was on the line. It was a dramatic thought to have . . . but his future was on the line too.

———◆———

Mindy and her grandfather entered the spacious dining room of the Peony Inn, the aroma of Thanksgiving filling their nostrils. She was happy her grandfather was feeling well and wanting to celebrate the holiday. She was also sure she'd never seen a more beautiful holiday setting. Sunrays beamed through sheer white curtains covering two large windows overlooking the pond in the distance, the water sparkling like fairy dust. There was a beautiful oak grandfather clock in one corner and a huge matching hutch against the wall nearby filled with various china and serving dishes. But it was the table setting that took Mindy's breath away.

She eyed the oblong table with enough seating for at least twelve but with only four chairs and place settings. White plates and bowls, white tablecloth, white napkins. The walls in the room were white, too, but Lizzie and Esther had turned what could have been nothing fancy into an elegance that Mindy loved. Beautiful white vases—three of them—were spaced along the middle of the oak table, each bursting with a glorious display of silk peonies. Large silver candleholders held white candles, and round silver holders enclosed the napkins laid crossways over the plates.

"Wow. Everything looks just beautiful," Mindy said as she took it all in. As lovely as the table was, the massive display of food was divine—turkey, dressing, and all the fixings, mashed potatoes with browned butter drizzled on top Amish style, which Mindy loved. And there were peas, carrots, various casseroles, relish trays, chowchow, jams, jellies, homemade bread, and two pies.

Her grandfather put a hand across his stomach. "And look at all that food."

Esther and Lizzie beamed as they smiled. Mindy was so glad she wasn't spending the day alone, doubly glad her grandfather was feeling well, but one person was still missing. She pictured Gabriel dining with his large family. She wondered if he thought about her at all.

"Where would you like us?" Mindy's grandpa waved an arm over the beautiful display. Lizzie rushed to him.

"Here." She pointed to one of the settings at the end of the table, then grabbed his arm and practically pulled him to the spot where three glasses had been set out. "One is sweet tea," she said, "one is cranberry juice, and, of course, the third one is water."

Her grandpa smiled. "Very well. Thank you."

Mindy couldn't help but smile. The women were going to make sure her grandfather had plenty to drink. "And where would you like me?"

"At the other end of the table," Lizzie said, pointing. Esther kept her hands in her apron pockets, and Mindy wondered if that was due to her shakiness.

"Well, okay, but it seems like you ladies should be at the heads of the table." Mindy slipped into the chair anyway.

"We like to sit in the middle so we can hear everyone." Esther took a seat.

Lizzie sighed. "I don't know why you say things like that. We aren't hard of hearing." She turned to Mindy's grandfather and smiled. "I'm not, at least."

"Let us pray," Esther said after she rolled her eyes at her sister.

After everyone had prayed silently, Esther spoke first. "I know it's not always traditional at an *Englisch* Thanksgiving to have jams, jellies, and chowchow, but . . . Lizzie makes the best chowchow in town, and we serve it at every meal, Thanksgiving included."

"And Esther is known for her dressing that she makes for Thanksgiving and Christmas. She also makes the best pies." Lizzie glowed as she talked about her sister. She was cute, so tiny. Esther was lovely as well, although more refined, for sure. It was sweet the way they bragged on each other. "But Gus did say he liked *mei* bread better." Lizzie chuckled. "He admitted that near the end."

"Why do you think that fellow, Gus, is haunting you at the cottage?" Mindy's grandfather took a large drink of water. "If he said you baked the best bread," he added.

"Because he was a cantankerous old coot." Lizzie scowled.

"We don't need that language at the table, especially today, when we have much to be grateful for." Esther glanced at Mindy, then at her grandfather. "We are so happy to have you here."

"Thank you for inviting us." Mindy reached for the bowl of mashed potatoes in front of her, which she knew would be heavenly. Even thoughts about Gabriel were not going to keep her from enjoying this meal—at least not too much.

They passed around the delicious foods and settled into

eating and conversation peppered with laughter and occasional requests for seconds. But when Mindy's grandpa covered his mouth and broke out into a coughing fit, it caused Lizzie to drop her fork on her plate, Esther to stop chewing, and Mindy to hold her breath.

When he finally got control of the cough, he laughed. "Now, ladies . . ." He glanced at each one of them. "You can't look so panicked when a fellow coughs. I am feeling fine, no issues at all. So, everyone please relax and enjoy this fine meal."

Mindy dabbed at her mouth with her napkin, then cleared her throat. "What do you think about Grandpa's beard?" She glanced back and forth between Lizzie and Esther.

"You look like one of us," Lizzie said, grinning.

"It suits you well." Esther leaned over the table, picked up a pitcher, and topped off Mindy's grandfather's water glass.

Mindy dove into the last of her pile of mashed potatoes and pulled up a large forkful. "Why is it that Amish mashed potatoes are the best? I mean, I know you drizzle browned butter on top, but there is something else." She ate the bite she'd been staring at, letting it rest on her palate, savoring the delicious flavor.

"If we tell you, we'd have to kill you." Lizzie cackled, and Mindy almost spit those wonderful potatoes out when she had to stifle a giggle. The comment was just so un-Amish-like. Most of the Plain people she knew were refined like Esther. Lizzie was anything but. She glanced at her grandfather, who smiled, then pointed his finger at himself like a gun.

"Bang. I'm dead. Now give my granddaughter your recipe secret."

The room went silent, and her grandfather sighed. "Seriously, ladies, you're going to have to lighten up. Please don't make me worry that I'm going to say something that leaves you all with looks on your faces like the ones you're wearing now."

Esther smiled as she turned to Mindy. "I'm happy to share with you, hon. The secret ingredient is—"

"Esther!" Lizzie slapped both palms to the table, hard enough to rattle a few dishes. "Are you out of your mind? I won first place for that recipe at the county fair." She turned to Mindy. "I'm sorry, dear."

"*Ach*, Lizzie. You're being ridiculous." Esther shook her head.

Mindy loved watching the sisters interact. Apparently, her grandfather did too. He was grinning ear to ear, but then his smile faded and he cupped a hand to his ear. "Is that a lawn mower I hear?"

Lizzie went to the window. "Now, why is that boy mulching leaves on Thanksgiving Day?"

Mindy's heart flipped in her chest.

15

―❈―

Gabriel had not given in to his earlier convictions about Mindy, but when he rode his buggy by the Peony Inn and saw her little red car out front, he was drawn in that direction and turning into the driveway without considering the outcome. He wasn't invited, and he didn't want to interrupt the meal, but he had to see her. Mulching leaves was an excuse, and when she came out onto the porch, he couldn't take his eyes off her. When she motioned with her finger for him to come onto the porch, he killed the engine on the motor and headed toward her.

"Happy Thanksgiving," she said, barely smiling.

"And to you. I, uh . . . didn't mean to interrupt the meal. We eat earlier than most families, around eleven. I just thought I'd get some mulching done and make sure the new blade was working okay."

"Lizzie sent me out here to invite you in for pie. There's also tons of food left if you're still hungry." She tucked her hands in the back pockets of her jeans. "So, are you coming in?"

There were plenty of warning bells going off in his mind to say he couldn't, but he nodded. "*Ya*, sure."

He followed her through the living room and into the dining room, where everyone greeted him.

"I'm sorry to interrupt," he said, although it looked like they were mostly done. Mr. Stoltzfus had two slices of pie on his plate. "We ate early, so I thought I'd get a little mulching in."

Esther was attempting to lift a chair that sat against the wall. Gabriel rushed to her. "Let me get that." He carried it to the table and placed it between Esther and Mindy.

"We have two kinds of pie, Gabriel. Apple and pecan." Lizzie stood, went to the china cabinet, and took out a plate, returning to place it in front of him. She put her hands on her hips. "I made the apple pie. Esther made the pecan pie. If I were you, I'd play it safe and have a slice of both. Otherwise, you risk hurting one of our feelings."

Gabriel grinned. "I *lieb* apple and pecan pies. A slice of each would be *gut*." He glanced at Mindy, who also smiled.

"I'm guessing you had a big Thanksgiving feast at your house?" Dr. Stoltzfus asked him once he'd been served.

Gabriel finished his first bite of apple pie. "*Ya*, yes, sir, I did. *Mei mamm* and sisters worked hard, and it was a fine meal, Dr. Stoltzfus."

"I'd be happy for you to call me Ben." Mindy's grandfather took a sip of cranberry juice from one of three glasses in front of his plate, which was a little odd. Dr. Stoltzfus must have noticed him staring at all the glasses. "These ladies are making sure I have plenty to drink."

Mindy cleared her throat. "Grandpa was in the hospital a few days ago for dehydration." She lowered her head.

"And a little touch of cancer," Lizzie said before she sighed.

Gabriel slid his gaze in Mindy's direction. She was still looking down and picking at her pie without taking a bite.

Dr. Stoltzfus didn't look sick today, but he recalled his uncle having cancer. There were good days and bad. He wasn't sure what "a little touch of cancer" meant, and he didn't want to pry.

"Sir—I mean Ben—I'm sorry to hear that you're ill." Gabriel would leave it up to Ben to elaborate or not.

"Thank you, Gabriel. I'm taking treatments and hoping for the best."

"I will keep you in prayer."

Gabriel enjoyed the pie as much as he could after hearing this news. Mindy was surely upset and still wasn't looking up. Even though he knew it was a bad idea, he was busy trying to figure out a way to spend time alone with her and to learn more about her grandfather.

He was lost in thought when he looked up and caught Lizzie staring at him, smirking. He needed to figure out a way to leave before Lizzie and Esther put their heads together and started plotting ways to play matchmaker for him and Mindy. Two single people were up for grabs in the widows' eyes, no matter the circumstances surrounding any potential relationship.

Gabriel kept his head down, but hard as he tried, he couldn't stop sneaking peeks at Mindy, and when he glanced at Esther, she grinned, then looked at her sister. The wheels were in motion. Gabriel ate faster until he'd finished both slices of pie. "*Danki* for the pie. Both slices were delicious, but I guess I better get back to work."

He eased his chair back, wiped his mouth with his napkin, and stood.

"Nonsense," Lizzie said. "It's Thanksgiving. Sit down."

She spoke firmly, and Gabriel wasn't sure how to argue with her, so he complied, slowly lowering himself back into his chair.

"Mindy, just so you know, if you come by tomorrow, I might not be home. Esther is taking me to visit their bishop and hired a driver for us to meet with my doctor for that follow-up visit he mentioned." Ben smiled. "I'm not supposed to drive until after we have a consultation."

"Grandpa, I would have taken you to the doctor." Mindy frowned.

"I know you would have, but Esther offered, and I didn't want you to miss school or work."

"Why are you taking Ben to see the bishop?" Lizzie directed the question at her sister as she lowered her eyebrows into a frown, exaggerating the wrinkles along her forehead. "And you hate hospitals, Esther. I could have gone with Ben."

Gabriel covered his mouth with his napkin so he didn't

grin. Maybe Mindy was right. Could the sisters be in competition for Ben's affections? Mindy believed Ben felt more fondly toward Lizzie. Gabriel couldn't wrap his mind around that. Esther seemed more his type.

Esther shrugged, smiling at her sister. "That's up to Ben how much he wants to tell you."

Lizzie's expression darkened as she shuffled her teeth around in her mouth, which was the first time he'd seen her do so since he sat down.

"I'm curious, too, Grandpa. Why the bishop?"

Lizzie gasped. "You're turning Amish, aren't you? You don't want to leave for heaven without being one of us. That's it, isn't it?"

"*Ach*, Lizzie, hush." Esther sighed. "You'll have to excuse Lizzie, Ben." She glared at her sister.

Ben chuckled. "*Turn* Amish? I didn't know a person could *turn* Amish. But I'm happy to explain." He focused on his granddaughter, and since Ben had her full attention, Gabriel embraced the opportunity to gaze at Mindy. How was he ever going to walk away from her for good?

Ben turned to Gabriel. "I'm participating in a clinical trial, and I'm hopeful for the outcome. But I want to cover all my bases." Then he glanced at everyone there before continuing. "I would like to speak to a member of clergy. I'm sure I could speak to Mindy's pastor at her church, but my only friends here are Amish." He smiled at Esther, then Lizzie, and Gabriel tried to read his expression. Did he look at one woman more than the other? He wasn't sure. "Esther said Bishop Lantz is a fine man and that she was sure he would speak with me. That was confirmed yesterday when Esther talked to him. I just want to have all my ducks in a row when I get to the pearly gates."

Everyone went uncomfortably quiet.

Ben looked directly at Gabriel again. "I have explained to the ladies not to react so negatively when I say things like that." He chuckled again. "Look at them all." He shook his head, still smiling.

Gabriel opened his mouth to say something, but he was at a loss for words.

"I can't imagine you'd have any problems at the pearly gates." Lizzie smiled in a way that left no doubt she was smitten with Mindy's grandfather. It was amusing and sad at the same time. Both women obviously wanted someone to live their final years with, and it didn't sound like either one of them would be able to for long if the clinical trial didn't work. Although, looking at Ben today, Gabriel wouldn't have known he was sick. Still, it didn't sound like just a touch of cancer if he was in an experimental trial.

"Excuse me." Mindy blinked back tears as she stood and quickly left the room.

Ben lowered his head. "Uh-oh. I better go talk to her."

"This is a lot for her to process. I don't think she's ready to joke about it," Esther said.

Gabriel stood. "Ben, if it's all right, I'll go talk to her."

All eyes were on him as he waited for Ben to answer. The older man nodded.

He found Mindy outside. She was standing in the front yard hugging herself with her back to him. She didn't turn around when he walked up to her. Her shoulders were shaking, and he instinctively wrapped his arms around her waist and put his cheek next to hers, which was moist.

"I could lose my grandpa," she said. "I'm not ready, and I don't like to hear him joking about it."

Gabriel eased her around until she was facing him. He brushed loose strands of wavy brown hair from her face, then kissed her gently on the lips—the last thing he needed to be doing, but this was a time to push his own worries aside and offer comfort. "But *he* seems ready and also hopeful, and I think he probably wants to keep everyone's mood up, not down. I know how much the thought of his passing hurts you, though."

"He hasn't even lived here very long at all." She sniffled, her eyes pleading with his to make it right.

"I know." He eased her away and took off his black jacket, which he hadn't removed when he went in the house. He draped it around her shoulders before pulling her close to him. *Don't say it, don't say, don't say it.* "I've missed you. And I'm sorry I haven't been there for you these past couple days. If I had known about your grandfather . . ." He sighed. "I just—"

She covered his lips with her finger, her eyes still moist with tears. "I know why."

He edged back a little and rubbed both her shoulders. "Logically, I know this has heartbreak all over it, but we've barely said hello, and now it's time to say goodbye? I'm having trouble accepting that."

"I've missed you, too, especially your laughter." She swiped at her eyes. "Especially now, at a time when I could really use some joy in my life."

When she smiled a little, all sense of reason abandoned him, and he kissed her with all his heart involved. His mother's words echoed in his mind. Maybe she was right. Maybe he needed to find out why Mindy was in his life and why he had become attached to her so quickly.

———— ◆ ————

Esther followed Ben to the window in the living room, and Lizzie was on his heels. They all tried to stay out of sight while spying on Mindy and Gabriel. Esther stuffed her shaky hands in the pockets of her apron. They'd been better today, and she was grateful for that, but the trembling was getting worse, and she was more tired than normal.

"Mindy shouldn't get involved with that boy," Ben whispered even though there was no way the young people could hear them.

"It's too late," Lizzie said. "They are already involved. Did you see the way they looked at each other in the dining room?"

"Not to mention now." Esther lifted her brows when the kissing became heavy. She took a step back. "We shouldn't be spying on them."

"Sure we should." Lizzie kept her face near Ben's as they both peered outside, and Esther recalled the comments she and Lizzie had thrown around earlier, each trying to build up the other in Ben's eyes. Esther had caught Ben gazing at Lizzie several times. It was sweet of Lizzie to want romance for Esther, but the romances today didn't involve Esther, and she was fine with that.

Ben moved away from the window and joined Esther a few feet away. "You're right. We shouldn't be spying." He rubbed his beard, which was fully covering his cheeks and chin now, completely gray and untrimmed. Lizzie had been right. He looked like one of their people. "And we shouldn't be encouraging either of them to let this blossom into something that can't be," he said.

The irony, Esther thought as she considered the possibilities for Lizzie and Ben.

Lizzie walked away from the window, huffing like a child. "Those two are already smitten with each other. Maybe we give them a little nudge and—"

"No" and "*Nee*," Ben and Esther said at the same time.

Lizzie frowned.

Ben pointed a finger at Esther, then Lizzie. "I know about you two. You like to play matchmaker, but Mindy knows nothing about the Amish way of life, and unless Gabriel could leave all he's ever known, they are going to get hurt."

"Not necessarily," Lizzie said as she tapped a finger to her chin. "Esther and I have helped several couples find love when one of them wasn't Amish." Lizzie's gaze lingered in

Ben's direction for a long while. "*Gott* always has a plan, and sometimes it's impossible to know which way the tide will turn, so to speak."

"She's right," Esther had to admit as she watched her sister keeping her focus mostly on Ben. "But in this case, I think Ben is right too. Mindy has a lot to process." She glanced at Ben, who was also staring at Lizzie. The groundwork for further development had been set for those two. But Mindy was young and probably letting her emotions control her sense of logic. "She doesn't need our help by putting more on her plate."

Lizzie walked back to the window and peeked out. "Her plate looks plenty full when it comes to that boy."

"I might not be around to take care of her, to see her get married, to see my great-grandchildren." Ben's voice broke as he spoke, and a knot grew in Esther's throat. She wasn't sure she could say anything without crying. She cared for Ben, even if it wasn't the same way she suspected her sister felt about him.

Lizzie shuffled back over and put a hand on his arm. "Esther and I will keep a close eye on Mindy and make sure she's okay. Don't worry about that. But I'm sure you'll be fine." There was a desperate sound in Lizzie's voice.

Esther put a shaky hand to her chest. All of Lizzie's nonsense—or her whimsical demeanor, as Ben had said—was only a veil for the compassion her sister carried in her heart.

"Lizzie's right, Ben," Esther finally said. "We will keep

an eye out for Mindy for as long as we are able." She paused, looking away for a moment. "If need be."

"It'll probably be longer than me." Ben shrugged.

"Stop it!" Lizzie stomped a foot, her bottom lip trembling. "Please stop saying things like that."

Ben's face clouded with regret, and Esther stayed quiet, a little stunned at Lizzie's outburst, but it served as confirmation. Ben and Lizzie were growing into a couple whether they realized it or not.

"Okay," Ben said barely above a whisper as he kept his eyes on Lizzie.

When they all walked back to the window and saw Mindy and Gabriel laughing, Esther's heart sang, despite the risks for the young couple. But when her hands began to shake worse than they ever had, the music in her mind quieted. All the laughter in the world couldn't cure what was slowly happening to her. She sighed.

Ben and Lizzie exchanged glances, then stepped to either side of Esther. Lizzie reached into Esther's pocket and took out both of her shaking hands.

"It's getting worse," Esther said softly.

"I know." Lizzie latched on to one hand, and Ben took Esther's other hand in his. They stood like that for a while until Ben broke the silence. He squeezed Esther's hand until she turned to him, and then he winked at her. "Well, aren't you and I a mess?"

For no other reason than the silly expression on Ben's face, Esther laughed. "We really are."

Esther silently prayed that all their souls would be soothed, including Mindy's and Gabriel's, no matter the outcome for everyone.

———◆———

Mindy and Gabriel had made their way to the barn, where it was warmer, and after they had finally separated from each other, Mindy shakily walked to the stalls where Lizzie and Esther's horses stood. "I've always wanted a horse."

"Maybe you should get one." Gabriel cozied up beside her while she rubbed the muzzle on one of the animals.

"Maybe I will." Her long-held vision of herself in a buggy came into view, but it wasn't as cloudy as it had once been, which was confusing. She pushed the images from her mind.

As they left the barn and walked across the yard, Gabriel held her hand. When they got to the front door on the porch, she wondered if this would be another goodbye. She didn't know how many she could take, especially considering what was happening with her grandfather.

"I know this is hard, having just found out about your grandfather. I know you need to focus your attention on that." He let go of her hand. This did sound like another goodbye. He kissed her on the forehead. "I will be keeping you and your grandpa in *mei* prayers."

She tried to keep her bottom lip from trembling. "Thank you."

Gabriel stroked his clean-shaven chin. "I should probably go mow."

"Okay." She handed him his jacket.

He draped it over his arm but didn't make a move to leave.

"I know this is probably contradictory to what I just said about you focusing on your grandfather, but . . . do you want me to come over tonight?"

"Yes." She didn't hesitate. "I mean . . . if you want to. If you're not bored hanging out at my house."

He smiled. "Bored? Never." He didn't care where they were as long as they were together, and meeting at her house had become their thing. He was comfortable there. And Montgomery was a small town. Gabriel was surprised that no one had spotted them when they had gone out to eat twice. If they ventured out too much, word would get around, and rumors would fly. The community would speculate about a situation that neither Gabriel nor Mindy had a handle on yet.

He stared into her eyes. "*Mei mamm* said something to me today that I feel like I need to explore. It didn't make sense at the time, but now I'm thinking maybe she was right."

Mindy tipped her head to one side, a little confused.

"Never mind." Gabriel shook his head as if he were shaking his thoughts away, then kissed her the way she would recall in her dreams tonight.

"I'll see you later." He started down the steps, then

turned round. "*Ach*, and can you tell Lizzie and Esther I'll finish the mulching another time. It's Thanksgiving."

Mindy smiled. "Yes, I will."

She burst in the door, her emotions spiraling all over the place, but when she laid eyes on her grandfather, Lizzie, and Esther, she laughed. They stumbled all over each other as they hurried to move away from the window.

Mindy pointed a finger at them. "You three were spying on us, weren't you?"

Her grandfather and Esther exchanged "We've been caught" looks.

Lizzie shrugged. "Of course we were." Then she walked over to Mindy, took her by the arm, and led her to the couch. "Now, tell us everything," she said as they sat.

So Mindy did. She confessed her feelings for Gabriel after knowing him such a short time, how they were both aware that it was a difficult situation due to her not being Amish, and how Gabriel made her laugh.

Lizzie patted her on the leg. "*Gott* always has a plan."

Her grandfather chimed in with a warning. "Just be careful."

Esther said, "Laugh a lot. I hear it soothes the soul."

Mindy nodded. Then she blew her grandfather a kiss, determined to keep her spirts up for his sake.

16

━━━━◆━━━━

Esther made introductions at the bishop's house the next morning, then accompanied the bishop's wife to the kitchen. Ben was glad. He needed this to be a confidential conversation, at least for now. He sat on the couch when the bishop motioned for him to do so, and the bishop took a seat in a plush but worn chair to his left. Ben assumed the man had probably counseled a lot of people while sitting in that chair.

"Thank you for taking the time to see me, Bishop Lantz. I know it's probably not customary for an *Englisch* person to seek your advice."

"*Englisch*'? You must know a little about our people. I don't usually hear those who aren't Amish use the word." The bishop was a large man, tall like Ben but rounder in the middle. His gray hair was speckled with flecks of black. Ben didn't have a dark hair on his head or face. He'd gone gray like his father at an early age.

Thinking of his father caused him to circle back to the reason he was here.

"Actually, I know more about the Amish than I've let on, even to my granddaughter." Ben ran his hand the length of his short beard. No one had noticed that he had been shaving his mustache. "Because my last name is Stoltzfus, I've been asked my entire life if I'm Amish."

Bishop Lantz nodded for him to go on as he pushed dark-rimmed glasses up on his nose. "I'm not a practicing Amish man, but I was born into an Amish family. My parents were Amish, and for the first fifteen years of my life, I was raised according to the *Ordnung*. Not here, though. We lived in Lancaster, Pennsylvania." He let the bishop absorb that information, knowing the man was surely wondering where he was going with this. "It pains me to talk about this, but . . ."

Cloudy recollections of his parents screaming at each other assaulted the pleasant memories Ben wanted to hold on to, but the truth couldn't be told without including all the facts. "My father had an affair with an unmarried schoolteacher in our district. My mother found out." Ben paused and took a deep breath. "Actually, everyone found out." He struggled to gather his thoughts, not expecting the subject to be so hard to talk about. It had been so long ago.

"That must have been difficult for a boy your age to handle." The bishop was a soft-spoken man.

Ben nodded. "It was. And it turned out to be way too much for my mother to handle, especially back then when times were different. That type of behavior was frowned upon even more than it is now. My parents ended up staying together, but we moved and never went back to the Amish way of life. I begged my parents to let me stay with my aunt and uncle. I wanted to be raised in the Amish community where I had grown up, but they wouldn't hear of it." He shrugged. "And back then, youngsters didn't buck up to their parents."

The bishop nodded again.

"I was still determined to return to the Amish faith when I was older and had saved enough money, even though I decided to not return to my roots in Pennsylvania. I wanted a fresh start in a new district. I had visited Montgomery when I was trying to decide on an Amish community that I might like to join. I ended up deciding on Montgomery after speaking with the bishop at the time. I was making plans to move here a few days before my twentieth birthday."

Ben paused, reflecting on the first time he saw his wife across the room at a wedding they were both attending. "But then I met Elsa, and everything changed. The woman swept me off my feet, and I couldn't think of anything but being with her. She didn't share my vision about moving to Montgomery to be baptized into the Amish faith."

He paused again, lost in memories for a few moments before he locked eyes with the bishop. "I chose her, and I don't have any regrets. We were married for fifty-two years, and we had a wonderful life even though our son, our only child, was taken from us way too young when his daughter was only four. Then my daughter-in-law remarried and moved to Texas with our only grandchild, Mindy, which meant I didn't really get to know my granddaughter."

Ben put a hand to his forehead. "My apologies, Bishop Lantz. I'm sure this is all more than you need to know, so I'll wrap things up. Mindy and I started communicating frequently when she got older, first via letters, then email the past few years. We visited each other a few times in Texas and Pennsylvania. We also made a trip here—although Mindy didn't know why I suggested it. Mindy fell in love with Montgomery. I was thrilled but unprepared to tell her about her family history since I hadn't before. And then I began dealing with health issues."

The bishop held up a hand, his palm facing Ben. "Wait. Why didn't you share your background with your granddaughter?"

Ben thought back, sighing. "Elsa asked me not to. She was worried our son might seek out his heritage, leave, and live an Amish life. She wasn't for that. Years went by, and my early years became distant memories. My son never knew his grandparents. They died young." He paused, considering his next comments.

"I know that fate probably shouldn't factor into any decisions, but windows opened during our visit here, then doors flew open. Whether it was fate or God's way of telling me that it was time to live the life I was meant to live, I don't know. But Mindy got a job, leased a house here, and country life suits her. And things just fell into place so easily.

I decided this is where I wanted to live, to be near her and the life that I once loved. I've just been waiting for the right time to tell Mindy everything."

The bishop nodded patiently.

"I've come to ask you if I can be baptized into the Amish faith. It's what I wanted as a boy, and I still do. Life got away from me, but my faith held strong. I had a wonderful life with my wife, and I wouldn't trade a day of it, but I feel like I am finally home here."

Bishop Lantz ran his hand the length of his long black and gray beard that ran to the middle of his chest. "I'm afraid it isn't as easy as that. There is much work to be done to live in accordance with the *Ordnung*. You probably remember that. And we like new members to know our native dialect. Do you remember any Pennsylvania Dutch?"

Ben shook his head. "Not much. And I'd need a big refresher on the *Ordnung* as well."

"We welcome new members to our district, even outsiders, who are willing to put in the work, and you probably have a slight head start since you remember some of the *Ordnung*, but it could still take a long time." He smiled warmly. "But I hear *Gott* in your words and ambitions. I think we could have you baptized next spring or summer."

Ben's heart sank. "With all due respect, Bishop Lantz, I need to make that happen sooner than next spring or summer. I'm not well."

He held his breath and waited for the bishop to give him an answer.

———◆———

Mindy sat next to Gabriel on the couch, the television on, but neither of them paid much attention to the old Western that played. Mindy had never been a TV addict, but sometimes the background noise was comforting. Everything was like the night before when he had come over. They hadn't talked about their situation, and they'd spent the evening enjoying each other's company, snacking on leftovers Lizzie had insisted Mindy bring home. Tonight Gabriel had brought a pizza again.

"What's the history on this house?" Gabriel scratched his cheek. "You can tell it's older by the way it's built, and it has the original hardware on the doors and windows." He pointed to the shiplap that ran halfway up the wall in the living room. "Is that original, or did you add it?"

"It was here when I moved in. I had to repaint the entire house, and it was super dirty, but I fell in love with it the first time I saw it. I like that I see deer most mornings, I hear the coyotes howl at night, and sometimes, before dark, I just sit on the porch and listen to the crickets chirping." She shrugged, smiling. "Who knew I had always been a country girl at heart. I'm renting it, but I hope to buy it someday. I pay my rent to a trust, but whoever runs it lets me deduct any repairs or painting. The biggest expense was having electricity installed. I guess it must have belonged to an Amish family at some point. My grandpa was insistent on paying to have the electrical work done. I don't think I could have moved here if he hadn't helped me with that."

"I remember this house being vacant for a long time."

"I asked my grandpa if he wanted to move in with me, but he said he wanted a simple life and a small place, thus the cottage, I guess."

Gabriel twisted to face her on the couch, his hand holding hers. "He already knew he was sick when he moved here, didn't he?"

Mindy lowered her head. "Yeah, he did. And I knew he liked it here from our visit."

"Is the attic finished out? Our attic is a bedroom for *mei* sisters."

She shook her head. "No. There's lots of room, though. It could easily be made into two bedrooms, and there's room for another bathroom, but it just feels like too big a project, and I don't need all that room for just me. Maybe I'll tackle it when I have enough money saved to buy the place." She scrunched her face up. "There's a basement, too, but I never go down there. It's dark and musty. It creeps me out. Hardly anyone has a basement in Texas."

He chuckled. "Creeps you out? You're not like Lizzie and believe in haunted places, are you?"

"Of course not. But it needs windows."

Gabriel laughed again. "Basements are mostly below the ground, and you'll be glad there aren't any windows if you need to retreat down there when there's a bad storm."

Her eyes widened. "I've had to do that twice since I've

lived here. And there's only a single lightbulb hanging from a cord in the middle of the room." She shivered. "And it's super cold down there."

"Speaking of . . ." He let go of her hand, walked to the fireplace, and added a log from the carrier where Mindy had about six logs stacked.

"Thanks," she said when he returned to her side. "That's probably my favorite thing about living here—the fireplace. I've never had one before."

"I imagine it gets drafty in here." His eyes scanned the room.

"It was when I first moved in, but Grandpa suggested I have insulation blown into the walls, and he sent me money for that too." She paused. "I hate taking his money, but it sure made a big difference in my electric bill. Someday, maybe, I'll tackle the attic, but right now my schedule is full with work and school." She laid her head on his shoulder, and he kissed her on the forehead, something he did often. She'd never tire of the gesture.

"I could help you with that if you ever decide to take on the project." Mindy picked up on the fact that they were speaking as if they would stay together. "What made you want to be a nurse?" Maybe Gabriel had picked up on it, too, since he abruptly changed the subject.

She shrugged. "Honestly, because there seems to be a shortage of nurses everywhere. I didn't go to college, but I wanted to have a profession. To become a full-fledged RN, I must complete an associate degree. I'm about halfway there. I mostly answer the phone at the nursing home, but . . . sometimes I think I've chosen the wrong line of work."

"What makes you say that?"

Mindy rubbed her forehead. "Well, for starters, I can't stand the sight of blood. I thought that with training and school, I'd get better about it." She shrugged. "I haven't. And it's also hard to watch people die. I've held quite a few of the residents' hands when they were leaving this life."

"I bet that *is* difficult."

"It can be if they're scared. I try to talk to them about Jesus and how they will see their loved ones again. You wouldn't believe how many of them tell me they see their loved ones in the room, and it's usually within a few hours before they die." She gazed into his eyes. "I love when that happens and they drift away with a smile on their face. But the ones that drift away as if they've seen nothing and appear terrified . . . It upsets me. Death scares me even though I'd like to think I have a strong faith in God and the afterlife." She paused, thinking. "Are you ever scared? I mean, about dying. What do the Amish believe?"

"I think everyone is afraid of dying on some level. We're human. The *Ordnung* teaches us to lead the best life we can, with purpose and good will. We believe Jesus is our Lord and Savior, and I choose to believe that if I abide by those ordinances I will go to heaven. In any religion, no matter what it might be, I think people identify with the rules in their own way. Our simpler way of life also wards off temptations that might lead us down the wrong path. So, am I scared?" He paused. "*Nee*, not really."

"Wow. When you put it like that, it doesn't seem so scary." Mindy had another vision of herself in an Amish buggy, less foggy, but still not clear in her mind. She wondered what it meant, or if she was just willfully imagining her life with Gabriel.

They were quiet.

"You're wondering if your grandfather will see his loved ones when he passes, aren't you?" Gabriel squeezed her hand.

"Like I told you, I didn't know my grandmother. After my mom remarried, the distance between my grandparents and my mom grew. Maybe because my mom was his daughter-in-law, combined with the fact that she remarried . . . and Texas was far away. I kinda get it, I guess." She shrugged, then smiled.

"But when my grandpa reached out to me, I was thrilled. He's an old man, but he sure doesn't act like it. He's fun to be around, witty, and kind." She blinked back tears. "And he might be taken away from me way too soon, and I'll be left with no one. But to answer your question, yes, I was wondering about that—if he would be reunited with my dad and grandma. I'm not close to my mom or stepdad, I'm sorry to say."

"Sometimes family is who we make it." He said it so sweetly that she struggled not to cry.

She thought about that for a while. "Maybe so. And that reminds me of something. Grandpa asked me to meet him Saturday, tomorrow, at two o'clock at the Peony Inn. He said he wants to talk to me, Lizzie, and Esther at the same time. At first, I panicked, thinking his condition had worsened, but he insisted he felt fine and that it wasn't bad news at all." She sighed. "I can't imagine why he wants Lizzie and Esther there too. He said he didn't want to tell me about his news over the phone. It seems to me that if it's that important, he would want to tell me alone."

Gabriel smiled as he waggled his brows. "Maybe it's so he can be around his two girlfriends."

Mindy laughed. "Maybe. It's fun watching them all together. But I can tell Lizzie has stolen his heart. When you left last night, I walked into the house and all three of them were looking out the window, spying on us."

Gabriel cringed. "We were making out like teenagers."

She kissed him on the cheek. "Yes, we were, and I'm sure Lizzie and Esther are busy trying to find ways to get us hitched." She laughed but stopped right away. "Oh wow. I'm sorry. I didn't mean to say that. I just, uh . . . I mean, you said they play matchmaker, and . . ." She squeezed her eyes closed. When Gabriel didn't say anything but let go of her hand, she quickly looked at him. Rather than a casual smile, his face held a sober expression. She covered her own face with her hands. "Now I'm embarrassed."

"Don't be. I'm pretty sure I wanted to marry you the moment I laid eyes on you." His serious expression remained.

Even though she'd heard of love at first sight, Mindy couldn't tell him she had felt the same way. "And that's a problem."

He leaned in and kissed her, lingering for a long time. "A problem we aren't going to worry about."

"Might be kind of careless on our part," she said in between the tenderness he was showering on her.

"Probably so."

Mindy closed her eyes and went with it. She'd fallen harder than she could have ever imagined for a man she couldn't be with. "Careless" might be a huge understatement.

Gabriel eased away from her when he felt like they were getting ready to cross a point of no return. Premarital sex wasn't something he believed in, no matter how much he wanted to make love to Mindy.

"I should go," he said. "And it's not because of anything you said."

She was breathing as hard as he was. "Too bad. I was already planning our wedding."

He laughed. "Amish or *Englisch*?"

She shrugged. "I was thinking a combination of both."

Gabriel groaned. "*Ach*, I can see *mei* family now. Everyone sitting around after a grand meal and watching all your people dancing and partying."

"My people?" She giggled. "I can't see my family sitting through a three-hour church service."

The realization that her grandpa might not be around to see her get married someday slammed into her like a jackhammer to the gut, and the playfulness and joy she felt took a hike. "Wow. All I have is my grandfather. I mean, I have my mom, I guess, but . . ."

Gabriel stood, holding her hand and pulling her up with him. "You have me."

She was tempted to argue the point and ask him for how long, but instead she leaned in and hugged him.

After more kissing, he said, "There is nothing more I want to do than sweep you into my arms and carry you to your bedroom. I think about making love to you all the time. But I believe in waiting until marriage."

"So do I." *Which means we will never make love.*

He kissed her again before he left, without telling her goodbye. Was that because it was or wasn't another goodbye? As she watched him pulling away in his buggy, she wasn't sure.

Later, after she was in bed and had prayed for her grandfather, she closed her eyes and prayed that somehow her and Gabriel's situation would play out in a way that worked for them both.

17

⎯⎯⎯⎯⎯⎯◇⎯⎯⎯⎯⎯⎯

During her drive to the Peony Inn Saturday afternoon, Mindy continued to wonder what this special gathering was about. What could be so important that her grandpa couldn't tell her on the phone, and why did Esther and Lizzie need to be there?

After parking the car at the inn, she glanced at the time on her cell phone. She was a couple of minutes early, but as she went up the steps to the front porch, she heard people laughing. She knocked on the door, and Lizzie hollered for her to come in.

Her grandpa sat on the couch with Esther on one side and Lizzie on the other. Mindy walked to the rocking chair facing the three of them on the other side of the coffee table. She set her purse on the wood floor, sat, then raised an eyebrow.

"What's so funny? I heard you all laughing from outside." Maybe her grandfather had good news—that the clinical trial was working or that he was in some sort of remission.

"I was trying to explain to Lizzie why Gus isn't haunting her, but she has a comeback for everything I say." Her grandfather laughed, then shrugged. "Maybe the place is haunted after all."

"Rubbish." Esther playfully slapped him on the arm.

"Anyway, the haunted cottage is not why I called this little meeting." He pursed his lips as if in serious thought, and Mindy's chest tightened. Maybe she'd read the situation wrong, or he hadn't wanted to tell her bad news on the phone.

He took a breath. "As I told you, Esther took me to visit the bishop yesterday . . ."

Her grandfather then began to relay his conversation with Bishop Lantz. Somewhere along the line, her mouth fell open, and her eyes were surely bulging. Esther nodded occasionally. Lizzie just smiled, and Mindy wondered if both women already knew this news.

When her grandfather finally quit talking, he looked directly at Mindy. "Well, what do you think?" He waited. Mindy was still unpacking all the information he had thrown at her. "About me being baptized into the Amish faith."

Mindy's hands landed on top of her head. "I'm *Amish*?"

"Your heritage is Amish." Her grandfather smiled. "I wouldn't exactly call you Amish, since you drove here in your car probably listening to music, you're wearing blue jeans, you attend college, and you know absolutely nothing about the *Ordnung*."

She dropped her hands to her sides. "I know a little." She had picked up bits and pieces over the last few years through conversations with Amish who lived in southern Indiana. But as she recalled her conversation with Gabriel, it was hard not to see this as some sort of sign from above.

"Then you probably know that it's the unwritten rules we live by," Esther said as her hands shook in her lap. "We all know these rules by heart."

"Mindy?" Her grandfather lifted a bushy gray eyebrow. "Are you okay with this?"

She slouched into the rocking chair, her legs stiff in front of her. "Uh, yeah. Of course. You should be able to be baptized into any religion you want. Are you sure, though?"

"Yes. I mean *ya*." He winked at Lizzie, who smiled even broader.

"Why are you telling me all this now?" She sat up straight and crossed one leg over the other, unsure if she should be upset that she hadn't known all this before.

Her grandpa shrugged. "I guess it didn't seem important until now."

"Of course it was important. It's part of who I am. Like you said, my heritage."

———◆———

Ben was having a hard time reading his granddaughter's reaction to this news. He'd intentionally avoided telling her the part about his father having an affair. That was a private part of history that didn't warrant sharing and part of the reason he'd never shared his background—although it was mostly at Elsa's request that he had kept his childhood a secret from their son.

"Obviously, my dad wouldn't have told me at four years old, but why didn't my mom ever mention it?"

He shrugged. "Your father never knew. Your grandmother didn't want him to know for fear he might leave to seek out his Amish heritage. Your dad wasn't raised Amish. I was only raised in our Amish community until I was fifteen. Your father wasn't much of a history buff and wasn't interested in information about our family tree. I knew this would be a lot to take in, and I should have filled you in on your heritage a long time ago, but getting baptized is something I really want to do. I've wanted to be baptized into this faith since I was a young man."

"Grandpa, it really is fine. I'm just super surprised." She sighed, and Ben braced himself for disappointment as she cupped her chin in a hand and stared into space. "That explains our last name. I've been denying my heritage my entire life when people question me about Stoltzfus being my last name." She chuckled. "I feel this sudden urge to go buy a buggy and some new clothes." She nodded at Esther's and Lizzie's dresses.

Ben didn't say a word, unsure if it was sarcasm or if she was upset. But Lizzie jumped to her feet and lifted her hands above her head. "Then do it!"

Mindy shook her head. "I was kidding!" Ben was relieved

when she laughed. "Seriously, I'm in shock, but I want you to do whatever you want, Grandpa. And I mean that." She rubbed her chin. "I guess that explains the facial hair too."

"Did you have this planned all along, since before you moved here?" Lizzie was still standing, peering down at him but still grinning.

He nodded. "Yes, I did. Another reason why the cottage was an integral part of my planning. I wanted to get used to the lack of electricity before I got any . . . sicker. And I know Amish men don't normally grow a beard until after they are married, but I've never had a beard in my life. I'll shave it if the bishop asks me to, if he feels it isn't appropriate for my situation."

They were all quiet.

"So, there you have it. That's my news. And I need to speed up the normally lengthy process." He glanced back and forth between Esther and Lizzie. "I'm hoping you two will help me get up to speed on the *Ordnung* and Pennsylvania Dutch."

Both women nodded their heads and repeated in unison, "*Ya, ya, ya,*" with big smiles on their faces, which warmed his heart. He would be able to spend time with both women—whom he cared for in different ways—but would not allow himself to become a burden.

Mindy slowly stood up, then picked up her purse. "Well, as much as I'd like to stay for your schooling, I need to make a Walmart run in Bedford and run a couple errands. Grandpa, do you want to walk me out?"

That was a clear hint that she had something to tell him privately. Maybe his granddaughter wasn't okay with his decision after all.

"Sure." He told Lizzie and Esther that he would be right back, then followed Mindy outside after she'd told the ladies goodbye.

She waited until they were at her car before she said anything. "Well, you know what this means, don't you?" She cocked her head to one side and grinned.

"Uh . . . outside of everything I told you, I guess I don't know what you're referring to."

"After you've been baptized into the Amish religion, you can marry Lizzie." She tugged on his short beard. "And justify this."

He sighed. "In case you have forgotten, who would want to marry a man who might only be around for a short time?"

Her expression fell right away. "You're going to pull through this. I just know it."

Ben wasn't sure he was that lucky. He thought again about how he might miss Mindy's wedding someday, along with any future great-grandchildren he might have.

She leaned up and kissed him on the cheek before climbing into her car. "I love you, Grandpa."

"And I love you."

She was closing the car door when Ben said, "Mindy?"

She looked up at him.

"It was a lovely thought, though."

"What?"

"Getting married." He swallowed back the lump forming in his throat.

She smiled, then winked at him. "Like I said, doctors aren't always right. The trial might work, and no one but God knows when our last day is."

After she closed the door and blew him a kiss, he waved as she drove off, prolonging his time alone with his thoughts. *Married.* How he would have loved to have spent his final years with a companion who could possibly be more than a friend.

Lizzie.

When he walked back into the house, Esther and Lizzie were busy putting notebooks and pencils on the table. "I'm percolating fresh coffee," Esther said. "Lizzie, get that small tape recorder you have in your room. Ben can record our Pennsylvania Dutch and listen to it when he's not here." She glanced at him and smiled.

"What tape recorder?"

Esther's face reddened as she moved closer to Lizzie and whispered, but Ben overheard her say, "The one you used to tape record *mei* snoring so you could play it for the doctor."

Lizzie snapped a finger. "*Ach, ya.* That was a *gut* idea. Otherwise, they wouldn't have known you had sleep apnea." She wasn't whispering as she pointed at Esther. "And you don't wear that mask hardly ever, because I hear you snoring."

"*Ach,* hush, Lizzie. Besides, you snore too." Esther

clenched her fists at her sides, her hands shaking more than ever. It broke Ben's heart. He recalled Elsa toward the end of her life. Even though the Parkinson's hadn't been the cause of her death, she'd had good days and bad with the disease. And he'd known plenty of others who had suffered greatly. He would pray that Esther didn't have a hard time with it.

———◆———

Mindy was sitting on the porch step at her house when Gabriel pulled up in his buggy, as planned. She tried to imagine herself sitting beside him wearing a baggy dress and prayer covering. The vision was becoming less cloudy by the moment.

"*Wie bischt.*" Gabriel pulled his black jacket snug as he crossed through her front yard. She'd learned that *wie bischt* meant either "Hello" or "How are you?" "Why are you sitting outside? It's cold."

She stood, stuffed her hands into the pockets of her blue down jacket she'd bought recently. "Just watching the sunset."

"Can we watch it from inside?" He kissed her on the mouth, which had become the norm the past couple of days.

"Sissy," she said as she walked in and tried not to shiver in front of him.

"Ha." He poked her in the ribs. "I see you shaking."

After shedding their coats, they went to their spot on the couch. Mindy had already stacked two new logs on top of the orange embers left from earlier in the day.

"So, what was the big meeting about with your grandfather?" Gabriel took off his boots. "Sorry. I forgot to drop them at the door."

She'd told him he didn't have to do that, but it was customary in most Amish homes.

After he set the boots on the floor next to the couch, he kicked his black-socked feet up next to her pink-socked feet, and they crossed their ankles at the same time.

She had been thinking about how she would tell Gabriel about her grandfather's plans ever since she'd gotten home, deciding she might as well have some fun with the information. "Well . . . it turns out I'm Amish."

His head jerked to face her. "What?"

"Shocking, huh?" She laughed, but when he didn't, she went through as much of her grandfather's explanation as she could remember.

"I knew there had to be a story behind the last name Stoltzfus." He rubbed his jaw. "So, if things had turned out differently, you could have grown up Amish."

"I guess that's one way of looking at it. If I had grown up Amish, it probably wouldn't have been here in Indiana. I wouldn't have ever met you, and I could have saved myself a lot of nicks while shaving my legs, since I read Amish women don't shave their legs."

Gabriel laughed. "Don't believe everything you read.

Amish women shave their legs. Maybe not all of them, but . . ."

"And you know this how?" She raised her brows, grinning.

"I have two sisters, and we all share the upstairs bathroom. *Mei bruders* aren't using pink razors to shave, and neither am I." He shrugged. "And I've heard *mei* sisters saying they shave their legs. But if you ask *mei mamm* if married women shave their legs, she'll tell you it depends on how long they've been married."

Mindy laughed. "Like any other couple, I guess."

"Back to your grandpa. I don't know how to say this except to come out and say it. Learning the *Ordnung* is a lengthy process, and with him being sick . . ."

"Have you forgotten about the two lovely Amish ladies who seem to dote on him?"

Gabriel chuckled again. "*Ach, ya*, I guess he'll have plenty of help."

"I could hear sadness and regret in his voice when he was talking—not about being married to my grandma or anything like that, but I could tell it was hard to give up his dreams of being baptized into the faith when he was a young man. It does make me wonder why my grandma didn't convert for him if it meant so much to him." She turned toward him. "It seems like if she loved him enough, she would have at least considered it for fear of losing him."

The conversation was starting to hit a little too close to home, but Gabriel had an answer for her. "If you love someone enough, you give them the freedom to choose."

"Then Grandpa loved her more than she loved him. Is that what you're saying?" She twisted her mouth, seemingly thinking.

He shrugged. "I don't know." Gabriel was about to step off a cliff, but he had to know. "What if it was me and you, and I was madly in love?" He held up a finger when she grinned. "I know we haven't known each other that long, but hear me out. What if I told you that I could never live in the *Englisch* world, and you told me that you could never live an Amish life? Who loves who more? The answer is the person who bends to the other's needs and desires. That's true love—putting your partner first. At least in my opinion."

Gabriel heard the words come out of his mouth and realized at that moment he really didn't want to lose Mindy. Even though it was too soon to be having these thoughts or conversations—or maybe it wasn't—he would never make her choose. He would live her way of life, even though that went against everything he'd ever believed about himself as a person. Maybe he'd never been in love before.

Could I already be in love with her?

"All food for thought," she said, avoiding his eyes. The conversation had just become awkward. "Speaking of food, I made lasagna. I don't make it a lot because it is so rich, but I didn't think to ask you if you even liked pasta."

Because there are a lot of things we don't know about each other. "I've never had lasagna, but I like pasta."

"Really? No lasagna, ever?"

He shook his head. "*Nee, mei mamm's* never made it, and we don't really go out to eat a lot."

She patted him on the leg, and her touch sent a shiver up his spine, in a good way.

"Well, you are in for a treat, then. Grandpa says I make the best lasagna ever."

Gabriel was happy the subject had changed, but now he was confused. About her. About his future. About everything.

But he was hungry, and a few minutes later, she brought him a plate. He liked eating on her couch, and he was glad the television wasn't on. He enjoyed the movies they'd watched, but he preferred the faint howling of coyotes in the distance and the sound of the fire crackling. He briefly thought about what it would be like to live like this. To eat on the couch—which his mother would never allow—to watch television if he wanted to, and mostly, to be with Mindy. Forever. It was too much to think about now, so after they prayed, he dove into the lasagna.

"How have I missed this all *mei* life?" He closed his eyes and held the bite in his mouth before chewing and swallowing. He then threw her a big, deserving smile. "*Ach,* you're a super *gut* cook. This is the best thing I've ever put in *mei* mouth."

She laughed. "Yeah, right. You're probably just saying

that." She sighed, grinning. "Although I've been told by a lot of people that it's the best lasagna they've ever had. I found the recipe when I was a teenager. I was going through some of my mom's cookbooks that she had put together, and the recipe was handwritten on a yellowed sheet of paper behind a tab she had labeled as 'Favorites,' so I guess I can't take all the credit."

When her cell phone rang from its place on the coffee table, she leaned forward to see the number, then quickly took her feet off the table. Gabriel reached for the plate in her lap, catching it before it fell to the floor.

"It's Grandpa," she said. "He never calls this late."

Gabriel wasn't sure what time it was, but it was dark.

"What's wrong?" she asked in a shaky voice.

He couldn't hear what her grandfather was saying, but whatever it was, it caused her to lower her head and put a hand to her forehead. "Okay. Which hospital?"

Gabriel set his plate on the coffee table and turned to face her.

"What's wrong? Do we need to go to the hospital?" he asked after she had ended the call.

She shook her head. "No. He said there was no reason for us to go and that they don't really know anything yet."

Gabriel frowned, surprised she wasn't rushing to her grandfather's side. "What happened to him? Is he in the ER?"

She shook her head. "Sorry. No, I should have said . . . It isn't Grandpa. It's Esther. She apparently passed out, and

Lizzie called 911. Grandpa saw the ambulance and rushed over there. They are all at the hospital now."

"They let them all ride in the ambulance?"

She grunted a little. "No. They took Grandpa's car."

"I thought he didn't drive anymore . . . because of his eyesight or his diagnosis?"

"He doesn't." She tossed her hands in the air. "Lizzie drove! How does Lizzie know how to drive a car? At least they made it there safely."

Gabriel just shrugged. "Nothing Lizzie does surprises me. I just hope Esther is okay."

"Me too."

18

———— ✕ ————

Lizzie felt weak as a kitten as she sat in the ER waiting room at the Bedford hospital. Esther's heart rate had dropped when she got to the hospital, and they had rushed Lizzie and Ben out of the small room. Lizzie had no idea what was happening.

"She's going to be all right, Lizzie." Ben put his arm around her, and she buried her head against his chest. She hated crying in front of people and was determined not to give in to the sobs building in her throat.

"I thought she was dead." And then she exploded with all the emotion she'd been holding back. "I went to take *mei* bath, and when I headed toward the kitchen, she was lying face down on the floor."

"But she's not dead, and she's in good hands." He brought his other arm around and embraced her in a full hug.

Lizzie finally allowed herself to cry, but when his shirt became soaked, she eased away, swiped at her eyes, and looked up at him. "*Danki* for being here."

He stared into her eyes. "I wouldn't be anywhere else."

"Esther hates hospitals, and I know she's scared. I wish they would have let me stay with her."

"Hopefully you can see her soon."

Please, Gott, *don't let Esther die. Please,* Gott, *don't let Esther die.* She repeated the prayer in her mind. Ben kept one arm around her, and they were quiet until a doctor finally emerged from behind a closed door and asked for the family of Esther Zook. There was a young couple on the other side of the room, but he directed the question to Lizzie and Ben. They both stood right away.

"We are her family." She latched on to Ben's hand, more for stability than as a sign of affection. She trembled from head to toe. "I am her sister." The doctor glanced at Ben but refocused on Lizzie. Maybe he thought Ben was her husband. His beard wasn't very long, and he didn't have on a straw hat, but otherwise he probably could have passed as Amish.

"We are running some tests and have requested her medical records from Dr. Reynolds, but can you give me a brief rundown on her health? Her blood sugar is high, and she appears to have Parkinson's disease. Is there anything else you can tell me?"

Lizzie fought to control her trembling bottom lip. Ben squeezed her hand, and she took a deep breath. "Esther is diabetic, and she does have Parkinson's disease. She was diagnosed with a stomach ulcer a couple of years ago, and she has arthritis in her knees, hips, and back." She took a handkerchief from her apron pocket and dabbed at her eyes.

"She's stable right now. I think she passed out due to the high blood sugar," the doctor said. "I'll let you know more when we get her records from Dr. Reynolds and the lab results, including if there is anything else we should be concerned about."

Ben ushered Lizzie back to her seat and kept an arm around her waist. She felt weak in the knees again. He must have sensed she was at risk of falling. It sounded like Esther would be okay, but Lizzie would feel better once she saw her sister and knew for sure.

"You should go home," Lizzie said as they sat in the same two chairs as before. "You need to take your nighttime medications."

"Not a chance. The meds can wait." Ben spoke firmly, and although she was concerned about his health, Lizzie didn't want him to go. "Besides, I don't drive at night." He gently nudged her shoulder. "How did you learn to drive a car? I mean, the ride to the hospital was a little harrowing, but we made it."

"I've never driven a car in *mei* life. The hardest part was seeing over the dashboard."

———◆———

Ben didn't mean to gasp or for his eyes to bulge, which caused Lizzie to frown at him. "You got us here safely. That's what counts," he said as he silently thanked God for their safe arrival, glad he hadn't known that information on the way to the hospital.

"I have perfect eyesight." She stared straight ahead at the blank white wall.

Ben wasn't sure her first time to drive a car was the lesser of the evils. He couldn't see well at night and had been advised not to drive in case of a seizure, but it would have probably been better than a first-time test run with Lizzie. He said another prayer of thanks.

He searched his mind for any words of comfort, but when you loved someone as much as Lizzie and Esther did, there really weren't any. He could continue to tell her that everything would be okay, but the words would sound hollow until the doctor reported back to them. At least Esther was stable.

Movement out of the corner of his eye didn't faze him at first, but then Mindy and Gabriel came into view.

"What are you two doing here?" Lizzie huffed. "It's too late for you to be running the streets."

Ben looked at his watch. It was ten thirty, not late by young people's standards.

"We were worried." Mindy took a seat beside Lizzie, Gabriel on her other side. "Do you know anything yet?"

Lizzie shook her head, her bottom lip trembling.

Ben cleared his throat. "They are running some lab work since her blood sugar is high and waiting on records from her regular doctor." Mindy began chewing her bottom lip. "She is stable, and none of this sounds life-threatening."

Mindy nodded. "Well, that's good news."

"Why didn't you just call me for an update?" Ben looked around Lizzie at his granddaughter.

"Grandpa, your phone goes straight to voice mail, so I'm guessing it's dead."

Ben retrieved his jacket on the chair next to him and felt around in the pockets for his cell phone. "You're right. Sorry, hon."

Mindy reached in her purse and pulled out a charger.

"*Danki.*" Ben smiled at her, hoping to remove some of the doom and gloom from the room. Only Gabriel smiled a little.

Ben knew how these things went. They could be here for hours. "I don't see any reason for you and Gabriel to stay. My phone is plugged in now, and I can call you with any updates." It occurred to him that Gabriel was with Mindy this evening, and he wondered if that had become a nightly thing.

"Gabriel, do you need me to take you home?" Mindy asked.

"*Nee*, I'm fine."

"We're both fine right here." Mindy put a hand on Lizzie's shoulder. "Do you want us to go find you some coffee?" She glanced around the small waiting room. "I don't see any in here."

"*Ya*, coffee would be *gut*. Thank you, Mindy."

Ben wished he had thought of that.

"I don't think we can go through the main hospital from the ER, but there's a Taco Bell across the street."

"They stay open late. I know this because it's *mei* favorite fast-food place. Esther can't stand it." Lizzie sniffled a little.

"Huh. It's Grandpa's favorite place too. Do either of y'all want something to eat?"

Ben was starving, but it seemed inappropriate to eat at a time like this. He shook his head.

Lizzie sighed. "I'd like a coffee, two soft tacos, and an order of nachos—the little one, not the big ones with all that mush on it. Just the chips and cheese."

"Got it." Mindy and Gabriel turned to leave just as Ben's stomach growled.

"Uh, Mindy . . ." He stood and walked to her. "I guess a little food wouldn't hurt."

"Do you want your usual?" Mindy smiled.

Ben nodded. "Along with a coffee." He reached for his wallet in his back pocket, but Gabriel spoke up.

"Please, let me, sir." He cleared his throat. "I mean Ben."

They turned to leave before Ben could object, but they didn't wait until they were completely out of sight before Gabriel reached for Mindy's hand. He wished things were different for them so Mindy would have someone watching over her after Ben was gone. Esther and Lizzie would keep an eye on her, but they weren't spring chickens. He cringed when he thought about Esther alone in the ER room. She was probably terrified.

He returned to his seat, still surprised that Lizzie would be able to eat with all the worry in her heart. Esther was Lizzie's sister. Of course she was worried. Ben himself had been caught off guard by his own feelings for Esther. Different than his feelings for Lizzie, but he cared deeply for both women. Unusual how they had connected so quickly.

Lizzie had leaned her head back against the wall, her mouth slightly parted, her eyes closed. Ben sat two chairs over so as not to wake her. Ben hoped they would get word about Esther soon.

———— ◆ ————

Esther had been drifting in and out of sleep. She was in the hospital. That much she knew based on the constant beeping of monitors, the blood-pressure cuff, pulsometer, and IV—all things that scared her. But not knowing what had happened was even more frightening. She was awake when a nurse finally came in.

"Am I all right?" Her voice sounded hoarse to her, but her throat wasn't sore. It didn't seem likely they'd put anything in her mouth to help her breathe.

"Hi, Ms. Zook. I'm Janet. And yes, you are okay. We are still gathering your test results, but we think your high blood sugar had something to do with you passing out. The doctor will be in shortly to speak with you." The young woman, probably around Mindy's age, patted her leg. "Now that you seem fully awake, would you like for me to have a family member come sit with you? The doctor had an emergency, but it shouldn't be long before he comes to see you."

"*Ya, mei* sister, please. Her name is Lizzie." Esther groaned as she shifted her weight.

The nurse picked up a chart hanging on the end of the bed. "If you're sore on your right hip, we think that's what hit the floor first when you fell. You're probably going to have a nasty bruise, but the X-ray results don't show a break or fracture, so you're very lucky about that."

Esther hazily recalled having an X-ray when she first arrived. Maybe she had mentioned her hip. She didn't remember. "*Danki* . . . Thank you."

A few minutes later, Esther heard Lizzie hollering her name. She burst through the door and immediately laid her head on Esther's chest. "*Ach*, thank *Gott*. The doctor poked his head out to tell us that you would be all right and that he would be back to talk to us. He had an emergency. *Ach*, Esther . . ." Lizzie sobbed.

Esther wrapped her free arm around her sister. "Lizzie, I'm okay."

"I was so scared." She lifted her head. "You were face down on the kitchen floor." She grabbed Esther's cheeks and turned her head from side to side. "I was afraid you would be all busted up. And lying there on the kitchen floor . . ." She swiped at her eyes. "I thought you were dead!"

"Well, I'm not. Now quieten down. This is an emergency room. People are sick."

Lizzie sat on the edge of the small hospital bed. "I know

you were probably scared being in here by yourself. They threw me and Ben out." She scowled. "Mindy and Gabriel are here too."

"*Ach, nee.* What time is it? I don't want everyone making a fuss."

"It doesn't matter." She latched on to Esther's hand and squeezed. "I don't know what I would have done if anything happened to you."

Esther gazed into her sister's eyes. "Honey, we can't live forever."

"I know."

They were quiet, just sitting and holding hands. Then Esther said, "What is that all over your black apron? I didn't notice at first." She tapped her jaw. "And there is something red on your face."

Lizzie rubbed her chin. "*Ach,* it's Taco Bell sauce."

Esther grinned. "Tell me again how worried you were."

"Look. I needed *mei* strength in case I had to storm the joint to see you."

After sighing, Esther said, "Lizzie, please take back those books of yours. When you talk like that, you don't even sound like a normal woman, much less an Amish woman."

"*Ya, ya.* I am. Ben had originally asked to go with me." She paused, biting her bottom lip. "Is that okay?"

Esther sighed. "Of course it's okay. Why wouldn't it be? I took him to see the bishop." She assumed Ben had asked her to take him to the bishop instead of Lizzie because Lizzie would have grilled him or spoken out of place. Although

Esther had never seen Ben expend anything but admiration for Lizzie. He was getting to know the real person beneath the quirkiness.

"I mean, I know we're sharing him and all, but . . ."

Esther laughed, which felt good considering the situation. "He's not a toy, and we're not sharing him. We are both friends with him." She smiled. "Although I expect more than friendship is blooming between the two of you."

Lizzie grunted and waved her off, but she also blushed, something she rarely did. "I can tell he's worried about you," she said as she took her handkerchief from her apron pocket and swiped at eyes that were swollen from crying.

"Ben is a *gut* man, and he has been a *gut* friend to us in the short time we've known him."

Lizzie nodded, but her sister had gone to a place in her mind that often left her with a dazed and thoughtful look.

She finally snapped back. "Do you want me to go get Ben and let him come visit you?"

Esther shook her head. "*Nee.*" She looked a mess, hooked up to all these machines. And she didn't have a prayer covering on. Not even a scarf. It wouldn't be appropriate. "Just stay with me awhile."

"I'll stay with you forever." Lizzie smiled.

———◆———

It was nearing midnight when Esther was released, and Mindy offered to drive everyone home. It was a tight fit in her small car with Lizzie, Esther, and Gabriel in the back seat. Her grandpa, the largest of their group, rode in the front passenger seat.

They dropped off Esther, Lizzie, and her grandfather at the inn. Her grandfather said he would walk to the cottage after he helped Lizzie get Esther settled. Esther had dozed on and off during the ride from Bedford to Montgomery.

Mindy's house was the last stop, and the first thing Gabriel did was exit the car to check on his horse. "Still plenty of water, but I best get him home, fed, and in the barn."

As they stood at the horse's side, Mindy scratched his nose and recalled her conversation with Gabriel when he'd said she should get a horse if she wanted one. Then she glanced at the covered black buggy nearby. That could have been her life if things hadn't happened the way they had.

"Thank you so much for coming with me tonight. I care a lot about Esther and Lizzie, but I was also worried about Grandpa. He really likes both women, and I was concerned how Esther's condition might affect him."

"I didn't mind at all." Gabriel pulled her close and kissed her tenderly. "Tomorrow is supposed to be a day of rest." He rolled his eyes. "But I promised *mei mamm* I would help her make some minor repairs around the house. I haven't exactly been pulling *mei* load when it comes to chores." Grinning, he kissed her again. "I've been busy with someone else."

"I'll go check on the three of them after I go to church

tomorrow. I've got some things I need to handle around here before I go back to work and school Monday."

He nodded. "But I'll be calling you if that's okay." He kissed her again, longer this time. The heady sensation filled her with longing, the way it always did when he held her.

"I'll talk to you soon."

She watched him hook the horse to the buggy, looking more intently than she had before.

After he left, she went inside but didn't go straight to bed, even though she couldn't stop yawning. Her mind was filled with ifs. But God always had a plan, even if He hadn't completely clued her in on it yet. She was getting to know her grandfather better. There was a nice Amish man who had taken an interest in her—although it might leave her with a broken heart. But as she glanced around the farmhouse, she couldn't imagine being anywhere else.

She had colleagues at work that she was friendly with. Some of the patients too. But she hadn't felt a sense of family until her grandfather arrived in Montgomery. And Esther, Lizzie, and Gabriel were starting to feel like part of that family.

But Esther and her grandfather weren't in good health, and she and Gabriel couldn't be together the way they wanted to be unless one of them made a drastic lifestyle change. How long would her little family thrive under the circumstances? Would God intervene in time for Mindy to capture the peace she was searching for?

19

⤬

Esther had been home from the hospital almost a week when Lizzie decided to return her murder books. Esther scolded her continuously about her language derived from her reading habits. It wasn't all that bad and certainly nothing derogatory about the Lord, but she wanted to make Esther happy, and Ben clearly wasn't a serial killer.

She, Esther, and Ben had been gathering daily for lunch and Ben's lessons on the *Ordnung* and practicing Pennsylvania Dutch. He was a quick study, and he remembered more than he thought from his Amish upbringing. They all felt a sense of urgency for his learning to progress as quickly as possible, even though Ben didn't look like a sick man. He'd followed up with his doctor on Monday and reported that his condition was the same. Not getting better, but not getting worse. Lizzie knew that could change on a dime. Esther's new medications had fixed her right up, although the doctor stressed the importance of avoiding sugary foods.

"Do you still want to go with me to the Donation Spot to get rid of some books Esther doesn't feel are appropriate?" Lizzie raised her chin with a pile of books in her arms. Esther was sitting on the couch next to Ben. They'd wrapped up school for the day.

"*Ya*, I'd like to get out and about." He turned to Esther. "Are you up for a ride?"

She shook her head. "*Nee*, not at all. This cold weather does not appeal to me."

The temperature had dropped into the thirties overnight but had warmed up to around forty-five degrees. Lizzie set the books on the coffee table, then slipped into her heavy black coat and tied her bonnet under her chin. "Do you need me to pick up anything while I'm out?"

"*Nee*. No weekend guests, and we're fully stocked. If I feel up to it, I'm going to make a pumpkin pie." Esther crossed her legs as Ben stood up. As he reached for Lizzie's stack of books—about seven of them—he flipped through them and frowned.

"What made you choose these books? I understand about the ghost ones, but serial killers and murder?"

Lizzie shuffled her teeth back and forth even though she tried not to do it in front of Ben. It was a hard habit to break since her dentures had never fit right and no one could fix them. Ben had offered to have a look several times, but

Lizzie wasn't going to have him staring into her toothless mouth and playing with her fake teeth.

"We didn't know anything about you when you moved into the cottage."

Ben laughed. "So, you thought I might be a serial killer?"

"You were so elusive, never left the cottage." She raised her chin. "Two single women can never be too careful."

Esther rolled her eyes, something Lizzie disliked but tolerated. She imagined Esther tolerated a few things she did.

"Well, let's go." Lizzie opened the front door and Ben followed.

"Are you going to let me drive the buggy?" he asked as she opened the driver's side.

"You don't know how to drive a buggy. That lesson isn't until week after next." She crawled onto the seat. Ben stayed standing as he placed the books on the floorboard.

"Well, that doesn't seem fair. I let you drive my car, and you didn't know how."

Lizzie huffed. "Fine." She jumped down from her seat. "I'll go ahead and put *mei* life in your hands." She circled around to the other side of the buggy, nudged him aside, and got in.

Ben stared at her, grinning.

"What are you waiting for?" Lizzie scowled. "And stop smirking at me like that." If he only knew how much his smile warmed her heart, but he had this funny little grin he threw her way when he seemed amused.

"Not a thing," he said, closing the door to the buggy after she was inside.

He managed to back up the buggy and get them on the road without any problems. "Not too bad for your first time," Lizzie admitted.

"It's a little like riding a bike. It's coming back to me." He picked up speed until they were in a steady trot. Lizzie slid the books over and reached for a blanket down by her feet, then draped it across her lap.

Ben adjusted the small battery-operated heater so that it faced her way. "Warm enough?"

"*Ya, danki.*" She eyed him up and down. "I'm glad you remembered a heavy coat." Even with his thick jacket on, Lizzie could tell he had lost weight. She worried there was something he wasn't telling her and Esther. He didn't seem to be eating as much at lunch either.

Lizzie said a silent prayer that Ben wasn't slowly going downhill. Her heart sank just thinking about it.

———◆———

Esther had just put a pumpkin pie in the oven when there came a knock at the door. Taking slow, easy steps, she shuffled to the door. She'd fallen shortly after Lizzie and Ben left and landed on her knees. Luckily, she'd been able to get herself up and was only a little sore. She didn't see a need to mention it to them, but she was being careful not to lose her balance again, something that was happening more often.

"Mindy, *wie bischt*." Esther motioned for her to come in. "Warm yourself by the fire."

"Thanks." Mindy walked to the fireplace, her back to the smoke shimmying upward. "I thought maybe Grandpa might be here. I knocked on the door at the cottage, and when he didn't answer, I got worried and went inside. But he's not there."

"He went with Lizzie to donate some books to the Donation Spot. I know it's not that cold outside to most people, but when it gets below fifty, my knees start acting up. So I stayed home. I'm baking, enjoying a warm fire, and relieved not to have any guests staying at the inn. Usually, the holidays are slow. Occasionally, we've been booked up with entire families coming to stay, but I think most people enjoy Christmas at home."

Mindy closed her eyes, and Esther watched the girl inhale. "Whatever you're baking smells so good."

"Pumpkin pie." Esther smiled when Mindy did. "The recipe is a family secret, if you ask Lizzie." She laughed. "But I'd be happy to give it to you." She winked at Mindy. "When Lizzie isn't around."

"I'd love that. Every time I've had a meal here, it's been fabulous. I have a few things that I cook, but it's not the same as the way you and Lizzie cook. More homestyle, I guess you could say. Maybe you could show me how to cook some of the things you make?" She grinned. "When Lizzie isn't around."

Esther laughed. "*Ya*, of course, dear. With Lizzie around or not, I'd be happy to."

Mindy took off her coat. "Can I talk to you about something?"

"*Ya*, sure. Let's sit. Do you want some coffee or tea?"

The girl shook her head but sat on the couch beside Esther with her coat folded over in her lap. She paused before she looked right into Esther's eyes. "The house I live in, the area, everything about this place has always felt perfect to me, like I've belonged here since the moment I laid eyes on the property. Do you think there's anything to that?"

Esther wasn't following. "What do you mean?"

"I don't know. I took a vacation day today because I don't have school, and maybe I've just had too much time to think. But . . ."

It clicked for Esther. "Are you trying to ask me if being born Amish is ingrained in you at birth and maybe you were meant to live an Amish lifestyle?"

"Yes. Yes. That's exactly what I'm asking." She searched Esther's eyes for an answer Esther didn't have.

"Hon, I don't know. But I have a question for you." She raised an eyebrow. "How much does this have to do with Gabriel?"

Mindy cradled her chin with her hands. "I don't know. Maybe some. I'm trying to decide if I'm reading some hidden meaning into my being born Amish because I'm scared of losing him."

Esther had been through this with more than one couple. Some worked out, some didn't. "My only words of advice would be that a person should only convert to our way of life if they are doing it for themselves, not another person."

Mindy blew out a breath of frustration. "I knew that's what you would say, and I appreciate you confirming what I already think. It's just that before I knew my heritage, it hadn't really crossed my mind to change my religious preferences. I mean, I've fantasized from time to time about what it would be like to live a simpler life. But now I'm not sure if I'm having these feelings because of everything Grandpa told me or because I am . . ."

"In *lieb* with Gabriel?"

She nodded. "It's too soon to be in love, though, isn't it?"

Esther smiled as she recalled falling in love with her husband all those years ago. "I think it's different for everyone. But the romantic in me does believe in love at first sight. Does Gabriel know how you feel?"

"Probably. When we get too close to the subject, we both seem to veer away."

"Do you think he is in *lieb* with you?" Esther could feel a matchmaking spark kindling. Could this be a couple that needed Lizzie and Esther's expertise?

"I want to say yes, but we've never said the words to each other. We haven't seen each other as much this past week because of my work and school, but he came over on my early days home from school, and we talk on the phone at night, sometimes for hours."

Esther recalled that in-love feeling—the newness, the heady sensation of it all.

"On a totally different topic, how do you think Grandpa is doing?"

"He's a quick study, and much of what he had learned as a child and young man is coming back to him. I even saw him take off in the buggy with Lizzie, and he had the reins." Esther snickered. "I can't believe Lizzie let him drive."

Mindy smiled. "That's nice, and I'm glad to hear that, but I mean his health. To me, it looks like he's lost weight."

Esther folded her hands in her lap and looked down. "*Ya*, I think you're right." She met Mindy's gaze. "He has been doing so well that I think we all forgot he has cancer. His doctor says he isn't any better, but he isn't any worse either. I've noticed his weight loss also."

"I suppose we should be grateful he isn't any worse." Mindy laid her coat across her arm as she stood up. "I should probably go. Thank you for talking to me."

"Anytime, hon. It sounds like you have a lot to think about."

Mindy nodded, then hugged her goodbye. A first. Esther liked that girl.

———◦———

Gabriel lingered in the den after his brothers had gone upstairs and his father was bathing. His mother and sisters were still cleaning the kitchen. He'd helped at first, but they seemed to have a system that didn't include him, so he waited patiently. After his sisters went upstairs, he joined his mother in the kitchen. She was drying and putting away the last of the supper dishes.

"What's on your mind, *sohn*?"

He told her everything Mindy had told him about her grandfather and her family history. "And what that all means is that she actually has an Amish heritage." He waited for his mother to tell him that didn't mean anything.

"I thought so," she said as she lifted on her toes to put a dish in the cabinet.

"What? Why?"

"With a name like Stoltzfus, I assumed she was of Amish heritage somewhere down the line. It's one of the reasons I thought maybe you should see what *Gott* had planned for the both of you since you were so instantly attracted to each other. I didn't tell you because I didn't want her possible Amish heritage to influence your feelings."

Gabriel took off his hat and hung it on the rack behind him, then scratched his head. "Is this some kind of sign from *Gott* that Mindy and I would have found each other one way or another?"

"I don't know. But *Gott* always has a plan." She smiled before she left the kitchen, stopping at the doorway to the living room to look over her shoulder. "Follow your heart."

———◆———

As she stirred a pot of chili on the stove, Mindy was filled with speculations about the different turns her life could have taken at any given time.

She lowered the burner to simmer, covered the pot, and went to the door when Gabriel knocked three times.

He pulled her close and kissed her, the way he always did, but something felt different tonight, and she couldn't put her finger on it. Not better, not worse. Just different.

Gabriel added logs to the fire until it roared in a glowing blaze of warmth, and without either of them saying anything, they opted for no television tonight. They ate bowls of chili in their laps on the couch with their feet on the coffee table, mostly making small talk. Something was on Gabriel's mind, and Mindy wondered if it was the same thing on her mind.

"Do you want to go first or me?" Gabriel grinned. "I can see the wheels spinning in your head, and mine seem to be on overdrive too."

"You know me so well." She nudged him with her shoulder. "Although you really haven't known me long at all."

He wiped his mouth with his napkin after finishing off the last of his chili. "Do you believe in fate?"

She suspected his speculations were in line with hers. "I believe that God controls fate. If it's meant to be, it will be, but we still have free will." She paused. "And sometimes that's confusing, because if everything is on God's time frame and He knows the outcome, then how does free will fit into the big picture?" She grinned. "That's not answering your question, is it?"

He shrugged. "Kind of."

"Maybe we're just not meant to know, but to trust the Lord to guide our steps onto the path He's chosen for us."

"I agree with that." He eased his feet from the coffee table, set his bowl down, then twisted to face her. "I need to tell you something, even though I know it's way too soon."

Mindy held her breath. Did he feel the same way about her that she did for him?

"When I'm around you, Mindy, I feel like I'm floating a foot off the ground." He grinned as he eyed the coffee table. "Except I guess *mei* feet are mostly on your coffee table."

She laughed and appreciated him infusing a little humor into the conversation. "Go on," she said softly as she tried not to sound too anxious.

"I'm just going to have to blurt it out." His face turned redder than she'd ever seen, but he gazed right into her eyes. "I feel like I'm in *lieb* with you." He waved a dismissive hand. "I take that back. I *know* I'm in love with you. I realize we haven't known each other long, but I feel it as sure as I've ever felt anything. I think I'd do just about anything to be with you, even if it meant leaving *mei* way of life. I'm not asking you to marry me. I guess I'm asking you to trust me with your heart and wondering if I can trust you with mine."

He chuckled. "*Ach*, that wasn't exactly the way I meant that to come out."

Mindy smiled, the way she always did when Gabriel was

around. Her heart pitter-pattered in a new way hearing how he felt about her. "Gabriel, I am in love with you too. We aren't teenagers. It isn't puppy love. And you *can* trust me with your heart, because I trust you with mine. I believe that God will lead us to make the best decisions, and it's up to us to hear Him and follow His guidance. When something good is on the line, there are always risks and potential missteps, but I'm not scared. Maybe I should be, but I feel safe with you. I trust you with my heart."

He nodded as she scooted her legs off the coffee table, set her bowl of half-eaten chili down, then tucked a leg underneath her and faced him. She looked down for a couple seconds before she searched his face. "I'm *really* questioning my life choices right now. I don't know how much of it is because of everything Grandpa told me or my discontent with my job and career path. I've always felt like I belonged in this house." She smiled. "A country girl at heart. But I think there has always been more to it, feelings buried beneath the surface that I didn't have a reason to confront . . . until now."

His brows lifted, but he wasn't smiling. "I think I know where you're going with this, and any choice you make about your future, particularly religious aspects, can't be based on your feelings for me." He shook his head. "That might sound contradictory to everything I have said, but if you are contemplating an Amish lifestyle, it has to be your choice and for the right reasons. Do you understand what I'm saying?"

"Yes, I totally understand."

"Even if you're thinking about it, exclusive of me, you'd be giving up a lot." He waved an arm around the room. "I'd be lying if I said I haven't enjoyed watching television with you, but not only would that become a thing of the past, but so would electricity, your car, your makeup, your clothes . . ." He put a hand to his forehead. "I'm voicing a lot of things I said I would keep to myself. But you said you trusted me with your heart. I'm making sure you think things through before you make any rash decisions based on our feelings for each other."

"I hear everything you're saying, and I agree. Any decision I make must be between me and God." She shrugged but grinned. "Being with you would be a bonus."

He laughed. They were back on familiar ground and in sync. Now she was ready to share with him.

"I think I have a plan that will work for both of us."

20

By the time Christmas rolled around, Ben had gained four pounds since his last checkup with the doctor only a month ago, after having lost some weight prior to that. His numbers hadn't shifted. He'd simply maintained his levels. And for that, he was grateful. He didn't feel at the top of his game all the time, but he didn't know many men his age who did. He had his moments, but it didn't appear he was going to go anytime soon.

He spent most of his time at the inn these days, usually having dinner—the word for Amish lunch, he'd recalled early on—and supper with Lizzie and Esther. He thought he would miss having a Christmas tree, but there was no lack of decorations or festivities inside the Peony Inn. As was customary, packages were beautifully wrapped and placed throughout various places in the house. They were empty, simply for decoration. Holly lined the mantel, along with red bows and three angel figurines—one playing a harp, another a flute, and the third looking up with her hands in the air and her wings spread as if offering glory to God through music. It seemed odd at first since the Amish didn't listen to music, and songs in church weren't really sung as much as the words drawn out without changing much in key. Ben supposed everyone had a song in their heart.

"It's Christmas Eve." Lizzie clasped her hands, and Ben wondered if she knew her black apron was covered with flour. She, Esther, and Mindy had been cooking all day long in preparation for the next two days of celebration. Tomorrow, they would dine together as the family they had become. The following day, they would take food to those without family or who couldn't get out on their own. Lizzie said she planned to visit Gus's grave and leave all his favorite foods in an effort for him to rest easy and not haunt the cottage anymore. She still refused to go inside, which wasn't an issue these days since Ben was always at the inn. He did hope that Lizzie could put the notion to rest for her own peace of mind.

"Is Gabriel joining us?" Ben added a log to the fire. Mindy had told him that Gabriel came to her house most evenings. The Amish were private. Ben suspected the youngsters were comfortable in the warmth of the farmhouse, but Gabriel probably didn't want folks to see him out with Mindy on a regular basis. He still had worries about their relationship, but they were adults, and Mindy had begged him not to be concerned.

"Tomorrow," she said. "He will be here for dinner." She laughed. "After he eats dinner with his family. He never seems to get full."

"And remember . . . no gifts." Lizzie pointed her finger at Ben, then at Mindy and Esther, who had each slipped into one of the rocking chairs. "We are each other's gifts this year."

Esther grinned at Ben and winked. She had already warned Ben that Lizzie said that every year, and that each year she had presents for anyone in attendance. Nothing big, and mostly handmade. Ben was prepared. He'd made each of the women a little something, and he also had a small token for Gabriel.

Lizzie bounced up on her toes with the energy of a teenager. "I almost forgot the silver candleholders for the dining room. I polished them yesterday." She whizzed away, and as always, it amazed him how much energy she had. Her zest for life was contagious. Maybe that's why he'd been attracted to her from the beginning. And soon he would be baptized into the religion he'd always been a part of in his heart. That had been his plan long before he fell for Lizzie.

His thoughts swirled back to Mindy. Her situation was the exact opposite. She had fallen for Gabriel, and Ben wondered how much her feelings for him would sway her decisions about her future. Again, he reminded himself that Mindy and Gabriel were adults. His only job was to pray for a happy outcome.

Ben had been watching the three women all day, busy

with cooking, cleaning, and laughter. General good tidings abounded. Esther tired easily and took breaks. Lizzie was Lizzie. But Mindy was the one Ben was keeping an especially close eye on. She appeared ready to burst with happiness, and he didn't think she'd stopped smiling all day long. He thought about all the Christmases he had missed sharing with her. Mindy had also been unable to spend holidays with her father following his death. Although Ben had heard her stepfather had been good to her. But they had never been close, and had mostly lost touch after Mindy was grown and moved out. As best he knew, she wasn't close to her mother, either, which was upsetting, but Ben still fought resentment that his daughter-in-law hadn't put forth any effort for him and Elsa to be a part of Mindy's life.

He reminded himself that it was Christmas, a time for absolute thankfulness, not bitterness. Today would be a good day.

———◆———

By Christmas morning Mindy thought she might explode with joy. She walked into the inn empty-handed, the way Esther and Lizzie had made her promise to do. *No gifts. Don't bring any food.* Her grandfather was already there, sitting in the middle of the couch, which had become his spot. Esther and Lizzie always sat on either side of him. Her grandfather cared about both women. They'd spent a lot of time together as Esther and Lizzie taught him their native dialect and schooled him about the *Ordnung*. Mindy was glad he had friends. She still suspected that Lizzie held his heart more than Esther, mostly by the way her grandfather's eyes twinkled when he looked at Lizzie. But her grandfather had a way of neither confirming nor denying his feelings for Lizzie if Mindy brought it up.

"Merry Christmas," she said to Esther, who had opened the door and ushered her in. The aroma of the food warming in the oven filled her senses with memories of Christmases past. She'd spoken to her mother yesterday, and even though she couldn't recall ever having a bad Christmas, she didn't think she'd ever looked forward to a holiday as much as she did today. The reason for the season had taken on a whole new meaning for her.

Their foursome snacked on light appetizers, enjoying the festive atmosphere, and Lizzie told tales from her and Esther's childhood.

"*Ach*, stop it, Lizzie!" Esther screeched through her laughter as her sister detailed a trip to school when they were eight and ten years old.

"Esther, that boy needed to be taught a lesson, and you know it. He was a bully." Lizzie raised her chin and pretended to be offended, but her grin gave her away.

"*Ya*, he was, but we weren't raised to fight, and you tackled that boy—who was twice your size—to the ground." Esther put both hands to her forehead and shook her head, but she couldn't hold back laughter.

"He called you a name that wasn't very nice," Lizzie

said, not smiling anymore, and she seemed momentarily caught in the memory.

Esther shook her head. "After the teacher told *Mamm*, I remember *Daed* hauling you behind the woodshed for a spanking. I could hear you crying from *mei* room."

"It was worth it. He didn't pick on you anymore after that." Lizzie's grin returned. "I got a lot of spankings when I was little."

Esther sighed, smiling back at her. "*Ya*, you did. But most of the time, your heart was in the right place."

Mindy glanced at her grandfather, and there was no mistaking the affection he had for Lizzie. He had that twinkle in his eyes when he looked at Lizzie.

Lizzie kept up with her stories, keeping them all in stitches most of the morning until Gabriel arrived at noon as scheduled. They all headed straight for the dining room.

"You were right, Mindy," Lizzie said halfway through the meal as she stared at Gabriel, who had a mouthful of food. "You never get full. I hope you ate a plentiful amount at your family's before you got here so as not to hurt your *mudder*'s or sisters' feelings."

He swallowed, smiled, and said, "What do you think?"

They laughed. It's what they did when they were all together. Mindy thanked God every day she was blessed with her grandfather, and she prayed for Esther and Lizzie too. Gabriel was always in her thoughts and prayers.

After the meal they went to the living room. Gabriel stoked the fire as Lizzie ran to her bedroom and returned with a large Christmas bag. She began doling out presents to everyone. "I know I said no gifts, but these aren't really presents, just some little things."

"What? No fair." Mindy folded her arms across her chest but still grinned as she glanced at Gabriel sitting on the floor near the fireplace.

"It's not a gift," Lizzie said as she handed Mindy a small box. Then she told everyone what was in their box before they even opened it. "Mindy and Esther, I knitted those mittens myself, but they aren't regular mittens. They are triple stitched and will last forever." Then she turned to Ben and glanced at Gabriel. "Yours are gloves, but they came from Walmart."

You would have thought Lizzie had given each of them a million dollars based on her own excitement. The woman lit up a room with her wacky ways, unpredictability, and a love that shone no matter what mood she happened to be in.

"I told you," Esther said as she walked to Ben and handed him one of the gifts that had been wrapped and set atop larger packages in the corner. "Lizzie always has something for everyone. And so do I."

Esther gave each of them a present, but unlike Lizzie, she didn't tell them what was in the package.

Mindy undid the shiny blue ribbon around a silver shirt-size box. She lifted three beautifully knitted potholders in various shades of blue. "I love them, Esther. *Danki.*"

"Look who else is learning the *Deutsch.*" Lizzie smiled at Mindy before she thanked her sister for a new black apron

Esther had made for her. Mindy had noticed that most of Lizzie's aprons were stained, thankfully not very apparent since they were black.

Practical gifts. And heartfelt.

Her grandfather blinked back emotion when he opened a box with a brand-new Amish straw hat inside. "You'll be needing that," Esther said sweetly.

Gabriel thanked Esther for a set of grilling tools. "These will be handy when I leave *mei* parents' *haus. Danki*, Esther."

Mindy's grandfather cleared his throat, then stood and retrieved a bag from behind the couch. "You didn't think I would let this day go by without a little something for each of you, did you?" He doled out small gifts, little things . . . all but one.

Lizzie and Esther each opened their gifts, both with awe in their expressions as they gingerly ran their hands over small trinket boxes with each of their names engraved on them. Her grandfather winked at Gabriel. "*Danki* for letting me use your father's workshop."

Gabriel nodded as he opened his present, his jaw dropping. "*Ach*, wow." He lifted a compass for everyone to see. "It's beautiful, Ben. *Danki*."

"It belonged to *mei daed*. I hope you will always receive God's guidance and stay on your intended path."

Mindy put a hand to her heart, elated that her grandfather cared enough about Gabriel to give him such a treasured gift.

"And there is one present left." He smiled at Mindy

as he handed her a package the same size as Esther's and Lizzie's. She was eager to see her trinket box, and it was as lovely as the others. "Open it," her grandfather said.

She undid the tiny latch, and the lid sprang open to reveal a folded piece of paper inside. "What's this?" As she opened up the document, tears fell instantly. "Grandpa!"

"It's the deed to your *haus*." Not one to have attention lavished on him openly, her grandfather blushed, his eyes moist. "It's the house I purchased as a young lad. When Elsa wasn't interested in moving here, I couldn't bring myself to sell it. When you spotted it and fell in love with it . . . Well, what can I say? *Gott* seemed to be leading us onto the right path."

She ran to him, taking Lizzie's usual spot on the couch, and threw her arms around him.

"There's one more thing." Her grandfather reached inside the pocket of his jacket and pulled out an envelope. "This is all the rent money you've paid since you moved in. I want you to have it. Think of it like a savings account you didn't know about. Now you can do some of the larger repairs on the place."

"*Danki*, Grandpa. I *lieb* you." Her heart melted like butter, sure she'd never be able to fully express how much this meant to her.

"I *lieb* you, too, Mindy."

"Good grief. Listen to everyone around speaking the *Deutsch*, like it's your native tongue." Lizzie laughed. "But what a blessed day this is." She began picking up crumpled wrapping paper and stuffing it into a trash bag she already had beside her for that purpose.

"Wait," Mindy said as she eased out of her grandfather's arms. She walked to Gabriel, who stood up and moved next to her. "Gabriel and I have a gift for all of you too." Finally, she could release the news she'd been hiding for weeks.

"What?" Lizzie asked as she stood with the bag in her hand, although she'd stopped stuffing paper inside.

All eyes were on her, and Gabriel's eyes twinkled, his face aglow with anticipation, like Mindy's.

"I quit school after Thanksgiving." She glanced at her grandfather, who frowned. "But for a good reason." Glancing at Gabriel, who nodded, she went on. "Gabriel is teaching me Pennsylvania Dutch. I'm doing this not just because we are in love—and we are—but because I feel like I owe it to myself to learn about my heritage. I can't make an educated decision if I don't understand what I might be embracing. If this isn't a journey that I feel I can take, Gabriel has offered to be baptized into the non-denominational church that I attend. He has been teaching me the *Ordnung* in the evenings, and I have been taking him to church with me."

She paused to look directly at her grandfather. "If I had never met Gabriel, I would still be quitting my nursing classes. I've known for a while that it wasn't for me. Gabriel and I will make the decision that suits us best, but we know that we want to pursue a life together." She paused again. "I've always been happy here, but deep inside I felt like something was missing. I want to explore that part of my life with Gabriel by my side."

Her grandfather's frown lifted. He raised a hand to his mouth, and his eyes were moist with emotion. He took a while before he spoke. "I think it is wonderful that you are approaching this decision with the seriousness it deserves, and I am proud of you both for putting in the work to decide what is best for you." He nodded in approval. "This makes me very happy."

Mindy couldn't believe the changes that had taken place in her little world in such a short time. She silently thanked God for the miracles in her life. Her grandfather was feeling well despite all earlier predictions. Esther and Lizzie were like the grandmothers she'd never known. And Gabriel was the man of her dreams. She wasn't sure things could be any more perfect.

———◆———

Esther poured herself onto the couch after Mindy and Gabriel left, unable to hide how exhausted she was as she leaned her head back and closed her eyes. She felt a gentle hand on her knee as a familiar person sat beside her.

"Here, hon." Ben used the endearment often with her, Lizzie, and Mindy. He handed her a cup of hot tea on a saucer. "No sugar, only Truvia. A splash of cream."

She smiled. "*Danki.*"

"I'm going to help Lizzie finish the cleanup. You should

go take a hot bath and get some rest." His hand was still resting on her knee. She put her hand atop his.

"I think I will."

Ben helped her to her feet, which had become more of a common thing. Esther hated being a burden, although Lizzie and Ben never made her feel like one.

After they stood, she went weak in both knees and would have fallen if not for Ben's quick reaction. He grabbed her around the waist and eased her back onto the couch, then sat beside her.

Ben chuckled. "Old age. It sneaks up on us."

They both knew that old age wasn't the only factor in play. Ben had cancer even though he'd been enjoying remission. Esther had Parkinson's disease, and between that and her knees, she lost her balance occasionally. Or more than occasionally, lately.

Her bottom lip trembled.

"Please don't be sad, Esther. I lose *mei* balance and get unsteady on *mei* feet too."

She glanced around at their Christmas decorations, the orange sparks from the fire disappearing up the chimney, and breathed in the aroma of the plentiful meal they'd all shared.

Turning to Ben, she smiled. "I'm not sad." She took a handkerchief from her pocket and dabbed at her eyes. "I'm happy. I'm grateful. And I'm blessed. This was a beautiful day, and I'm glad you're here to share it with us."

He returned the smile. "I wouldn't want to be any-where else."

———————◆———————

Lizzie peeked at her sister and Ben from the kitchen. She'd heard everything that was said, and it warmed her heart to see Ben giving Esther such comfort. Lizzie couldn't have loved him any more if she tried. And she knew how much Esther loved him too. He'd become such a blessing in their lives, and Lizzie knew that Ben loved them, too, even if he loved them in different ways. They all took care of each other, and that was important to Lizzie.

Last week Esther had fallen in the kitchen. It was Ben who kept her calm, reassured her that she was okay, then helped her to her feet.

Prior to that, Ben's doctor had changed his medication to reverse some unpleasant stomach issues he was having. It had had the opposite effect. Esther and Lizzie had taken him soup and a special herbal recipe that was their moth-er's, and he'd been back to himself in no time.

Lizzie watched for a few more seconds before she went back to what she was doing. She packed up turkey, dressing, mashed potatoes, peas, green-bean casserole, chowchow, bread, and three slices of different pies. She'd recently gone into the cottage when Ben had been sick to his stomach, and she'd briefly forgotten about Gus. Maybe because she'd been so worried about Ben at the time. She hadn't felt a sense of him there, but she wasn't taking any chances.

"I'm off to the cemetery," she announced to Ben and Esther, Gus's favorite foods in a Walmart bag she had draped over her arm.

"Lizzie, don't be silly. It's freezing outside, and it's supposed to snow."

"*Ach*, it's not snowing now, and I want to take Gus his meal before it gets dark. You two stay here where it's warm."

"Like the sick people we are." Ben sighed before he grinned and winked at her. "You sure you don't want me to go with you?"

Lizzie shook her head. "*Nee*, I'll be fine." It was something she wanted to do alone. Partly, it was superstition and an unjustified fear of his ghost, but it was also about paying respect to a man who had found peace at the end.

21

———— ✄ ————

ELEVEN MONTHS LATER...

Lizzie stood in front of the fireplace that hadn't been lit in months. Winter had left them, and spring had blown in. They'd endured another unusually hot summer, and with the arrival of fall came the baptisms of Ben and Mindy. Lizzie was happy they had all been able to witness the baptisms and Mindy and Gabriel's wedding last month. And today they would attend another holy event that Lizzie hoped to get through without collapsing.

She'd left the three angel figurines on the mantel after she'd taken down the Christmas holly, bows, and other decorations last winter. As she homed in on the angel with her arms in the air, she gingerly ran a hand along the wings spread wide and thanked God again for another day.

"Are you ready?" Ben asked as he opened the front door and stuck his head in.

Lizzie nodded as she swallowed back a lump in her throat. She couldn't believe this day had arrived. She put on her cape and bonnet. November had come back around and brought cooler temperatures.

They were quiet as Ben drove the buggy, dressed in his black slacks and dark-blue shirt. He'd donned a black hat for the occasion, as most of the men would be wearing. Lizzie was in her Sunday best too.

Upon arrival, Lizzie was certain that the entire community had shown up for this occasion. Buggies stood end to end up and down the road.

Lizzie didn't move as Ben tethered their horse in a reserved spot up front, then came around to her side of the buggy. He opened the door and waited patiently. No words were necessary. He knew how she felt. But the reality of the situation left her feeling surreal.

She recalled a conversation she'd had with Esther several weeks ago.

"It's time, Lizzie," her sister had said over coffee at the kitchen table early one morning. "You and Ben are in *lieb* with each other. You should get married."

Lizzie had tried to deny their feelings at first, for fear of hurting Esther, but Esther had chuckled. "*Ach*, stop it, Lizzie. I know Ben *liebs* me, and I feel strongly for him too. But he *liebs* you in a different way, and we aren't all going to live forever. I want to see you have your happily ever after, a second chance at romance. Don't wait until I'm dead because you think I won't be happy for you. It's what I want for you.

I'll move into the cottage or the other guest *haus* so you and Ben can have the main *haus*, but I'll still help you run the inn for as long as we're able."

Lizzie had slammed her coffee down on the table so hard that liquid spewed across the table. "Are you out of your mind?" she'd blasted at her sister.

"Stop being dramatic." Esther had reached for a napkin and begun cleaning up the spilled coffee. "If you don't marry Ben, I'm going to haunt you when I die, and it will be much worse than Gus."

Lizzie had smiled at that point, mostly because Esther laughed. "If I do marry Ben," she'd said, "I would only do so if you promised to keep living at the inn with us." She'd shaken her head so hard she'd knocked her prayer covering off. "Otherwise, it won't happen." She'd pointed a finger at Esther. "Do you hear me?"

Esther had grunted. "*Ach*, Lizzie. Don't you want to be alone with Ben after you're married?"

Lizzie recalled herself raising an eyebrow, knowing what her sister was insinuating. "Do we really need to have this talk?"

Esther had smirked. Lizzie could still see the mischievous look on her face. "I don't know. Do we? As the older sister, I feel it's *mei* responsibility to chat with you if you have any questions." Esther's forehead creased as she scrunched up her cheeks in an effort to keep a straight face, but she couldn't hold it and burst out laughing.

"*Ach*, good grief." Lizzie had chuckled. "I guess I better

agree to marry Ben before you drag me into a conversation I am not prepared to have."

Ben's experimental medications had kept him from getting any worse, and Esther's doctor had put her on a new medication for her Parkinson's that was a tremendous help. They'd all had good and bad days, even Lizzie, who found herself slowing down somewhat. But they took care of each other. Ben might be the man she would marry, but Esther would always be her best friend.

Lizzie finally stepped out of the buggy. Ben put an arm around her and walked her to the building as a light snow began to fall. She stopped a few feet from the entrance.

"Are you all right?" Ben asked for the tenth time this morning.

"*Ya.*" She stared into his eyes. "I am."

They took the steps up to the old farmhouse together. Mindy and Gabriel had done wonders with the place and had even added on to the living room, which was packed to capacity as Lizzie and Ben stepped over the threshold.

He'd been blessed to attend Mindy and Gabriel's wedding here only a few months ago. The couple had carried out their plans to explore both of their religions. Ben had secretly been hoping Mindy would choose the Amish lifestyle, although he had never voiced his thoughts. He smiled every time he saw her riding her horse out in the pasture. It seemed to represent a newfound freedom for his granddaughter, just a small part of the life she'd chosen with Gabriel.

Perhaps a few folks older than her and Ben weren't there, those who couldn't get out due to health reasons, but it was a large gathering with lots of familiar faces in the crowd. Esther and Lizzie had played matchmakers for plenty of the young people in attendance. Jake Lantz and his wife, Eva, were across the room. Benjamin and Rose stood nearby, as did Evelyn and Jayce—all couples Esther and Lizzie had played a part in nudging toward romance. But the one person Lizzie needed to be there wasn't in view.

"You look lovely," Mindy said as she pushed through the crowd toward Lizzie and Ben. "Both of you," she added before she kissed each of them on the cheek. "I know it's crowded, but we are making it work."

Lizzie felt weak in the knees as she scanned the room, all the chatter like background noise as she searched and searched. Then . . . There she was, coming toward her.

"I didn't see you at first," Lizzie said in a shaky voice, but a feeling of comfort began to sweep over her.

"You didn't think I'd miss *mei* baby sister's wedding, did you?" Esther leaned in for a hug. "For the second time," she whispered as she held Lizzie tightly.

Lizzie's bottom lip trembled. "Do I look okay for an old lady about to get married?" she said as she eased away.

"Stunningly gorgeous." Esther cupped Lizzie's cheeks and kissed her on the forehead as all of Lizzie's nerves began to settle.

Ben was casually talking with another guest, a man Lizzie didn't know.

"This is all silly, me being so nervous." Lizzie scowled. "What's wrong with me? I *lieb* Ben. I want to marry him." She envisioned lying down beside Ben this evening for the first time and gasped. "What if *mei* snoring bothers him?"

"Everything will be fine." Esther grabbed both of Lizzie's hands in hers. "The bishop is ready, along with the elders, and as soon as everyone gets seated, we're ready to begin."

Lizzie nodded. Ben was still chatting with the same man. She tugged on the sleeve of his jacket. Ben excused himself and leaned down to hear Lizzie amidst the chatter.

"Let's do this thing," Lizzie said in a whisper.

Ben smiled. "*Ya*, let's do it. I'm ready for you to be *mei fraa*." He winked at her, then held her arm as they walked to the middle of the living room, where the men were taking their seats in chairs on one side and the ladies were sitting on the other side, everyone facing the middle section where the bishop and elders stood. Furniture had been relocated to other rooms to accommodate the crowd. Some folks were standing in the back.

Lizzie walked on shaky legs to her spot in the middle with Ben. She felt like a teenager as she briefly recalled her wedding to Reuben. They'd had a wonderful life, and she was sure he would want her to be happy. But her focus immediately returned to the man by her side, her second chance at love.

For a moment her chest tightened as if she was missing something—a limb or something. Then she saw her. Esther, sitting in the front row.

"I *lieb* you," her sister said as she smiled.

"I *lieb* you too," Lizzie mouthed back at her just as Ben latched on to her hand. Everything was perfect.

Normally, an Amish wedding would last three hours. But it was only two hours later when Lizzie and Ben said their vows to each other. The bishop then blessed Ben with a holy kiss, and his wife did the same with a kiss on the cheek for Lizzie. Maybe the bishop had rushed it along due to the age of the bride and groom, Lizzie thought, somewhat amused.

After the ceremony the younger men in attendance headed outside to finish setting up the large tent and fire up the propane heaters. The snow earlier had prevented them from finishing the setup, but the clouds had parted, and sunbeams shone into the living room, lighting the crowded space and setting the scene for a lovely day. The aroma of baking filled the area, and as women bustled about and made their way to the kitchen, Lizzie stayed by her husband's side as they walked to the window and gazed at the activity outside.

"It's a perfect day," Ben said as he squeezed her hand.

Lizzie's heart was full. "In every way," she said as three young men arranged the bridal table where she and Ben would be seated soon.

They both turned to their right when a man cleared his throat.

"Ben, are you going to introduce me to your lovely *fraa*?" The man was tall like Ben, with a long gray beard that reached almost to his waist. He had to be roughly their age, and he had hazel eyes that twinkled beneath bushy gray brows. Ben had a much shorter beard, but otherwise, the two men could have been brothers as far as looks went.

"This is *mei* beautiful bride, Lizzie." Ben sounded so proud that Lizzie didn't think she could be any happier.

"Lloyd." The man nodded at Lizzie, which was more customary during an introduction, and Lizzie did so as well.

"It's a pleasure to meet you." She turned to Ben. "How do you two know each other?"

"We met at the hardware store. He is interested in renting the cottage." He grinned at Lizzie. "He's a widower who has moved here from Ohio to be near some of his family. Sound familiar?"

Lizzie only heard one word: *widower*.

Esther couldn't have picked a better time to walk up to them, and her eyes widened when she met Lloyd, who shook her hand . . . for an unusually long time, Lizzie noted. Ben and Lizzie exchanged glances, and Ben winked at her.

When Lloyd and Esther began their own conversation, Lizzie and her husband sidestepped away until they were semi-alone. "Back in business," Lizzie said with an added excitement. Just when she'd thought the day couldn't get any better.

Lizzie and Ben bundled up and made their way toward the bridal table. Once there, she found there was enough warmth from the propane heaters to shed her cape, and Ben removed his jacket. Various gifts lay on their table. Lizzie knew they would be candies, cookies, and small sentimental items.

"This *is* a perfect day," she whispered to her husband, who blinked back tears.

Ben nodded, and Lizzie reached for his hand under the table and squeezed. "I remember the first time I looked at this place and decided to buy it. I could have never imagined that I would be getting married here."

Lizzie struggled to control her own emotions on and off throughout the rest of the day. But every tear that threatened to spill was a happy one. Their blessed day was filled with merriment and good wishes.

When it was time for Ben and Lizzie to take off on their own as husband and wife, a crowd gathered to walk them to their buggy. The snow had continued to give them a reprieve, and the clouds had parted again, as if to lay a path for Lizzie and Ben—a path meant for them.

Lizzie turned when she got to the buggy, scanning the crowd until she found Esther. She had every intention of running toward her sister, embracing her, and telling her how much she loved her. Esther was staying at Gabriel and Mindy's house tonight to help with cleanup the following day and to let Ben and Lizzie spend their wedding night alone. But her sister was conversing with Lloyd. Lizzie smiled, waved to all their guests, and let Ben help her into the buggy.

As they pulled into the driveway at the Peony Inn, it began to snow again. Lizzie had originally assumed they would have their wedding at the inn, but Gabriel and Mindy had offered to play host, and Ben was thrilled to be married in the house he'd bought all those decades ago, even if he hadn't been the first in his family to do so.

Ben hurriedly tethered the horse, opened Lizzie's door, and ushered her toward the house. Inside, Ben shed his coat and rekindled the smoldering fire as Lizzie slowly took off her cape and bonnet and placed it on the rack by the door next to Ben's jacket.

They fell onto the couch, exhausted but exhilarated. They'd sneaked a kiss here and there when no one was around, but when Ben leaned over and kissed her the way a husband kisses his wife, it was everything she'd dreamed of. They might have been two old folks in their seventies, but there were still fireworks.

"You're pretty *gut* at that," she said before she kissed him again . . . and again. Afterward, breathless, she added, "That's all I can handle."

"Me too." Ben winked at her. "For now."

She turned and gazed at her husband. "Was it everything you thought a kiss should be?"

He laughed. "Everything plus some."

Lizzie smiled, still caught up in the euphoria of the day, but fighting sleep. "Coffee?"

Ben nodded as Lizzie stood. "But wait. There's one more thing I want to ask you." He sat taller on the couch, grinned his silly grin, and said, "Will you please let me have a look at your mouth and your dentures? I'm sure we can get them corrected so they're more comfortable."

Lizzie threw her arms in the air. "I'm speechless. I give you *mei* whole heart, agree to marry you, and smother you in kisses . . . and now you want *mei* teeth? *Nee!*"

She stormed into the kitchen, thought for a few seconds, then took out her dentures. She stomped back to the living room and handed them to him. "There." She flashed him a toothless smile. "Now you've seen me naked too."

They both buckled in laughter.

Because laughter and joy truly do soothe the soul.

Acknowledgments

———— ⋈ ————

As I've said before, it takes a team to get a book onto the shelves and in the hands of readers. This isn't a solo project, and I am so grateful to have masterful players on my team.

God is at the forefront of everything I do, and without Him, there wouldn't be any books. He feeds me stories that I hope glorify Him and entertain my readers. Thank you, my Heavenly Father.

All the folks at HarperCollins Christian Publishers deserve a huge round of applause. They work tirelessly behind the scenes to make my books shine. I'm deeply appreciative of all that you guys/gals do . . . from editing, marketing, distribution, and everything before, after, and in between. You all rock.

Janet, you remain—and always will be—my voice of reason, sounding block, proofreader, and way too many other things to list here. I value our business relationship, but it's our friendship that I cherish even more. I love and appreciate you.

Natasha, you are the best literary agent ever, but it is our friendship that I hold dear to my heart. We've laughed, we've cried, we've celebrated, and we have comforted each other during difficult times. You are very dear to me and always will be. Love you bunches.

To my street team, Wiseman's Warriors, you ladies are amazing. Thank you for everything you do to promote my books and for your friendships. May we carry on together for years to come!

And without my family and friends to support and encourage me, I'd be lost. Thank you to my husband, Patrick, and to all those I love for walking beside me on this journey.

Discussion Questions

1. In the beginning of the book, Lizzie and Esther are both infatuated with Ben. Initially, did you feel that Esther was a better fit for Ben?
2. Have you experienced or known anyone to find love late in life? How was that romance different from a younger version of love? Discuss the differences.
3. Mindy and Gabriel develop a close friendship quickly. Even though Gabriel is Amish, and Mindy is not, what are some of the traits/characteristics that draw them to each other besides physical attraction?
4. In the parallel developing romances between Mindy and Gabriel and the love triangle with Lizzie, Esther, and Ben, which character could you relate to the most and why?

5. Readers often tell me that they enjoy the escapism they feel while reading Amish novels. But there are also traditions and restrictions that some folks might find difficult to adhere to. What are some of the challenges you might face if you were suddenly living an Amish lifestyle?

6. It's obvious that Esther and Lizzie love each other very much. What were some of your favorite scenes that display the sisterhood the women share?

7. Based on various circumstances, key players act out of character sometimes. What are some examples of these unlikely shifts in behavior?

8. Did you foresee a joyous wedding at the end of the book, or did you fear it might be a funeral that the characters were attending?

9. Mindy is working at a nursing home and going to community college to pursue a nursing degree. What were some early indications that she might not be suited for a career in the medical field?

10. In addition to some tender moments, there were also humorous scenes between the characters. Which scene did you find the funniest and why?

11. If you could insert yourself into the book as one of the characters and rearrange the outcome of the story, who would you be and how would you change the plot and/or ending? Or would you leave the story as it is written?

12. Lizzie believes the cottage is haunted by their previous renter, Gus, with whom she'd had a tumultuous relationship. When does Lizzie make her peace with Gus's passing?

From the Publisher

GREAT BOOKS

ARE EVEN BETTER WHEN THEY'RE SHARED!

Help other readers find this one:

- Post a review at your favorite online bookseller

- Post a picture on a social media account and share why you enjoyed it

- Send a note to a friend who would also love it—or better yet, give them a copy

Thanks for reading!

The Amish Bookstore Series